MARKED I

Angela Caldwell

DEDICATION

I want to thank my amazingly supportive husband AJ and my equally amazing and supportive son Kylar. Thank you both for all of your love and encouragement. Also, thank you for being so understanding when I have to lock myself away for days at a time to write. I love you both with my entire heart.

This is a work of fiction. All of the characters, names, incidents, organizations, and dialogue in this novel are either the products of the author's imagination or are used fictitiously.

Cover Design: Lacey O'Connor

All inquiries should be made to 8th Street Publishing
sales@8thstreetpublishing.com

I never would have completed Marked without the support and encouragement of my family and friends. I am so blessed to have such amazing people in my life. Thank you all.

CHAPTER 1

Sitting back in her chair, Jacinda continues to stare at the name plaque on her desk. *Jacinda Kilmeade*, she proudly reads over and over. While she's been married almost six months, seeing it in writing still gives her butterflies. She took her husband's last name when they married, but this is the first time she's used his name professionally. The Kilmeade name rivals that of Kennedy in terms of political influence and power.

How little Jacinda Wright, a preacher's daughter from Texas, became Mrs. Gregory Kilmeade--wife of a respected U.S. senator, still baffled her.

It was all such a whirlwind--the romance, the marriage, the job offer. She understands why people criticize her for getting involved with

Gregory so soon after losing her husband and son, but they didn't understand the loneliness.

She knows her colleagues will question her merit, being that she was plucked out of virtual obscurity to become the newest on-air reporter at *Your Nation Now.*

I deserve to be here, she willed herself to believe, while using her finger to trace her name on the plaque. She could already foresee the hype surrounding her employment at the most influential television news program in the nation. She could visualize the smirks and imagine people attributing her career advancement to the popularity and influence of her husband. Sometimes she wonders if there is truth to those claims, but remains determined to show the world that she, Jacinda Kilmeade, deserves to be here.

*****

Thirty feet from Jacinda sits Keith Ludwig, one of a handful of college interns that graced the grounds of the newsroom. Most of the show's interns are legends in their own minds. They all jockey for rank during the three months they are released into the real world from the campuses they feel they have outgrown. They all look for *the* power play that will get them noticed and no doubt hired once they receive their degree. Keith is no exception. He doesn't have the classic good looks that some associate with broadcast news, but he's creative and capable of spinning anything into a masterpiece. A college professor once said of Keith, "Give that kid some yarn, and he will spin you a new reality." Keith never really knew exactly what his professor meant, but he liked the way it sounded. Of course, that was same professor who suggested Keith was better suited for public relations than journalism.

As he sat punching the numbers into a cell phone, he felt resentful. *Internship*, he thought to himself, *they should call it slave labor*. In the days leading up to his arrival in Washington, D.C., he dreamed of exclusive interviews, important leads, and power lunches. He was humbled after being assigned to such mundane tasks as proofreading, checking emails, and confirming appointments for the already established reporters. In the small town where he completed an internship last summer, he was treated no differently than the reporters on the payroll. He was in for a rude awakening when he signed up to intern in such a large market. His latest monkey-level task was programming a new phone for the show's top reporter, Rob Livingston.

Keith shifted his weight, and spun his chair to face the computer. He begrudgingly clicked on the messages icon, preparing himself for what he considered his next menial task of the day. Today he was assigned to help Rob Livingston--reporter extraordinaire. *Rob couldn't possibly be bothered to check his own company email*, thought Keith.

He was constantly irritated by the lack of learning his internship provided. It was his opinion that the point of an internship was to obtain real world experience, and he wondered how running others' errands and programming other people's phones fit the bill. He completed his tasks without complaining, knowing he had to pay his dues. He secretly longed for the day that he had his own intern to boss around. Sometimes, when he got bored, he daydreamed about the monkey tasks he would shove off on the newbies. Although he didn't consider himself a newbie, this place had a way of making him feel like one. He stared at the tiny puddle of condensation his drink left on the desk. *It looks like a little pond,* he thought to himself. He began studying it and realized what the big fish, small pond--small pond, big fish nonsense was all about. This was a big pond--an ocean if you will, and he knew he was viewed as little more than a single-celled organism. *What did they call those in school*? he wondered, *amoby, apony, no--amoeba*! If his short, stubby arms could reach the center of his back, he would most definitely pat it.

Why do I let my random thoughts distract me? He asked himself. This is a problem he's wrestled with since childhood. One word or symbol would act as a puzzle piece that would invade his head until he figured it out. The puzzle could be a thought, but that thought was often a recollection of a memory that was sparked by sometimes the most random of things. *They've got to have a pill for that*, he thought. Keith stared at Rob's computer screen, and clicked on the mail icon. A list of incoming messages filled the computer screen. Keith was to write down any lead that might turn into a good story and flag any message that warranted a response. Most messages were press releases that he forwarded to the assignments desk. He always rolled his eyes at the audacity of PR agents who tried to bypass an entire step, by sending their releases straight to the reporters. Still, he waded through email after pointless email. Finally, he clicked on an email with the subject line reading: **URGENT.** *Aren't they all*?, he thought sarcastically, as he opened the message. The email was short but desperate; it simply read:

It is happening. You have known this for years. They meet again this month. Expose them now before it is too late. The time has come. Think of all the souls you can save. Please do not continue to ignore me. The desperate note was simply signed **Mitch**.

Keith's curiosity was too much to contain. He quickly did an old mail search, using *Mitch* as a keyword. His eyes doubled in size, when he saw the list of equally desperate sounding subject lines that appeared before him. Not realizing he was about to open Pandora's box, he clicked on one of the six emails. Hearing Rob Livingston's voice, he closed his mail and spun the seat around. Keith was sure he looked like a deer caught in headlights. He prayed Rob didn't see him snooping in the old messages, but it's not like he had time to read them. *It figures*, Keith thought, *he's out of the office ninety percent of the time, but the one time I'm doing something sneaky, he appears out of thin air*. Okay, thin air wasn't the most accurate description of the newsroom's air; in fact, it was thick with negativity and greed. Keith has never seen such a selfish bunch of narcissistic toe-steppers in his entire life. The reporters here seemed a tad more arrogant than the reporters at his last internship. *Oh well*, he shrugged, *D.C. is a self-important town*.

"Hi Mr. Livingston," Keith said, trying to sound as casual as possible.

"Um. Hi. Logan is it?"

"It's Keith."

"Of course it is, it's just the last one was Logan or Lance or...."

"It's okay, I know we come and go at Mach speed."

"Yeah," Livingston replied, without taking his eyes off the screen. "Could you get up for just a minute, Lance?"

"Sure, it's your desk. I was just checking your email like the producer asked. There is this one email from a guy named Mitch that looks really interesting. Well, it either looks interesting or completely psychotic."

"The latter," replied Livingston, as he leaned toward the screen, seemingly looking right through it. "Mitch is crazy. He's a conspiracy theorist whom I imagine lives in his parent's basement and brews his own beer. If you ask him, he probably has theories about aliens, Scientology, and black helicopters. You can't take nut jobs like him seriously." Keith felt as if Livingston was talking at him, rather than to him. Keith smiled and walked away. *Brews his own beer? That was random,* he thought. Something about the email intrigued him. He had a gut feeling, and when it came to stories, intuition has never steered him wrong.

CHAPTER 2

Jacinda slowly sank into her plush sofa, as the soft velvet of her white, overstuffed couch hugged her tired legs. The cold air trickling down from her ceiling vents made the sweat on Jacinda's forehead feel cool. She dabbed at the sweat with her sleeve, staining the cuff of her blouse with makeup. *Great,* she thought as she noticed the smudge, *just great!* The commute is enough to make anyone's feet ache, but to make that commute in three-inch heels was just stupid, she silently acknowledged. *Rookie mistake*, she thought to herself, and made a mental note to wear tennis shoes on Monday. She decided to stick her heels in her bag, and not change into them a moment before she had to. She jokingly referred to them as her power heels. She had to give them a snazzy title, to justify paying $800 for a pair of shoes.

Her in-laws spend money like crazy, but she still feels uncomfortable shelling out massive amounts of money for something she could get cheaper somewhere else. To the Kilmeades, eight hundred dollars for a pair of shoes was a bargain, but to Jacinda, it was obscene. Growing up a preacher's daughter, money was always in short supply. After putting herself through college, she learned to live on a meager broadcasting salary, which sometimes barely reached poverty levels. She always had a difficult time believing that a degreed position paid minimum wage, but that was the reality of small market news.

Her wardrobe allowance was usually a joke. She was lucky if she even got an allowance from the frugal networks. Now, as she sits in her upscale Washington D.C. apartment, looking at her expensive shoes, she feels a little guilty for not cherishing her beautiful things more. It's not that she didn't appreciate her things, she was just never able to get wrapped up in all the labels and pricey objects that other people, like her mother-in-law, held so dear. It was her opinion that a shoe was a shoe. She didn't know Prada from Payless, but thanks to a few shopping trips with Chandra, her mother-in-law, she now possessed a few designer items to call her own. The need for a wardrobe allowance was a thing of the past. She didn't know how deep the Kilmeade well ran, but it seemed endless. If their credit cards had limits, she certainly didn't know about them.

She rubbed her burning, throbbing feet acknowledging her twenty-dollar, budget shoes never ate her feet in such a cruel manner. "Dahling, you must have them," she could hear her Chandra say in her faux British accent. Knowing her mother-in-law was born and raised in Connecticut made the accent all the more ridiculous. Jacinda loved her husband dearly, but could never really picture herself getting too close to her somewhat chilly mother-in-law. She felt guilty about the negative thoughts that seemed to escape her when thinking of Chandra, so she always forced one nice thought to counter each negative one. It might have been a pointless exercise, but it made her feel better. *She has a nice smile*, Jacinda offered up as a positive thought, before returning her attention to her aching feet.

Her thoughts turned to Kyler, the baby who was taken only hours after she gave birth to him. She thought about Kyler at least one hundred times a day. She wondered if he was happy, hungry, or being cuddled. She prayed that God would send him a protector—someone to love and nurture him. Of course, she'd do anything to be able to do those things herself, but until she found him, she just hoped that somebody was tending to his needs. The helpless tears began welling up in her eyes, and she willed herself to think about something else.

Grabbing the remote control, she flipped on the television. She heard Gregory's voice echoing in the hall outside of her apartment. His voice grew louder, with each step that he took towards the door. Sounds of a key fighting the lock reverberated in the empty entryway, seconds before the door swung open.

"Hello Angel," Jacinda said in a singsong voice, as she switched off the television, and dropped the remote control. She was doing her best to hide the sadness that crept over her just seconds earlier. She knew he was on the phone, but she couldn't bear him entering without a proper greeting. He winked at her, before managing a polite goodbye. He kicked off his shoes, as he made his way from the doorway to the couch. "How was it?" Gregory asked, a smile beaming ear to ear. It was the same magnetic smile Jacinda found so enchanting the first time they met.

It was almost a year ago that Jacinda landed an interview with the Congressman, although he was campaigning for senate at the time. He took time out of his busy campaign schedule to receive the F.J Bailey award in Texas. The F.J. Bailey award honored the foundation's Man of the Year. He was nominated Man of the Year for his part in pushing new energy legislation. Jacinda could still remember how excited she was to interview the senatorial candidate. Although Gregory was a politician, he was viewed as a celebrity. The interview turned into dinner, which turned into a whirlwind romance, which turned into the fastest marriage in Kilmeade history. The quickie wedding sparked rumors of a pregnancy, but such rumors were ridiculous. Her rumored pregnancy was even analyzed on nightly news programs, which only added to Jacinda's distaste for sensational journalism.

Jacinda found the pregnancy rumors especially cruel, so soon after losing Kyler. She thought of him almost every minute of the day. She thought about her late husband too, but not nearly as often. Losing both of them in the same month was almost too much for her to bare. While her husband's funeral helped to bring her closure, she knew she wouldn't find peace until she had Kyler safely back in her arms. She is a woman of Faith, but that Faith has been severely tested by an anger towards God that she's been unable to resolve.

Gregory was such a pillar of strength. He came into her life offering so much support and hope. He always knew just the thing to say to ease her pain.

He was even working on legislation that would fund the search and recovery efforts for missing children. He was truly trying to make a difference, and she found so much comfort in that.

Gregory gripped a package in one hand and dropped his phone on the coffee table with the other, before sitting down next to Jacinda. He sank down next to her on the couch while holding up the package for her to take. "What is it?" She squealed. "Open it," he said, handing the package to her. She reached into the thin, plastic bag, and felt the familiar texture of leather against her hand. She pulled out a soft, black briefcase and immediately noticed the *Our Nation Now* insignia emblazoned on the front. It was a triangle with a small eye in the middle, centered on top of the world. *Oh my gosh--how cheesy!*, she thought to herself, but did her best to look thrilled. Even if it was flashier than what she would have liked, it was a sweet thought, and she knew she would cherish it forever.

"So, tell me?" Gregory said, his big green eyes searching hers inquisitively. Jacinda's finger ran along the insignia on the briefcase, while she looked at him. Even after six months of marriage, she couldn't help but admire his beauty. He was blessed with the genetically superior Kilmeade genes. He was tall and naturally muscular, with chiseled cheekbones, and full, soft lips. His large green eyes danced, and came alive when he smiled. His smile could light up the darkest heart. When he looks at you, it's as if he can feel your pain, and instinctively knows how to fix what ails you. He has the type of charisma that transcends the television screen, which is why he's considered a national sex symbol. While he is no doubt beautiful, it wasn't his movie star good looks that got him elected. Jacinda believed he was the smartest, kindest, most compassionate man alive-- a belief shared by many. Jacinda was proud to share her husband with the masses, and became giddy when imagining all the good he could accomplish through politics. She thanks God every night for blessing her with such an amazing man. A man who could still make her heart flutter when he appeared on her caller ID.

Although people constantly rave about Jacinda's beauty, she always wonders if they are empty compliments. She doesn't see beauty staring back at her when she looks in the mirror; she simply sees herself. Her long, brown hair always makes her blue eyes pop. Her small, upturned nose delicately punctuated her naturally berry-tinted lips. Gregory gently brushed her lips with his thumb, and said, "Well?"

"Well, what?" Jacinda playfully responded, inching closer to him on the couch.

"How was your first day?"

Jacinda planted her head on his shoulder and sank

her body into his arm. She breathed in the faint scent of cologne, and lovingly wrapped her arm around him. "It was great, but it was pretty much just an orientation day. I didn't expect you to be home for a few more hours."

"My six o'clock meeting was cancelled, so I thought I'd take the nation's prettiest newscaster to dinner to celebrate."

"Celebrate?" Jacinda seemed confused. "Did something happen?"

"To celebrate your first day on the show!"

Jacinda smiled, feeling embarrassed that she didn't make the connection. She was still a little distracted by the gaudiness of the insignia on the briefcase; it must have been six inches tall. She moved her finger, tracing the insignia. "Oh that," she said, her smile transforming into an accomplished grin. "Well, let's go!"

*****

Keith's stomach growled loudly, as he checked the watch on his wrist. It was already one o' clock, and he was starving. He found it highly unfair that reporters came and left as they pleased, while interns had to sneak in a lunch break. After almost a month of working at *Your Nation Now,* Keith couldn't get over how glamourless the office was. Not only was it too chilly for his taste, but it reeked of mildew and new paint—a combination he found especially vile. He looked around, noticing the large, framed pictures of the newscasters that the show made famous. He rolled his eyes, while noticing the uniformity of each picture. Each reporter stood with their shoulders back, and had their arms crossed in front of them. Their arms looked as if they were resting on the show's insignia. He could just imagine the memo each reporter must have gotten before the photo-shoot. *Remember to look official and hard-hitting. Cross your arms and look important.*

Most of them look so pretentious, he thought. You would think they *were* the news, instead of just newscasters.

He stared at the picture of Rob Livingston, until he tricked his mind into seeing a picture of himself instead. *I'll be up there one day*, he assured himself. The telephone snapped him back to reality, and he dutifully picked up the line saying, "Your Nation Now, this is Keith, how may I help you?" Answering the phone like that made him feel like he worked at a fast food restaurant, but he did what he was told to do. A gruff voice came from the other end. It was Bertha, a producer of *Your Nation Now.* "Did you not see the double blink?" she asked in a gruff tone, not giving him time to respond. "It's in-house, you don't need the whole answer spiel. I need you to get the number off of Livingston's email of a man named Bruce Polanski," she barked before hanging up the phone. *Was it really necessary to use the phone?* Keith wondered. After all, she was only sitting fifteen feet away. Of course, maybe giving an order without using some form of technology would be a bit too personal for Bertha.

Keith dubbed her Big Bertha upon meeting her, and the name stuck. He was convinced that if Satan had a henchwoman, she was it. She was a dreadful woman, always barking orders and eating a seemingly never-ending supply of corn chips that she kept stashed away in her desk drawer. She didn't seem to care about her appearance, or hygiene for that matter. She towered over him at about 6'3", and never bothered combing her tangled, grey-streaked hair. If he felt the need to invest personally, he would have already named each rat in her hair. While he guessed her to be about forty-five, he decided she had the social skills of a two-year-old. She always failed to say please and thank you. He determined right away that she obviously never read the book *How To Make Friends And Influence People*, and daydreamed about leaving it on her desk.

After getting past his irritation with Bertha's lack of phone etiquette, he snapped his attention back to the task at hand. He considered the request, and found himself annoyed yet again. *Why can't Rob Livingston check his own email?* He knew Livingston was equipped with a handheld device that allowed him to access all of his mail. Oh how

Keith longed for the day that he had his own intern.

Keith stood up, grabbing his soda and phone, and made the 30-foot trip to Rob Livingston's desk. He had this thing about his phone and pockets; he refused to put his phone in them. He didn't know why he had an aversion to putting his phone in his pocket--he just did. Not only would he not put his phone in his pocket, he'd rather wear a dress and sing the theme song to My Pretty Pony, while applying lip gloss, than put his phone in one of those little belt clips. He didn't know why, but he found them entirely too feminine. It was his inability to come to terms with his phone storage issues that made losing his phone a daily occurrence. This station-issued phone was a life-saver, since he had no idea where he lost his personal cell last week.

Today, he hasn't lost his station phone once. In the mind of Keith Ludwig, even if nothing else went his way today, he still had his phone. Keeping track of his phone was a tiny bit of personal victory that no one else would even pretend to understand. Sitting his phone by the keyboard, he touched the mouse, bringing Livingston's sleeping computer back to life. Back home, at the University of Texas, where he was entering his senior year, checking someone else's email would be considered a criminal offense. Here at *Your Nation Now,* it's just one more mo nkey task the big wigs pass down to the interns. Oh well, Keith would rather do this than program phones or log story ideas that will never see the light of day.

He plopped into the seat, and pulled the little knob to lower the hydraulic chair down about six inches. *Clearly, Livingston was the last person to sit here*, Keith thought. Livingston is crazy tall. Keith opened the incoming messages, wondering what kind of people don't password protect such information. There was no shortage of messages filling the screen, as usual. Most looked run-of-the-mill, benefit tonight, blah, blah, blah. We Cordially Invite You, blah,blah blah. One, however, caught his eye. His attention focused on a subject line that read: **The time is near.** Keith clicked on the message.

Mr. Livingston,

I have tried over and over to contact you. I have called your personal numbers; each time being met by a rude response followed by a dial tone. I've left messages on both your work email and private email. It has become quite clear that you have decided to betray, not only me, but your entire country. If I don't hear from you, I will be forced to bring what I believe to be a prophesied evil to light by way of another outlet. I will be forced to expose your

involvement with The Brotherhood, as I feel you are a traitor not only to me, but your entire nation. I fear their power and influence steered you off the righteous path.

I have attached a picture. You will recognize yourself in the middle. I do not want to go this direction, but you are leaving me no choice. The truth must be told, for the freedom and soul of every American citizen is in grave danger.

If you change your mind, you can give me a call at 555-2211. I have left the number dozens of times, but I will give you the benefit that perhaps you have lost it.

Mitch.

Wow, Keith thought, *this guy does sound a little loony.* He clicked on the attachment and saw Rob Livingston along with four other guys in red, hooded robes. It was definitely disturbing. He didn't remember graduation robes having hoods. In fact, they looked more like KKK costumes. The men all had ear-to-ear grins, each putting their arms on the shoulders of the men next to them. Keith recognized the man on Livingston's left as being Senator Kilmeade. The man on Livingston's right was African-American, which kind of ruled out his KKK theory. There were several men in the background. They all looked like they were having a good time. It looked like a celebration. Sure, a group of middle-aged men in hooded robes seemed a little weird, but he didn't really see it as blackmail material.

There's got to be a great story here, thought Keith. *I mean, even if this Mitch guy does have alien tea parties in his parent's basement, there's got to be a kernel of truth.* Keith has always given in to his own curiosities. Keith believed it was his curious nature that made him a great reporter. He quickly forwarded the message and picture to his own email, deleted his tracks in Livingston's sent folder, and closed out of the messages. Without a second thought, he grabbed his phone and stored Mitch's number. He would devise a plan on how to approach Mitch later. Right now, he had monkey duties that included getting a number for a woman whom he seriously doubted knew how to use email.

CHAPTER 3

Jacinda was running late, as usual, speed walking from the subway to street level. The July heat in Washington, D.C., was almost unbearable. Her husband didn't understand why she didn't just drive to work, but she insists some of the best story ideas come from public transportation. Back home, she rode the bus to work every day. Someone always recognized her from television, and there were no shortage of story suggestions. She thought of it as keeping her finger on the pulse of the community.

She'll make it just in time for the assignment meeting, if she jogs the entire way. Each Monday, the producers and reporters meet to discuss story ideas and assignments. Today will be her first assignment, and she's ready. Usually she would arrive prepared, bringing several story ideas to the table, but this is a national news program. She feels certain they already have the assignments set in stone.

Maybe it's her lack of self-confidence that has kept her from choosing ideas to bring to the table. *This is NATIONAL news*, she reminds herself; *THE BIG TIME!* She knows she doesn't have the experience to be here, but tries to convince herself that she deserves it just the same. *You deserve this*, she told herself with every long stride; *you deserve to be here. Please God. Please give me the confidence I'm going to need in there*, she prayed, feeling a little guilty for asking God for a favor, despite her anger toward him.

She opened the office doors and took a deep breath, as the cold air-conditioned breeze surrounded her face. It felt like a hundred degrees outside, and sweat beads were forming above her top lip. *What a great first impression*, she thought, as she dabbed at her face. While yesterday was technically her first day, she wasn't able to meet everyone. Today would be the first time everyone would be gathered together, allowing for a formal introduction.

She turned the corner to see everyone sitting at a long table in the meeting room. "There she is now," said George, the News Director. in a less than friendly voice.

Everyone, this is Jacinda Kilmeade; Jacinda Kilmeade, this is everyone," George offered in a pathetic attempt at an introduction. "Sit down and we'll get straight to business," he continued.

Jacinda wondered how someone so socially uncouth could climb to the position he's achieved. He was obviously good at his job. He would be even better, if his job did not involve actual living, breathing people. George always looked cross and irritated. She heard he was in his early sixties, but he looked closer to seventy. She attributed his hyper-aging to his pack-a-day cigarette habit. He was short and squatty in stature, and always smelled like a chimney. He had this irritating way of never looking directly at the person he was speaking to. Of course, what he lacked in the social department, he made up for with skill. He was, after all, running the top-rated news program in America.

Jacinda took a seat next to Keith, which just happened to be the one closest to George. The assignment meeting at the show was pretty similar to what she was used to back home. Reporters grumbled about story assignments, and producers told them to make it work. The meeting was winding down, when someone whispered something to George. "Oh yea," said George, "don't forget about the awards show a week from today. Everyone can bring one guest." *Here it comes*, thought Jacinda. *Everyone is going to want to know if I'm bringing Gregory.* As much as she loves Gregory, she gets tired of everyone acting like he's a celebrity. She knows that technically, he is a celebrity, but she does not understand how public servants can incite the same kind of frenzy as movie stars.

"Will you be bringing Senator Kilmeade?" asked Livingston. *It's nice to meet you too*, she thought. "Yes, that's the plan," she responded.

"Good, I can't wait to meet him; he's some guy-- your husband."

Keith looked at Livingston and then back to Jacinda. He just saw a picture of Livingston and Senator Kilmeade together. *What did he mean he couldn't wait to meet him? How can you not remember hanging out with a senator while wearing a hooded robe?* He couldn't imagine people found themselves in that situation every day. Plus, he's the most established television reporter in D.C. How could Livingston's long career as a journalist in Washington, D.C. not have him cross paths with its most celebrated senator?

"He's very excited to meet everyone," Jacinda said politely.

"That's it," said George. "Get to it." Everyone stood and quickly scattered. Jacinda hadn't been assigned a story so she quickly approached George. "I didn't get a story," Jacinda said. "What would you like me to do?" George didn't even look at her, as he breezed past.

"Walk and talk with me," he ordered. "We're not going to give you a story this week. We're going to have you sit in on an editing session while you get used to the place. That will give you a feel for how the stories are cut around here." Jacinda felt insulted. It's not that she wasn't interested in how the stories were cut, but she knew she was being put off. Was it possible that George didn't have faith in her? "Sure," Jacinda said. "Show me to it."

Jacinda begrudgingly stepped into the tiny, dimly lit editing room. The editing monitor illuminated the darkness, but it took her eyes a moment to adjust. Sitting at the editing bay was a man in his mid-fifties with long grey hair pulled back into a low ponytail. He wore a Grateful Dead t-shirt and camouflage cut-off shorts, which Jacinda found highly unprofessional.

"Hi," said Jacinda. "I hate to bother you, but George said I needed to spend some time in here to see how things are edited."

"You have a story to edit already?"

"No. George just wants me to watch you do whatever you're doing, I guess."

The man gave her a confused look and said, "But you're the Kilmeade lady, right? You're the new reporter. Why are they sending you in here without a story to edit?"

"I don't know," she replied with a shrug. "Is that not standard for new reporters?"

"Nope," he said. "Bbut take a seat. The name's Jack, but they call me Jerry. You can call me Jerry." Jacinda was curious. " Why do they call you Jerry if you'r e name is Jack?"

"They say I look like Jerry Garcia. They've called me that for years and it just stuck."

Upon closer examination, she could absolutely see the resemblance. The thick, full, grey beard and chubby cheeks did resemble that of The Grateful Dead's deceased front man. The tie-dyed shirt with the band's name didn't hurt either. She took her seat and looked around. "How come there is only one editing bay?"

"There are three editing rooms," he answered. "Each bay gets its own room. I like it that way because I like to work alone. Um, no offense."

"None taken. Don't reporters usually sit in to make

sure their package is edited the way they envision it?"

"Sometimes, but they usually just give us their scripts and footage. I've been here for so long that most of 'em just trust me to get it right."

"So what are you working on now?"

"A package about RFID/GPS chips and how they're supposedly revolutionizing modern society," he said with a roll of his eyes.

"What was that for?" Jacinda asked, after noticing the eye-roll.

"I can't believe I'm putting this story together, man. I guarantee this technology is going to be the way The Man is able to oppress us. It's all about control. And before long, you won't even be able to walk to the mailbox without someone knowing what you're up to."

Jacinda smiled, sensing he was a little out there, and said, "I've heard a little about RFID and GPS but refresh my memory."

"It's like this, RFID stands for Radio Frequency Identification. It's an automatic identification method that relies on storing and remotely retrieving data using devices called RFID tags called transponders. GPS just stands for Global Positioning System.

"Sounds complicated."

"Not really, the technology is everywhere. They put transponder chips in cats and dogs to identify them if they get lost. They also use the technology for toll tags, and keyless entry systems. Here in D.C., they introduced the SmarTrip card for the Metrorail in '99, so it's nothing new. Shipping companies use it to track packages and the list just goes on.

"GPS is the same technology they use for automobile navigation systems. They use it to find the position of stolen cars. It's everywhere, man. What's scary is there are people who are having chips implanted in their skin for this reason or that reason. No way would I ever let them put that in me, man. Uh-uh, no way am I going to let The Man know every move I make. It's bad enough this cell phone the bosses make me carry has a chip in it. They can pull it up on the computer at any time and see where I am."

Jacinda looked at the phone she was issued, "You mean they can always see where I am as long as I'm carrying the phone?" she asked, feeling a little unsettled.

"Yup, and if you read the contract, you always have to have the phone on you unless otherwise cleared by the execs. It's crazy, man. I'm tellin' you, it won't be long until we all have to have one implanted in our skin to even use a credit card. One day drivers licenses and passports will be a thing of the past because all they need to do is scan the chips in our hands."

"That sounds a little far-fetched" Jacinda said, but somehow didn't totally rule out the possibility. Being a Christian, she's heard about the Mark of the Beast, but seriously doubted it would take place in her lifetime. In the Bible, it says in Revelations that everyone will be forced to take the Mark of the Beast, which sounded a lot like what Jerry was describing. *Of course, that will happen in the end times*, she assured herself, *not in my lifetime*.

Jerry looked at the script in front of him and shook his head. "Can you believe they are suggesting that people get this thing called the BARAchip that has both RFID and GPS technology implanted in their skin?" Jerry asked, unable to hid his disgust.

Jacinda shared his distaste. She couldn't imagine what good reason anyone would have for implanting a computer chip in their skin. "Well, let's see what you've got so far, said Jacinda, pulling her seat up to the monitor.

"I just started, I don't have much yet. Paula Strong is the reporter. She never leaves me in or out points on the video she wants me to put under her voice-overs.

Jacinda looked at him blankly.

"You know, in and out points, man. The numerical point on the tape that she wants me to capture for editing purposes at different points to go along with her voice-over."

"I know what in and out points are," Jacinda said, half insulted. "I just can't believe that a reporter isn't required to do that. If we didn't do that at my old station, the editor would mess everything up."

"Like I said, I've been here forever and they know I'll find the best video to match the audio. It's just irritating that they think I don't have anything better to do with my time. It's part of their job, but you'll find that every reporter here pushes most of their work off on other people. I don't say a word, man. I just keep to myself and do my job."

"Well, I'll never do that," Jacinda assured him.

"Give yourself a year. You'll see. Laziness is like a disease around here. Everyone catches it.

CHAPTER 4

Lucio sat in the back of a limousine holding his cell phone, while tapping his knee with his finger. He looked like any other businessman, dressed in an expensive Italian suit. He was meticulous about his appearance. He'd just left his Manhattan penthouse and was heading to a meeting near Times Square. His cell phone hadn't even had a chance to complete a full ring when he answered. "This is Lucio." He continued to tap his knee, as he listened. "So the woman of God, Jacinda, is learning of The Mark?" He smiled, pleased that everything was going according to plan.

*****

Keith sat at Livingston's computer, hoping against hope that there would be an email from the mysterious Mitch. He didn't know why he had become so fascinated with a man whom, for all he knew, could be a complete loon. He had always fancied himself a Sherlock Holmes, and thought detective work was the cornerstone of any good reporter. Nothing intrigued him like a good mystery, and ever since Livingston's sudden amnesia about meeting Senator Kilmeade, he was certain there was something to this Mitch guy.

His redundant intern duties were making his summer crawl by, and he needed something exciting to distract him from his boredom. He needed to feel like a reporter again, not the station lackey he felt he had become. He took a good look around, making sure Livingston was out of sight, before logging into his email. He was disappointed to find nothing from the mysterious Mitch, and quickly logged out before anyone noticed.

He looked down at his watch and noticed it was quitting time. Usually, he would ask one of the producers if it was okay to leave, but today he didn't feel like asking anyone's permission. He felt restless, and couldn't figure out why. He grabbed his phone and backpack and headed for the exit.

He couldn't get Mitch off his mind, and figured now was as good a time as any to get to the bottom of things.

As he made his way to the underground rail system, he scrolled down his phone list to find Mitch's number. He clicked on the number, took a deep breath, and nervously pushed send.

"Hello," said the voice on the other end of the phone.

"Um, hello," said Keith. "May I please speak to Mitch?"

"This is Mitch. Who's calling?"

That's a good question, thought Keith. He hadn't worked this part out beforehand. He searched for an answer, needing to end the awkward silence. "My name is AJ—AJ Lovely." *UGH*, Keith thought. *Lovely? LOVELY?! Why did I say Lovely? Whose last name is LOVELY?*

"Well, Mr. Lovely, what can I do for you?"

Keith's hands were shaking. He hated being this openly deceptive. A million thoughts were running through his head, none of which stopped long enough for him to get a handle on an answer. He was usually not at a loss for words, but he hadn't thought this one through. He'd always been impulsive, and now he was kicking himself for calling Mitch before figuring out the best way to approach the situation.

"Um, I guess the question is not what you can do for me, but what I can do for you. I'm a reporter and I understand that you have a story to tell."

Again, there was a long silence. "How do you know that?" Mitch asked.

"Like I said, I'm a reporter. I have sources."

"Really? And just who are these sources?"

"A good reporter never reveals his sources, Mitch."

"Please, call me Mr. Tatum."

"Mitch Tatum?" Keith asked, sounding completely taken aback. "Senator Mitch Tatum?"

"I was," he replied. "Who did you think you were calling?"

Keith frantically searched for a response, before saying, "My source just didn't mention that you were Senator Tatum. He just said your name was Mitch."

"What is this about?" Mitch demanded. "I really don't have time for…"

Keith reached deep, and found the confidence for which he was known. Determined to take control of the situation, he changed his tone. "Mr. Tatum, I'm a reporter, and as I understand it, you have a story that needs to be told. I would be more than happy to meet with you and get your side of the story."

"What story?" Mitch asked, sounding annoyed. "You have no idea what you're talking about, do you?"

"Look, all I've been told is that you have a story worth telling."

"How do I know I can trust you?"

"Trust me?"

"Yes, you call me on the phone saying that you're a reporter I've never heard of. You say you want to tell my story, but how do I know you aren't one of them?"

"One of who?" Keith replied; his interest was now at an all-time high.

"Oh never-mind," Mitch responded. "I'm not interested, but thanks for calling."

Keith heard the call disconnect and jerked the cell phone away from his ear like it was on fire. *Senator Tatum*, he thought. *This just keeps getting better and better!*

Keith made his way down to the subway, intrigued now more than ever. Loony Mitch, just became ex-U.S. Senator Mitch Tatum. This story just grew legs. Senator Tatum may have left office disgraced, but he certainly didn't leave it crazy.

Keith suddenly felt excitement tingling through every last nerve ending in his body. He didn't know the story, but he knew he was going to get it— whatever it took. He smelled a scandal. *This is it*, he thought to himself. *My own Watergate*. Of course, this is an ex-senator, not a president. Plus, his handle was Lovely, not Deep Throat. *Lovely?* Keith cringed. *I can't believe that was the best I had! I might as well have called myself Princess.*

Keith's forty-minute commute to his shabby efficiency apartment in Tyson's Corner was made impossibly longer by his own unanswered questions. Keith was simply too young to care about politics when Senator Tatum resigned. Senator Tatum's name saturated the news during the scandal, but Keith hadn't heard the name since. It's almost as if Senator Tatum vanished into obscurity. He desperately tried to remember the circumstances behind the resignation, but to no avail.

He jogged up seven stairs to his apartment, unlocked the door, and flung it open. He couldn't wait to sit down with his computer and research Mitch Tatum. He couldn't remember the last time he was this excited about a story. He grabbed his laptop, typed *Mitch Tatum* in the search box, and hit "Enter."

*****

Jacinda sat watching Jerry edit Paula's computer

chip story, while peeling her nail polish off in sheer boredom. She was itching to get out there and start reporting. She felt sitting at this editing bay watching Jerry edit someone else's story was a complete waste of her time. What made it worse was that Jerry had on headphones, so she couldn't hear anything he was editing anyway. She was well aware of how to edit. She's been editing her own stories for years. She didn't need a refresher course, and found it a tad bit insulting.

"I gotta run to the little boy's room," Jerry said, pulling Jacinda away from her thoughts. Jacinda realized she was peeling her nail polish, and quickly covered her half-painted nails in embarrassment.

"Go ahead and play with the system," Jerry offered. "Have you ever edited with this program before?"

"Oh, yes," Jacinda replied. "I know it well."

"Good, then make yourself at home. Don't mess with what I have saved and don't save anything, but feel free to check it out. I could be awhile."

Ew, she thought. Hearing him say he may be in the restroom awhile created mental images she quickly kicked out of her mind. "Take your time," she said "I'm not going anywhere."

Jacinda scooted over to Jerry's chair and scrolled though the raw footage on the DVR tape. She didn't even know why she was bothering to scroll through the footage, but supposed it was less boring than doing nothing. She fast-forwarded the tape, watching everything go by at a super-fast pace. It always amused her to watch people's mannerisms in hyper-speed. This particular interviewee was very animated. Jacinda giggled, watching the woman jerk her head, flail her arms, and exaggerate her facial expressions. She kept fast-forwarding, hoping to see the woman again, after some of the basic establishing shots. She kept her hand on the fast forward knob, until she recognized a face that made her jerk her hand away from the equipment. It was her beloved Gregory.

"Imagine if we could locate missing children as easily as we can locate stolen cars," Gregory said confidently. Hearing her husband's words made her heart ache for her own missing child. Although she hasn't felt complete since his abduction, some moments were more gut-wrenching than others.

He continued. "Take for instance, the High-Star tracking systems that many of you have installed in your automobiles. With the High-Star system in place, your car has a ninety-nine percent chance of being located. That's right, High-Star locates ninety-nine out of a hundred stolen cars. Imagine if we had a ninety-nine percent recovery rate for missing children." Jacinda was intrigued. She hung on every word Gregory spoke, not realizing Jerry had returned from his break and was now standing behind her. She was devouring Gregory's every word. "The BARAchip is a simple solution to a problem that devastates hundreds of thousands of families each year. Did you know that over eight hundred thousand children are reported missing each year? Eight hundred thousand is a number too high to ignore. With a tiny, painless implant, the recovery rate could be as high as ninety-nine percent."

Jacinda's eyes swelled with tears, as she watched her husband talk about the enormous amount of missing children per year. She knew the statistics all too well. In her quest to recover her own missing child, she met many other parents of abducted children. Suddenly this once ridiculous computer chip seemed invaluable. The chip seemed ingenious, once it was connected to child recovery. She lived with the grief of a missing child every moment. She knows she isn't alone, but can't help feeling like she is the only person on the planet who experiences this kind of heartbreak on a daily basis. She sees Kyler in every infant that crosses her path. Every toddler makes her wonder what Kyler looks like, now that he is two years old. She wonders if he's warm and safe, or scared and hungry. How her heart aches for her child every minute of every day.

She knew that Gregory supported legislation to fund the search for missing children, but he hadn't mentioned anything about RFID/GPS chips or implants. Why was he keeping her in the dark? Why did he fail to mention something that could make such a difference, and keep other parents from feeling the torment she's been living with for years? She felt a slight tinge of jealousy while picturing the lucky parents reuniting with their missing children due to this new technology, but quickly corrected herself. After all, she would trade her own life if it meant nobody else would have to experience the pain of losing a child.

Jacinda still spends hours each day on the internet writing emails, checking data bases, and desperately searching for her baby. Although every lead has always ended in disappointment, she is determined to search for him until the day she dies. She also calls Pastor Rick at least once a week. Pastor Rick was her pastor back home in Texas. He's always been such a wonderful support to her, always referring her to scriptures that bring her comfort. She's new to the D.C. area, but is determined to find a church that she likes as much as her old one.

Feeling a tap on her shoulder, she spins around to see Jerry standing behind her. Removing her headphones, she apologized. "Sorry, I didn't hear you come in."

"It's all right, I never hear anything with those things on either."

Jacinda averted her eyes, hoping Jerry wouldn't

notice her tears, as she slid from his chair to her own. She desperately tried to collect herself, not wanting to appear weak or vulnerable. Having to explain why she was crying would lead to even more emotions and tears.

"Excuse me," she said, while rising from her chair and heading for the door. Jerry seemed oblivious as he placed the headphones on and got back to work.

Jacinda opened the door to the ladies room and rushed to a private stall. Once she felt hidden, the tears poured down her face. She dabbed at her cheeks with toilet paper, hoping it would save her makeup, thereby avoiding an explanation. She didn't want to even think about having to step back into the office and explain why she was crying. For now, she knew she was alone in the stall, alone in the bathroom, and at that moment, alone in the world.

CHAPTER 5

Lucio sat inside the temple watching Lyla, the maidservant, play with the toddler they simply referred to as *child*. The toddler giggled as he and Lyla rolled a rubber ball back and forth. He was a beautiful boy with light brown curly hair and big blue, inquisitive eyes. He was dressed in white from head to toe. Like the child, Lyla was also beautiful. She too had brown curly hair, a small, delicate nose and high cheekbones, but her eyes were green, not blue. She let her long, soft curls spill over her delicate shoulders and was constantly brushing her hair from her eyes. At twenty-one, she has yet to outgrow her childhood habit of twisting her hair around her finger; a habit she's been determined to break for years.

"I'm glad to see the child is still happy," Lucio said to his assistant, looking quite pleased. Even though he looked pleased, his very presence frightened Lyla to the core. She'll never forget the day Lucio barked the orders, "Venus is making the transit, the child must be born tomorrow. Induce labor if you must. Ancient prophecy says the child *must* be born tomorrow."

Lucio looked at his driver, "You may now take Lyla and the child back to their home." Lucio nodded, before focusing his attention back to the ancient scrolls that laid before him. Lyla felt relieved his attention was no longer on her and the child. She felt satisfied he was pleased, but only because she feared seeing him angry.

Lyla's assistant helped her collect the child's toys. Lyla scooped the giggling toddler into her arms and kissed him on his cheek. Lucio looked up from the scrolls, "Remember, Lyla, it is you I hold responsible to keep the child happy."

"Of course Your Highness," she said as she bowed to him. "His happiness is my only reason for breathing." The way Lucio looked at Lyla worried her. Could he tell she had become attached to the child?

*****

Keith sat on his small bed, balancing his notebook computer on his lap. The internet search for Mitch Tatum yielded thousands of results. Not knowing where to start, he clicked on the first one, and waited for it to load. There in big, bold letters read: **Senator Tatum Resigns**. The accompanying article read:

U.S. Senator Mitch Tatum resigns after being implicated in a drug scandal. Tatum was arrested two weeks ago after three law enforcement officers allege they saw him exchange money for cocaine. The alleged exchange occurred outside of the Ronald Reagan building in Washington, D.C. Jacob Dyess admitted to selling Senator Tatum the cocaine, as part of a plea bargain with prosecutors. Dyess also claimed that Tatum was a regular customer. Senator Tatum strongly denies these charges, but says he is resigning to protect the American people from a lengthy, public trial. If convicted, Tatum could face up to one year in prison.

Keith couldn't remember what the outcome of the trial was, but didn't remember hearing that Tatum went to prison. He typed in the keywords *Tatum* and *Trial,* but all the search results were very similar to the article he just read. *Why isn't there anything during or after the trial?* Keith wondered.

Tatum's arrest was eight years ago, which would have made Keith thirteen. He wished he would have paid more attention to the news back then, but he was more interested in playing video games than keeping up with current events. He couldn't understand why there were no news articles following up on the Tatum trial. It seemed that the story just died after Tatum resigned. It's like he just disappeared and nobody noticed or cared. Growing frustrated with the lack of answers the internet offered, he phoned his father. If anybody would know anything about the Tatum scandal, it would be his dad. His dad followed politics more closely than anyone he knew.

"Hello," said a voice on the other end of the phone.

"Hi Dad."

"Keith!" his dad said behind a smile. "I was just talking about you. How's D.C.?"

"It's good. Hey--I have a question."

"Shoot."

"Do you remember a Senator Tatum? He was arrested about eight years ago."

"Sure, I remember him. Why? Did you meet him?"

"No, not exactly. Hey, I was wondering what ever happened to him? Was there ever a trial or anything?"

"No, there was never a trial. He always said he was innocent. He ended up striking a deal with the prosecutor. The media just moved on after that. I don't remember hearing anything else about it. Why do you ask?"

"I just heard his name, and knew it sounded familiar. Oh hey, that's my other line. I'll talk to you later," Keith said and hung up the phone. Nobody was on his other line, and while he felt bad lying to his dad, he didn't want to explain his fascination or get into a lengthy conversation. He's always been guilty of having a one-track mind, and right now, that focus was on Mitch Tatum.

Could it be that Mitch wanted to clear his name? Is that why he's been contacting Livingston? If so, why did he send that picture of Senator Kilmeade and Livingston wearing the robes? What did that have to do with anything? Furthermore, why was he talking about souls being saved? Keith was both confused and intrigued. He picked up his cell phone, scrolled to Mitch's name, and pushed send.

"Hello," said a voice that Keith recognized as Mitch's.

"Hello Mr. Tatum, it's AJ Lovely again." He cringed as the word Lovely jumped off his tongue. He quietly scolded himself for not using a manlier alias.

"I already told you, I have nothing to say. Please

stop calling this number. Good bye."

"Don't hang up! Please! I know you don't want to talk to me, but I want to talk to you. You're right, I don't know what your story is, but I'm fascinated." Keith knew that honesty was the best policy, and thus far, his AJ Lovely ruse had gotten him nowhere. "The truth is that I want to hear your side of the story. I want to know what happened."

"Well, as much as I'd love to feed your fascination, Mr. Lovely, give me one good reason why I should trust you."

"I can't. I can't convince you to trust me, but what could it hurt? If what you want is to tell the truth about what happened, then what can telling your side of the story hurt?"

"What happened? What do you mean when you say 'what happened?'"

"Well, you know—the false charges. Well, assuming they were false."

"If you are referring to the drug charges, of course they were false, but the story I wish to tell is so much bigger than that. The story I wish to tell will turn the world on its head. You have no idea what you're getting into, Mr. Lovely."

"I'm up for it," Keith replied. "Just tell me when and where to meet you."

"I never agreed to meet with you, Mr. Lovely."

"Just give me twenty minutes of your time. Meet me outside the Ronald Reagan building at the table by the..."

"Is that supposed to be a joke?"

Keith realized his mistake, temporarily forgetting that the Ronald Reagan building was where Tatum was arrested. "Forgive me, I wasn't thinking. Then you name it, tell me where you want to meet, and I'll be there."

"Meet me at Swift Coffee shop on Maryland Avenue tonight at 9:30. Do you know it?"

Keith's heart sank to his stomach, causing a fluttering sensation in his belly. He never expected Mitch to agree to meet with him. It was all he could do to reply. "I'll find it. See you there." Keith hung up the phone. A million thoughts were competing for attention inside his head. What would he say? Would Mitch realize he was just an intern? Would Mitch even show up? Should he bring an audio recorder? What did Mitch mean when he said that his story was much more than just the drug charges? Keith felt drunk with excitement and anticipation. He couldn't believe his luck. Glancing at his watch, he realized he only had one hour to get to the coffee shop.

*****

Jacinda dreaded going to her in-laws for dinner. Visiting their home for dinner was always such a show. She had to dress to impress, in order to escape sharp barbs of criticism from Chandra, her mother-in-law. She slipped into a beautiful, silk dress she felt was far too formal for family, and finished her look with the expensive designer shoes she bought at Chandra's insistence.

"We're late, love!" Gregory shouted from the living room.

"Two more minutes," Jacinda assured him, as she stared at herself in the full-length mirror of their posh bathroom. Their bathroom was larger than her childhood bedroom. She spun on the tips of her toes, scanning herself from top to bottom. She searched for anything Chandra might criticize. While she couldn't find anything, she was sure Chandra would.

Jacinda joined her husband in the living room. His eyes lovingly looked her up and down. "You look gorgeous, my love. It was well worth the wait."

Jacinda smiled. She never tired of him charming her. She loved that about him. He always made her feel like the prettiest woman in the world. "You think so? You don't think I should change?"

"Don't you dare. You look perfect."

"Well then, let's go," Jacinda said, slipping her tiny hand into her husband's and heading out the door.

Jacinda used the short drive to Virginia as an opportunity to approach Gregory about the BARAchip implants he discussed in the interview. "I just don't understand why you never mentioned it," she said.

"I just didn't want to get your hopes up, in case the legislation doesn't get passed," Gregory explained.

"Legislation? What legislation? Why would putting a tiny implant in your child for their protection require legislation? Is it Illegal or something?"

"No, it's not illegal. What *should* be illegal is any parent refusing to allow the implant. I didn't want to talk to you about it until I knew for sure our legislation would be passed, because I know how emotional you get. I know the subject makes you miss Kyler."

Jacinda felt her heart skip a beat at the mention of her son. "I always miss Kyler, Gregory. It doesn't take a subject to make me miss him. How did you think I wouldn't find out? You gave an interview to *Our Nation Now*. I want to know everything. What kind of opposition could the legislation face? If this technology is going to save children, how could anybody be against it?"

"I was hoping you would see it that way."

"How else is there to see it?"

"Knowing you feel the same way I do makes me

want to push the legislation that much harder."

"Wait, you're the one responsible for this legislation? This was your idea and you didn't tell me?"

"No, it certainly wasn't my idea. I can't take credit for that part."

"You know what I mean, Gregory."

"A lobby group approached me about the idea because they knew how near-and-dear the subject is to my heart. They knew I would listen to them. They explained it, and it made perfect sense to me. I thought if we can spare just one person from having to go through what you're going through, it would be a success."

"When Gregory? When did they approach you?"

"About six months ago. Like I said, I wanted to tell you, but didn't want to get your hopes up."

"I wish you would have told me. I just want you to feel like you can share things with me. If there's any technology that can help find missing children, I will be its biggest supporter. You of all people should know that. It's not about getting my hopes up. It's about joining you in making the public aware of the technology. I want to do whatever it takes to make sure every parent has the option to safeguard their children."

"You have no idea how happy that makes me."

Jacinda leaned over and gave her husband a kiss on the cheek.

They rolled into the long, winding driveway of the Kilmeade's Virginia estate. It was magnificent. The colonial-style, white brick home stood three stories tall. It was surrounded by manicured hedges, and was beautifully lit from the ground up on all sides but one. "Look, the lights are still out on the entire north side," Jacinda pointed out to Gregory. "When are they going to get it fixed, it's been like that since we first met."

"Oh, you know my parents, they are slow to get anything done."

"Since when? They certainly never waste any time getting their handy man to fix anything else."

"Oh look, there's Mom," Gregory said, pointing to the front door. Chandra stood on the front porch, waving to them as they rolled to a stop.

"Your mom is wearing jeans!"

"So?"

"So, she never wears jeans!"

Gregory stepped out of the car and waved to his mother. "Hello dah-lings," Chandra cooed in her faux semi-British accent.

Jacinda followed Gregory to the front porch while putting on a big, fake smile to greet her mother-in-law.

"Well, aren't you fancy," Chandra said before kissing Jacinda's cheek. There's the barb she was hoping to avoid. She just couldn't win with this family! *I mean--jeans! When did she ever wear jeans?* Jacinda couldn't help but wonder if she did it on purpose. As more negative thoughts crept into her head, she pushed them out and said, "Dinner smells wonderful."

"Good, I hope you're hungry," she said while hugging Gregory, "I didn't know if you'd already eaten at the ball you just attended," Chandra sassed while eyeing her dress.

Gregory seemed to think his mother was complimenting his beautiful wife. "Yes, doesn't she look stunning?"

"Oh yes, Gregory. Stunning."

Jacinda dug her fingernails into the palm of her hand as a way to release the negativity that was dying to escape her. She didn't understand why every compliment her mother-in-law paid her had to be so backhanded.

"There's the lovebirds now," Gregory's dad, Nicholas, said as he rounded the corner of the entryway. "You married the prettiest girl alive, well except for your mother. What the heck do you see in him Jacinda?"

Jacinda smiled and hugged her father-in-law. She never had to wonder where her husband got his charm. The apple didn't fall very far from the tree. Gregory seemed so much like his father. Nicholas spent years as a U.S. senator. While he no longer holds office, he still acts as a mentor to Gregory, and holds stock in more companies than Jacinda cares to count. Sometimes, Jacinda feels a little jealous that her husband always goes to his father for advice, instead of her. While she appreciates the relationship the two men have, she can't help but think Nicholas is a bit too controlling of Gregory. It seems that what Nicholas says goes, even if Gregory seems to have other ideas.

"So Jacinda, How do you like work so far?" Nicholas asked, while leading her by the arm to the living room.

"Oh, it's great, but I haven't gotten to do much yet."

"How's George been treating you?"

The question caught Jacinda off guard. She had no idea her father-in-law knew her news director.

"You know George? George Dittmeir?"

"Oh honey. Dad knows everyone," Gregory said with a smile.

"Oh, I've known George for years. He was a

reporter back when I was a senator."

"He was alive that long ago?" Gregory teased.

"Gregory, you didn't mention your dad knew George." She didn't know what shocked her more: the fact her father-in-law knew George, or that socially awkward George used to be a reporter.

"Must have slipped my mind," Gregory said, eager to change the subject.

"Oh dah-ling, are those the shoes you bought when we went shopping?" asked Chandra, in what seemed like an awkward attempt to change the topic. Jacinda smiled politely and nodded.

She wanted nothing more than this family gathering to be over. She was tired and had to be at work early in the morning. Tomorrow was another assignment meeting, and she hoped to finally be given a story. She missed being out in the field, and felt that she had wasted enough time hanging around the newsroom. Tonight was Thursday, the night *Your Nation Now* broadcasts all over the country at nine o' clock. After dinner, it was time to wrap up the evening and head home, but Jacinda suggested they stay and watch the broadcast. She didn't want to miss it while driving back to D.C., even if it meant staying at her in-laws another hour.

"Oh, of course," said Chandra. "Will you be on?"

"No, I didn't get a story last week, but Gregory was

interviewed in a wonderful piece that Paula Strong did about this amazing new technology called the BARAchip. You'll have to watch it. Gregory did a wonderful job during the interview, as usual."

Nicholas flipped on the television. They sat through the entire hour-long broadcast, but Paula's story never aired. "That's weird," said Jacinda. "They finished editing that piece days ago and it was great. I wonder why they didn't include it. Who knows, maybe they're saving it for next week's broadcast for some reason. I just wish you guys could have seen it."

"Well, it's a quarter past late," Gregory said, while helping Jacinda up from the couch. "We better get going."

.

CHAPTER 6

Keith nervously sipped his coffee, while sitting at a small, iron table outside of Swift Coffee Shop. He scanned the faces of everyone who walked by, looking for the mysterious Mitch Tatum. He saw pictures of him during his internet search, and hoped his appearance hadn't changed too much. As far as Keith could tell from his pictures, he looked like a very dignified man. He was a man in his mid-fifties with grey hair, and a clean-shaved face. Keith thought he looked like your run-of-the-mill politician. A man who appeared to be in his sixties stopped outside of Swift, and looked around as if he were searching for someone. *Could it be Mitch?* Keith wondered. This man didn't look like a politician. He had on a plain blue t-shirt, shorts, and a red baseball hat. The hat covered what was clearly dark hair, and this man had a dark mustache. Keith studied the man, wondering if it could be Mitch. It was just so hard to tell since he's only seen a few pictures. The man noticed Keith studying him and walked in his direction "You must be AJ," the man said with an outstretched hand.

Keith shook his hand and said, "Mr. Tatum, I barely recognized you."

"That's kind of the point. Call me Mitch."

"Here, sit down," Keith offered while pulling out a chair.

"I'd rather walk."

"Sure," Keith said, "Let's take a walk."

"Are you a Christian, Mr. Lovely?"

Keith thought that was a strange question. He had gone to church his entire life, and considered himself a Christian. It was the reminder of his Faith that made him feel even guiltier about lying to Mitch. "Yes, but what does that have to do with anything?"

"Oh, Mr. Lovely, you'll find it has a great deal to do with everything. So, you say you're a reporter. Where do you work?"

"I'm a freelance reporter, mostly."

"Mostly?" Mitch looked a little confused.

"Yea, I usually write freelance, but sometimes…" Keith realized that one lie had turned into another, and now he didn't even know where he was going with his story. "I am a reporter sir, but I'm also a student," Keith said, in a move he hoped he wouldn't regret. "This summer, I'm interning at *Your Nation Now*." Keith felt somehow relieved to be telling the truth, although he hoped his initial dishonesty wouldn't be held against him. He didn't know why he felt the need to confess his true identity--he just did. "My real name is Keith, not AJ."

"So, then I take it that your last name isn't Lovely."

Keith cringed upon hearing the word Lovely. He was happy to rid himself of the alias. "No, it's Ludwig, Keith Ludwig. I'm sorry I lied. I was…."

"No need to explain. I admire your honesty. It couldn't have been easy to admit that you're a liar."

Feeling a little offended, Keith retorted, "I'm not a liar, I just…"

"Lied?"

"Well, yes, I lied. But I'm usually very honest and..."

"No need to explain," Mitch assured him, giving his shoulder a squeeze that conveyed all was forgiven. "I admire your honesty, even if it took you awhile. I respect honesty; it's something you don't see a lot of in this town. So, what exactly did you want to talk to me about?"

"Well, since I'm being truthful, I might as well just tell you everything. I don't really know what I want to talk to you about. Part of my intern duties are to check Rob Livingston's email, and I saw the messages you sent him."

"What's your relationship to Mr. Livingston?" Mitch asked.

"I don't really have much of a relationship with him at all. Like I said, I'm just an intern at the show. He can't even remember my name."

"Which one?"

"I guess I deserved that. I ran across your emails and became fascinated."

"You mean nosey."

"I'm a reporter. I'm nosey by nature."

"So you want to know what those emails are all about. Well, you wouldn't believe me if I told you."

"Try me."

"You see AJ..."

"It's Keith."

"Right. Keith," he said with a smirk that let Keith know he was kidding. "You see Keith, what I have to tell can't be told in a simple news story. It requires proof and testimonies from people far more reputable than myself. It's so important that people become aware of what is about to happen, but it's going to take something far greater than a news story to convince anyone. I have knowledge of something so sinister that the public won't want to believe it. It's a conspiracy that pre-dates our very nation, but one that will affect every part of life as we know it. See, I can tell you all about it, but I run the risk of you thinking I am crazy. You could tell the entire world about it, but until you find the right way to do it, and have proof, you run the risk of everyone thinking that you're crazy, too. I don't have anything to lose by telling you what I know, but you do."

"What do you mean I have something to lose?"

"I mean my name is mud. I don't have a reputation to protect anymore. I suspect that as a reporter, jeopardizing your reputation could be career suicide. Not only that, but once you know too much you'll become a target, and not only risk your reputation and career, but quite possibly your life."

Keith couldn't believe what he was hearing. Maybe Mitch *was* crazy, after all. "I'm willing to take that risk," Keith assured him, deciding to play his game. *Maybe Mitch is nuts,* Keith thought, but he was still as curious as ever.

"So you say you're a Christian?"

"I did say that, yes."

"Well, is it true, or was it made up like your name?"

"No sir, that part is true."

"Have you read the Book of Revelations?"

"I'm sure I have, although I can't recall exactly what it said. It's a lot of gloom and doom Right?"

"I'll tell you what Keith--you go home and read the Book of Revelations. Pay particular attention to 13:16. When you're done, call me and we'll meet again."

Oh come on! Keith thought. *What does being a Christian or the Book of Revelations have to do with anything?* Without saying another word, Mitch turned and walked into the night.

Keith's mind reeled his entire walk home. Was Mitch crazy? How is being a Christian relevant? He was so lost in his thoughts his walk home flew by. After arriving at his apartment, Keith kicked his shoes off and flung himself onto the bed. He reached over and picked up the Bible his mom packed in his suitcase. He never really read it, but it comforted him just knowing it was there He didn't know why Mitch wanted him to read Revelations, but he was going to do as instructed. It was late, and he was tired, but wouldn't be able to sleep without knowing the significance of Revelations. He flipped his Bible to Revelations 13:16 which read:

And he causes all, the small and the great, and the rich and the poor, and the free men and the slaves, to be given a mark on their right hand or on their forehead.

Keith remembered learning about the Mark Of The Beast, although he never really thought it was something he'd have to deal with in his lifetime. He promised his mother many years ago that he would never take it--no matter what. His mother always worries about stuff like that. Sometimes he thinks she worries too much and that she is a little too fanatical. She reads the Bible for hours each day and is always praying for someone, but Keith just figured it's because she had nothing better to do.

He started at the beginning of Revelations and read it all the way through. Glancing at his alarm clock, he realized that it was time to go to work. He couldn't believe he stayed up all night reading the Bible. He smiled when he realized how proud that would make his mother. She was always trying to persuade him to read the Bible.

Keith jumped in the shower, then headed to the subway train to go to work. He only had to work for two hours today, and couldn't wait until his intern duties were finished so he could call Mitch. Maybe Mitch will finally tell him what the heck all of this is about. He couldn't imagine what Revelations had to do with anything, and wondered if Mitch was playing games with him.

Keith spent his entire time at the office thinking about what he read the night before. He wanted so badly to make sense of everything. His workday was finally coming to a close, so he grabbed his phone and headed out the door. He scrolled down to Mitch's name and hit send.

"Hello," he heard a voice say on the other end of the phone.

"Hi Mitch. It's Keith."

"Oh, hi Keith. Did you read what I told you?"

"I did Mitch, but I've got to tell you that I'm a little confused."

"Confused about Revelations?"

"Well yeah. But more specifically, what Revelations has to do with anything."

"Due time, Keith. Due time."

Keith was frustrated. *Why won't Mitch just spill it already! Why does he insist on stringing me along?*

"Mitch, I did what you asked, and I would love to meet up with you again. I'm in D.C. now, and want to know if you are free to meet this afternoon. I just wanted to touch base before I went all the way back to Tyson's Corner."

"Oh, so you want to meet right now?"

"Well, it doesn't have to be right now, but I'd like to meet soon."

"I don't have anything planned," said Mitch. "How about you meet me at Swift in an hour? That'll give me time to grab what I need and get up there."

"Sure, I'd love that. I'll be there in an hour."

"Great. See you then."

Keith hung up the phone and turned around, heading to Swift Coffee Shop. He was glad he called before making the long commute home. He wondered what Mitch meant when he said he was going to grab what he needed. What did he need?

Even at 10:30 a.m.., the D.C. morning was hot. He wiped the sweat from his brow, while dodging people coming from the opposite direction. The sidewalks were packed with wide-eyed tourists, and he wondered if there was anywhere that he and

Mitch could talk privately.

Keith arrived at Swift and ordered an iced coffee. He waited for a table to clear and jumped on the first one that became available. He looked at his watch, noticing that he still had about fifteen minutes before Mitch arrived.

"Hey, Keith," he heard a voice behind him say.

Keith twisted in his chair. "Hi Mitch. I didn't expect you for another fifteen minutes."

"I'm running early. I'm glad you are, too."

Mitch was carrying what appeared to be two maps in his hands. He set the maps down, and reached out his hand to greet Keith. Keith wondered if he was carrying maps to blend in with the thousands of tourists. "So, you claim you read Revelations?" Mitch asked.

"Yea, I stayed up all night reading. I can barely keep my eyes open, I hope this coffee will help."

"We'll make this quick then."

"No, that's not what I meant. I want to take as much time as we need today to understand everything."

"I'm afraid that would take a lot longer than today."

"Can you just give me some idea of what all this is about?"

Mitch opened what appeared to be a large aerial view photograph of Washington D.C.

"What do you see?" asked Mitch.

"A picture of D.C., I think."

"Right, that's what most people see, but there's more to it than that. Look closer."

Keith studied the picture but was unable to find anything out of the ordinary. "I'm not sure what I'm supposed to be looking for."

"Here's a map of D.C.," Mitch said, while unfolding the map on the table. "Would you say it looks similar to the photograph?"

Keith looked at the picture, then shrugged. "Sure."

"Using the pen I just gave you, I want you to mark some points for me. Okay?"

"Um, sure." Keith wasn't sure of the game Mitch was playing, but decided to play along anyway.

"Do you see Dupont Circle?"

Keith studied the map and said, "Yes. It's right there."

"Good, mark it." Keith did what he was told and

waited for further instruction.

"How about Logan Circle?"

"It's right here," he said, pointing at the map.

"Good now mark that one too." Keith continued doing what he was told, marking Scott Circle, Washington Circle, Mt. Vernon Square, and finally the White House. Keith wondered if he was playing a game of I spy. By the time Mitch took the pen from him, he was already feeling frustrated.

"These are all important places, are they not?"

"Yea, I guess so. What are you saying?"

"See what happens when I connect the dots that you just drew on this map?"

As Mitch connected the dots, a perfect star appeared on the map before him.

"Oh, that's cool. It forms a star."

"Oh, not just a star," Mitch said, continuing to connect the dots. "A pentagram."

CHAPTER 7

Jacinda felt especially excited as she pranced into the newsroom. She arrived early so she could talk to George before the meeting and let him know she was ready for an assignment. She smiled and greeted everyone as she moved across the newsroom, heading to George's office. The door to George's office was always closed, even though the walls were made of glass, and he never lowered the blinds. Jacinda never understood why he bothered to close his door, since everyone could see in anyway.

Jacinda knocked, to which George responded "Come on in. It's open."

Jacinda slowly opened the door and stuck her head in.

"Come in. Don't be shy. Have a seat," George

said to her with a smile.

Jacinda thought that he was being uncharacteristically nice. She took a seat in the black, wobbly chair facing George's desk. She tried to balance herself, to keep from rocking back and forth.

"What can I do for you, Jacinda?" George asked, never looking up from the papers in front of him.

"First of all, Nicholas says hello."

"Nicholas Kilmeade?"

"Yes, he said you two go way back."

"We do, indeed. He's a card, that one."

"Yes, I know. We watched the show last night. We were hoping to see Paula's story about the BARAchip."

"I scrapped her piece."

"Why? I thought it was wonderful. I mean--it's such an important story. It could mean so much to so many people."

"I agree; that's why I scrapped it. She didn't do it justice. I'm assigning the story to you," George announced, finally looking up to meet Jacinda's gaze.

"To me! Are you sure? I mean, how does Paula feel about this?"

"It's not Paula's decision, it's mine. Frankly, I don't care how Paula feels about it."

"It's just that I don't want to step on anyone's toes."

"Jacinda, this is a newsroom, not a high school. It's a place of business, not a popularity contest. If you plan to succeed here, or anywhere as a reporter, you need to start thinking less about other people and more about what's right for your career and the show." Jacinda didn't know how to respond. George's advice sounded a little cutthroat, but she understands it's the nature of the business. "I'll do it justice," Jacinda promised, as she got up to leave the office.

"I know you will," George assured her before adding, "I'll see you at the meeting."

Jacinda sat in the meeting room, waiting for the others to arrive. She was a little early, but had nothing else to do but sit and wait. She was brainstorming how she would handle the BARAchip story, when Paula Strong came breezing in. "Hello all," Paula said in a chipper voice. Paula was a fifteen-year veteran of the show. She looked like a typical anchorwoman. She was in her early fifties, and looked great for her age. She was tall, slim, and had chin-length bleached blonde hair. Her hair wasn't the only thing she bleached, which was evident when she smiled. She was attractive, but not what most would consider beautiful.

Paula chose the seat next to Jacinda and sat down. "Hi Jacinda, I haven't had a chance to introduce myself. I'm Paula Strong."

"Yes, I know. I've admired you since I was a teenager. I'm a big fan of your work."

"A teenager? Wow, I feel old."

"You're not old. You're fantastic."

"You're a doll. Tell that to George. Did you hear he scrapped my story? In the fifteen years that I've been here, that has never happened. Sure, I've had stories pushed back, or cut down in length, but never scrapped completely."

"I saw that piece while it was being edited. I thought it was fascinating."

"Thank you. You know your husband was a lot of help. He personally put me in touch with just about every source I used. I just can't believe the story was scrapped."

Jacinda didn't know how to tell her she had been assigned the story. She was squirming inside, searching for the best way to break the news. Paula being so nice made this even harder. She knew she had to do it. Everyone seemed to enter the room at the same time. Right as she was opening her mouth to tell Paula, George walked in. He took his seat at the head of the long, wooden table. He began popping his knuckles, one finger at a time and said, "Let's get to it," officially starting the meeting.

Jacinda had a sick feeling in the pit of her stomach. It's not that she wanted to tell Paula that she was given the story, but she didn't want Paula to find out from someone else. Paula had no intention of letting her story go without a fight. "So George," she said, taking control of the meeting. "Do you want me to rework the BARAchip story? What was it you didn't like? Do you want me to use different sources?"

"Yes, Paula, I want you to use different sources, with a different subject, for a different story. I'm taking you off the BARAchip story and giving it to Jacinda," George said with a coldness that made Jacinda wonder if he had a heart. She imagined him kicking puppies every chance he got. The man was ruthless. She wondered how her father-in-law could be friends with someone so insensitive.

Paula turned and glared at Jacinda. Jacinda gave Paula an apologetic look and shrank in her chair. *Great*, she thought, *I've already made an enemy. Did George really have to phrase it like that? Did he have to do it in front of everyone? How humiliating for Paula!*

Paula bolted from her chair to the door, as soon as

the meeting ended. Jacinda called after her, "Paula, wait!" Paula didn't acknowledge her, which made Jacinda feel even worse. She quickened her pace to catch up to the woman she's admired for so long. "Listen," she said, finally catching up to Paula, "I didn't even know he was going to do that until this morning. I really have no idea why. I thought your piece was wonderful. I'm as confused as you are." Paula didn't even look at her when she shot back. "I should have known George would play favorites when you showed up." The weight of Paula's words hit Jacinda square in the gut. She felt sick.

*****

Lucio stood facing members of his brotherhood inside the luciferian temple. "It has been confirmed, the woman of God will introduce The Mark to the United States. Her announcement will be next Thursday when Mercury transits the sun, as prophesized. Her announcement will be aired at 9:30 p.m. Eastern, which is halfway through the transit. Two hours later, upon completion of the transit, the child is to be sacrificed on the alter. The blood spilled from the child, born during the transit of Venus, will consecrate the earth for our Messiah Lord Maitreya.

*****

Keith sat staring at the pentagram before him. "That's crazy," he said.

"That's far from the last of it," Mitch assured him. "This is an inverted pentagram. It forms a goat head. The goat head is said to represent Lucifer. The three points that form the top of the goat head, or its horns, are Dupont Circle, Scott Circle, and Logan Circle. Each of these circles have six major streets coming into them from all angles."

"So then that's 666?"

"You catch on quickly, I thought I'd have to explain it to you."

"This is all very interesting, but I don't really see what it has to do with anything."

"This, Keith, is only one occult symbol in a town littered with them. You'll notice that in each triangle of the pentagram, there is a circle. Scott Circle and Washington Circle are easy enough to find. The point of the White House, the southernmost point in the pentagram, also has a circle. Its circle is formed by the ellipse to the south of the White House Lawn." Keith squinted his eyes and leaned closer to the map. "Each anchor point for the pentagram has a circle except Lincoln Square," Mitch said, while pointing to the map. "That was remedied by placing Thomas Circle at one of the points, which gave that triangle an all-seeing eye as well."

"All seeing eye?"

"What do you know about occult symbols, Keith?"

"Nothing really."

"You should study them. They're everywhere. I'll give you a crash course. In occult symbolism, the circle is sacred. It's often used to symbolize the sun or the Sun God. It's also used to represent the all-seeing eye. Of course, there are people who believe the Sun God and the all-seeing eye are one in the same. Everything I've studied suggests that Lucifer is the Sun God."

"So then you're saying that D.C. is satanic?"

"No, D.C. is just a place. A place can't be satanic, although the men who designed the city were said to be deeply into the occult," Mitch replied.

"So based on one thing that could quite possibly be a coincidence, you're saying that the people who designed our nation's capital were in a cult?"

"What do you know about the Illuminati?" Mitch asked, while looking pensively at Keith.

"Just what I've seen in the movies."

"Well, you can't believe everything you see in the movies. Some movies portray them as heroes. Throughout history, some of the most powerful men in the world have been involved in organizations that descended from the Illuminati. Their power extends to every continent. They have their hands in everything. In fact, some of our founding fathers were members of this group.

"George Washington was a member. He commissioned a man named Pierre L'Enfant, whom many believed was a member as well, to design the buildings and streets of D.C. The three commissioners hired to oversee the design had trouble with L'Enfant, so he was canned. Washington handed L'Enfant's plans over to another group member named Andrew Ellicott who completed L'Enfant's design.

"This group was said to study mysticism, and used many occult symbols that you still see everywhere." He pulled a dollar bill out of his pocket and handed it to Keith. "Look closely at the national seal, what do you see?"

"I see a pyramid with an eye."

"That's right. It's the all-seeing eye. It's the same all-seeing eye that is in each triangle of the D.C. pentagram. The national seal was designed by three men. All three men were said to be associated with the same group that descended from the Illuminati. You'll notice not only symbols, but also numeric patters on the seal. Since you aren't familiar with occultism, I will tell you that thirteen is the number value that many occultists assign to Satan. Now look at the seal." Keith looked intently. "Notice there are thirteen leaves in the olive branches. There are thirteen bars and stripes in the shield. Thirteen arrows. There are thirteen stars in the green crest, and thirteen granite stones in the pyramid.

"The pyramid is also significant. In Egypt, many believe that the pyramids were built to worship gods--Osiris specifically, which is how they referred to their sun god. We have another name for him; we call him Lucifer. Notice the pyramid is unfinished--there is no capstone. It's believed the pyramid was left unfinished, on the seal, to suggest there was still work to be completed. I believe that the work to be completed was written right there on the seal in Latin."

Keith looked at the seal. "Annuit Coeptis," Keith read aloud. "I don't know Latin, what does that mean."

"Some would argue that it means *he has prospered our undertakings*, but I, along with others translate it differently. It can also be translated into *announcing the birth of*."

"Announcing the birth of what?" Keith asked.

"That question is answered on the ribbon below the one that reads Annuit Coeptis."

"It says Novus Ordo Seclorum. What does that mean?"

"Roughly translated it means New World Order."

MARKED I

CHAPTER 8

Paula stormed into George's office, "What were you thinking? How could you take my story and give it to the new girl? I don't care if she *is* Senator Kilmeade's wife. She doesn't have the experience to be here in the first place, and you know it!"

"If you'll remember right, it was my story," George responded, in a tone so calm it sounded cruel. "I'm the one who suggested it to you. It was my idea. You didn't do the story justice, Paula. You didn't show the importance of the technology. You couldn't have garnered enough support."

"Do it justice?" Paula raged. "Garner enough support? What is this, a news program or an infomercial? Since when do we garner support for anything but ratings? We are a news program, George. We inform the public, we don't sell to them!"

"I've made up my mind," he said without looking up, "if you'll excuse me, I have calls to make."

Paula left his office looking defeated. Jacinda watched from her desk, but didn't dare approach Paula. She felt so torn. Jacinda was elated to have received such an important story. She knew she could do the story justice, not only for herself, but for all parents. On the other hand, she really did like Paula, and couldn't help feeling guilty. Of course, she had no choice. She was assigned a story and was obligated to complete it.

The phone on her desk rang in a tone that told her it was in-house. She answered, "This is Jacinda."

"Hi Jacinda--George. Come to my office, will ya?"

"Sure, George. Be right there." Jacinda hung up the phone, dreading the walk across the newsroom to his office. She didn't want to be seen entering so soon after Paula stormed out. She didn't want Paula to get the wrong idea. She wasn't just worried about Paula, but wondered how it would look to all the reporters. Like it or not, she knew she had to go.

She knocked on his door and turned the knob. "You wanted to see me?" she asked, choosing not to sit.

"Yeah, here you go," he said, handing her a bundle of papers. "In that stack, you'll find all the sources you need for your story. You'll also find all the information and statistics." Jacinda flipped through the stack of papers. She couldn't believe that he just handed her everything she would need to put the story together. Finding all of that stuff was supposed to be her job. After all, she was the reporter. She couldn't believe there was no legwork for her to do. It just didn't feel right. "Thanks," she said, turning to walk back to her desk.

She returned to her desk with the stack of papers. She took out a piece of paper to start making a rough outline of how she was going to format the story. First, she wrote down what she wanted to accomplish with this story. This story was unlike anything she's ever covered. Jacinda wasn't just reporting a story--she was selling an idea. She knew that as a journalist, it was unethical, but didn't care. This was too important for her to handle like a typical news story. She has to convince the country how important this technology is, and what it could mean for the future.

She flipped through her sources, but didn't see her

husband's name on the list. Of course, she knew using her own husband as a source would be a little unprofessional. She continued looking at the sources. One read: **Susie Dittmeir-Willis,** and the text next to it read: **mother of abducted child.**

She focused her eyes on the name Susie Dittmeir. *Dittmeir? As in George Dittmeir?* She could only imagine the name was a coincidence. In any case, Susie was the first source that Jacinda wanted to speak to. She wanted to build her whole story around the mother of an abducted child, to make it a human interest piece.

Jacinda picked up the phone, and dialed the number by Susie's name. "Hello," said a fragile voice at the other end of the phone.

"Hello, this is Jacinda Kilmeade. May I speak to Susie Dittmeir-Willis please?"

"Speaking."

"Hi Susie," Jacinda said with her mind reeling for a way to break the ice. "Dittmeir. That's a unique name. You know, my boss's name is Dittmeir-- George Dittmeir."

"Yes, I know," Susie said. "He's my father."

Jacinda skipped a breath. Her back and neck tensed. She gripped the phone so hard, she could have squeezed the life out of it, if it weren't inanimate. This means George's grandchild was abducted. Why had nobody mentioned this to her? Her own questions were cut short by her need to end the awkward silence. "Susie, as the mother of an abducted child, this story is extremely important to me. I'm so sorry for your loss, it's something I'm going through, too." Jacinda tried not to get into detail, in fear of becoming emotional. She wanted to be as professional as possible, and tried to emotionally remove herself from the situation, in an effort to keep her tears at bay. "I would love to get an on-camera interview with you, so that you can tell your story."

"I already gave an on-camera interview this morning. A man named Thomas Fields said he was taping the interview for you. He asked me questions, and I told my story. I told him all about how my son Ethan was taken while riding his bike outside. Even though it happened a year ago, I still find myself hoping that he'll come running through the door."

Jacinda closed her eyes, fighting back tears. In a weak voice, she responded, "I can imagine."

"I see the kids playing outside on their bikes, and each time, for a split second, I swear I see Ethan pedaling next to them. I'm sorry that I'm babbling, but I've been so emotional since doing the interview this morning." Susie began crying, and Jacinda felt tears running down her own face.

"Susie, I know how you feel. I do the same thing. I see my son Kyler everywhere. Even though there were no pictures taken of him, and he was taken only hours after he was born, I can still remember exactly what he looked like. I can see him in my mind as clearly as the day he was born."

"I know what you mean," Susie said. "I can close my eyes and see Ethan as clear as the day he was taken. I know he's a year older now, but I still picture him as the same ten year-old that I lost a year ago."

"Listen Susie, I don't know who Thomas Fields is, or why he taped the interview. I don't want to make you tell your story again, so I'll talk to your dad about how I can get my hands on the tape. Did my number pop up on your caller ID?"

"Yes, I've got it."

"Good, that's my cell number. If you ever want to talk, please don't hesitate to call me. Mothers like us need to stick together. I'm very excited about the BARAchip implant, and I only wish it could have been implemented earlier. I only wish it was around soon enough to save our boys. I know I can't wallow in what could have been, but I'm going to do everything I can to bring awareness to this implant. If one mother can be spared the grief that you and I have experienced, then it will have been worth it."

*****

Keith continued to study the map in front of him.
"So, who are the groups that descended from the
Illuminati? Have I heard of them?"

"Well," Mitch replied, "many believe that one such
group is the Freemasons."

Keith looked surprised. "So, I don't understand.
Are you saying the Masons worship Lucifer? I
mean; my uncle is a Mason. Does that mean my
Uncle Sam is a devil-worshiper?"

"Well, I don't know your Uncle Sam, so I couldn't
possibly say. My guess would be probably not. In
fact, most Mason's don't worship Lucifer at all. The
only requirement to become a Mason is the belief in
a supreme being. They simply worship the Great
Architect of the Universe as they call him. The
most recognizable Mason symbol is the set-square
and compass, which are both architect's tools.
Their very symbol represents The Great Architect.
People see their own god in the symbol."

"Well, if they use that symbol for God, what's the
problem?"

"Many believe that their god is not the Biblical God
that you and I worship, as Christians."

"How do you know?"

"I think Edward Ronayne, a former Mason said it

best when he said, 'An Architect is a man who furnishes plans for and superintends the erection of a building made from material already prepared; but God created of nothing the heavens and the earth, and all the host of them, and hence cannot be a mere Architect, and it would be a direct insult to call him such a nickname.'"

"You memorized that?"

"I think you'll be surprised at all the things I've memorized. I've gone over these texts so many times, they are embedded in my mind. Remind me to give you some reading material that I think you'll find very interesting."

"I'd love to read whatever you can give me," Keith said. He couldn't help but be a little fascinated.

Mitch continued. "I told you that numbers have significance in occultism. What I didn't tell you is directions, such as north, east, south, and west also have significance. You see, it's very complicated, and I can't possibly explain thousands of years of occult thoughts and theories in one afternoon, but I'll try to make it as simple as possible. In ancient occult mysticism, the north is a place of darkness. Do you know why?"

"No, should I?"

"Probably not, but in Isaiah 14:13 it states, *'But you said in your heart, 'I will ascend to heaven; I will*

*raise my throne above the stars of God, And I will
sit on the mount of assembly In the recesses of the
North.'*

"If you'll recall, the 'I' in that instance is Lucifer, the
fallen angel. He wishes to take God's place in the
north, but until then, the north remains a place of
darkness for those who worship Lucifer.

"One of the greatest Masonic writers was named
Albert Pike. In his book Morals and Dogma, he
wrote, *'To all Masons, the north has immediately
been the place of darkness, and of the great lights
of the Lodge, none is in the north.'*

"Each Masonic lodge is said to have a worshipful
master. This worshipful master always sits in the
east. The east is also said to be where Lucifer
resides. In ancient mysticism, the east is the
source of light and knowledge.

"Look at the Washington Monument over there. Do
you see it?" Mitch asked, while pointing to the large
memorial.

"Of course. You can't miss it," Keith responded.

"George Washington was a Mason. I'll give you
some facts about the monument that you might not
have known. An obelisk has an Egyptian origin.
Like the pyramids, it's said the obelisk was built to
worship the Sun God. In fact, many believe that
the very presence of the Sun God actually resides
in an obelisk. You'll remember than many believe

Lucifer to be the Sun God. Look closely at the
National Monument. Each side of the base
measures 666 inches and its height is 6,666
inches.

"There are eight windows atop the monument, two
facing each direction. Of the eight windows, six are
the same size. The two eastern-facing windows
are larger than the others. You'll remember the
east is not only where the worshipful master of the
Masons sits, but also where many who study
mysticism believe Lucifer resides. Now it's possible
that the Masons are so far removed from the
Illuminati in this day and age, that all symbols and
traditions are simply a leftover product of days past.
It's not the Masons that are the threat--just Masons
that are tied to the Illuminati. However, there are
members of the Illuminati who are not Masons at
all."

*****

Lyla sat rocking the child, inside the lavish
Manhattan apartment loaned to her during her time
as the baby's keeper. Despite the beauty and
ornate decor, she felt it was more of a prison than a
home. The expensive abstract art gracing the walls
might be cherished by most, but she is unable to
see beauty in anything these days. Her legs stuck
to the leather rocking chair as she stood to deliver
the sleeping toddler to his bed. She hated the way
the sticky leather made her exposed skin sweat
when she sat too long in one place.

She made her way to the child's bed, gently laying him down in an effort to not wake him. She covered his little body with his favorite blanket and sat next to him on the bed. She ran her fingers through the soft brown curls on his head and watched as the corners of his delicate mouth turned upwards. She wondered what wonderful dream was making him smile. "Continue to dream sweet, my angel," she said, as she kissed his forehead, before standing to leave the room.

She closed the door behind her, and leaned the weight of her body against it. Tears welled up in her eyes and began streaming down her face. Her body slid down the door onto the floor, where she buried her face in her trembling hands. In her twenty-one years of life, she has never felt such love for anything or anyone. Being chosen as the child's guardian was the proudest day of her painful, lonely life. She never expected to develop the feelings that now consumed her. She'd come to think of the child as her own, and her love for him has awakened feelings she never knew existed. She simply can't imagine that love will come to an end when the young boy they simply call, *child* is sacrificed at the altar. She's all too aware that when the child is sacrificed, she too will die. It may not be a physical death, but her heart and soul will cease to exist.

She wiped her face and tried to pull herself together before her guard could sense anything was out of the ordinary. With the guards that surrounded her and the child, she tried not to show emotion. She has come to believe that the only room not being monitored is her bathroom. She has felt like a prisoner since the day she was tasked with caring for the child. With little to no contact with the outside world, and at least one guard outside the apartment at all times, she's been given no room to escape.

*****

Jacinda entered George's office and took a seat. She was looking for the best way to approach George about what must be a painful subject for him. "I just talked to your daughter, Susie," she said. "I had no idea that your grandson was abducted. I'm so sorry." George looked at her for a moment, and then nodded his head, acknowledging what was said. "Now I understand that this story means as much to you as it does to me."

"It means a lot to a lot of people, Jacinda."

"I'm a little confused. Susie said a man named Thomas Fields interviewed her this morning. I was wondering if you knew anything about that."

George nodded and responded, "That's actually why I called you in here. I just got off the phone with Thomas, and he's on his way up here. I have editing room number three reserved for the both of you in thirty minutes." Jacinda couldn't imagine why they would need an editing room, unless it was so they could use one of the monitors to view Susie's interview. "Alright, well I have a few more calls to make regarding the story, so I better get back to work," she said as she stood up to leave.

Jacinda spent the next thirty minutes researching RFID and GPS technology on the internet. She couldn't believe how much a part of everyday life both technologies had become. She looked down at her watch, and realized she was supposed to have met Thomas Fields in the editing room five minutes ago. Time always seemed to pass by so quickly when she was on the internet. She sprang up and rushed across the newsroom, walked down a narrow hall, and turned the corner. She saw a man in his early thirties standing by editing room three.

The first thing she noticed was his height. Standing about 6'6", he was very handsome with dark features. He was the epitome of tall, dark, and handsome. He was holding a small, black leather bag, which she assumed was a man purse. "Are you Thomas?" Jacinda asked, extending her hand to greet him.

"Yes," the man answered in a thick Italian accent, "You are Jacinda, I presume?" His name didn't fit him, she thought. She would expect his name to be far more exotic.

"Yes. Hey, sorry I'm late. I can't wait to see the interview you taped. Let's go inside." She led him into the editing room. Trailing close behind her, he closed the door. Her stomach knotted when she heard the door click shut. Ashamed by her discomfort, she forced an awkward smile. "Why don't we keep that door open, it gets pretty stuffy in here." Without acknowledging her request he sat his bag on the table and pulled out a tape and some papers.

"Everything is on the tape, all it lacks are your voiceovers and your standup. Here is your script," he said, as he handed her the papers.

Jacinda was speechless. *Who does this man think he is? This is MY story! He can't just come in here and hand me a complete script.* "If you don't mind, I'd kind of like to put the story together myself," she said, handing the papers back to him.

"Not possible," he replied, in a slow steady voice, as he made his way to the chair in front of the editing bay. "We will tape your voiceovers now and shoot your standup immediately. Wardrobe, hair, and makeup have already been alerted.

"Wait just one minute," Jacinda said in a tone that bordered on yelling. "This is crazy, I'm going to go talk to George."

"Talk to him if you must. I've already spoken with him, and these are his wishes," the tall handsome man assured her.

"I'll be right back. I want to talk to him myself," Jacinda said, as she flung the door open just in time to see George walking down the hall. "George, Mr. Fields said the story has already been put together for me," Jacinda said in a loud voice that begged him to assure her she had been misinformed. George put his finger up to his lips, indicating she needed to lower her voice. He walked into the editing room and closed the door. Jacinda stared at him, in utter confusion.

"Jacinda, you know how important this story is to both of us. It's not that I don't trust your reporting abilities, it's just that this story needs to be presented in a way that will show the country how essential the BARAchip truly is."

Jacinda felt dissatisfied by George's explanation. "George, I feel like I'm being used less like a reporter, and more like a spokesperson. All I'm being asked to contribute to the story is my voice; it just doesn't feel right."

"You're contributing far more than just your voice, Jacinda, you're contributing your story."

"My story?"

"Yes, thanks to marrying Senator Kilmeade, you have become America's sweetheart. People love you, and they know the tragedy you've endured. Coming from you, this story will touch people in a way they won't be able to ignore. Everyone will want their children implanted with BARAchip. How could they not? What loving parent wouldn't want to protect their children with an implant the size of a pinhead. The implants are small, painless, and invaluable. Don't you want to be a part of something that will end up saving hundreds of thousands of children a year?"

Jacinda couldn't argue with that. She wanted to, but she simply couldn't. Maybe she was letting her ego get in the way of her better judgment. Maybe, acting as a spokesperson instead of a reporter was something she could do just this once. She turned to Thomas. "Can you pass me the script?"

"Wonderful, Jacinda. I knew you'd see it my way. Let's make a difference," George said as he placed his hand on her shoulder.

Jacinda read the script carefully. It was masterfully written. "This looks great," she told them. "Can I see the tape you put together?"

Thomas inserted the tape and said, "I think you'll be pleased."

Jacinda and the two men watched the tape. The first thing Jacinda noticed was that Susie's interview wasn't included. "Why didn't you use any of the interview you taped this morning?" she asked Thomas.

"It wasn't right for the piece, I thought the other

interview I included was much stronger."

Jacinda couldn't argue since she hadn't seen Susie's interview. "So Thomas, are you a reporter? Do you work here at the show? I've never seen you before."

George didn't give him a chance to respond, and answered the question for him. "He freelances,." George said in a tone that told Jacinda the topic was closed. He then looked at Thomas and said, "I feel confident you can take it from here. I'll be in my office if you need me." He turned to Jacinda, "Jacinda, I probably don't even have to tell you this, but I think it would be best if you don't mention how this story was handled to anyone else. Nobody here has gone through the pain of losing a child or grandchild. I'm afraid they wouldn't understand."

"Of course I won't," Jacinda assured him. She wanted to keep the handling of this story a secret as much as anyone. She already knew that nobody thought she was experienced enough to be reporting on a national level. She sure didn't want to prove them right by admitting her story had been written by someone else.

CHAPTER 9

Keith was riveted by everything Mitch was saying. He wasn't fully able to wrap his brain around all of Mitch's allegations, but he was fascinated. Keith loved puzzles and mysteries. He loved conspiracy theories and larger-than-life claims. He couldn't get enough. He couldn't wait to research the other occult symbols and structures in D.C. He didn't know what he intended to do with the information, but he wanted to know everything.

"Mitch, if you don't mind me asking, what were the emails to Rob Livingston about? What were you saying about saving souls? What was with the picture you sent with Senator Kilmeade, and some other guys wearing hooded robes? How did you even get that picture?"

Mitch smiled. "Wow, that's a lot of questions, but I'll start with what the picture is all about. Have you ever heard of Rhapsody Grove?"

"I don't think so, what is it?"

"Rhapsody Grove is a secluded campground in northern California. When I tell you what goes on there, you won't believe me. Nobody believed what happened there until it was infiltrated by a young reporter. He got the whole thing on tape. Watch that tape on the internet when you get home, you'll be floored. Anyhow, I'm getting ahead of myself. Some of the most rich and powerful men in the world meet at Rhapsody Grove every July—this week to be exact. The guest list is very exclusive, and if you aren't on it, you can't get anywhere near the action. The compound is heavily guarded by law enforcement and the Secret Service. It's a boy's club--no women allowed. It's a place for the powerful elite to get together, use drugs and alcohol, and be sexually immoral."

"Wait, I thought you said there were no women allowed."

"There aren't," Mitch said, with a knowing wink. "They bring in male prostitutes and engage in activities they may never think of doing at home. Anything goes in Rhapsody Grove. The scary thing is that this is where some of the world's biggest plans are hatched. It's where some of the most important political decisions are made. Some of the world's most important decisions are made in the den of the devil."

"What do you mean 'the den of the devil?'"

"This is the part nobody would have believed without the video. They participate in many occult rituals and ceremonies, but the biggest is the cremation of care ceremony. They burn the effigy of a child as a sacrifice to the demon Molech. In fact, on the tape you can hear the men scream 'Burn him again; give him what he deserves.' All of this is done in front of a large stone owl, which represents Molech. The demon Molech is commonly referred to as the Owl God. If you'll remember right, God forbade the sacrifice of children to Molech in the Bible. In *Leviticus 18:21 it states:* 'And thou shalt not let any of thy seed pass through the fire to Molech, neither shalt thou profane the name of thy God: I am the Lord'.

"Leviticus 20:2 states, *'Again, thou shalt say to the children of Israel, Whosoever he be of the children of Israel, or of the strangers that sojourn in Israel, that giveth any of his seed unto Molech; he shall surely be put to death; the people of the land shall stone him with stones'.*

"You have lawmakers, presidents, and heads of state participating in demon worship and mock sacrifices. I've heard rumors that real sacrifices occur there on occasion, but I never saw one myself."

"Wait," Keith said excitably. "You were there?"

"Who do you think took the picture of Mr. Livingston?"

Keith's eyes widened. "Even if everything you say is true, I don't see how that picture you sent Livingston would convince him to come forward with information. Aside from the hooded robe, it seems like a pretty harmless picture."

"That photograph isn't the picture he should be worried about. That photograph is merely a reminder of the other photographs that exists for blackmail purposes."

"So you're blackmailing him?"

"I wasn't referring to myself; I was talking about the Illuminati Brotherhood. You see, Rhapsody Grove is the devil's den. You couldn't possibly imagine the debauchery that goes on there, nor would you want to. Power and control is what those men seek. They dream of unlimited power and will spare nothing to achieve it, not even their souls. But you see, in order to maintain power, The Brotherhood must control their members through fear."

"Fear of what?"

"Well, you might think once you've sold your soul, there is nothing left to fear. But these men are ruled by pride and greed. They fear damaging their reputations. They fear losing their positions and wealth. If for some reason, one of these men decides to step out of line, The Brotherhood has ways of making them fall back in place. Most of the time, they are able to avoid such heavy-handed methods as torture or death, using simple blackmail techniques.

"You see, during their time at Rhapsody Grove, most men are told that there is photographic proof of their debauchery. Drugs and alcohol flow freely throughout the campground, and inhibitions tend to be checked at the door. Men are encouraged to do things they would never have dreamed of doing outside of Rhapsody Grove. Unfortunately for them, more than just jaded memories exist of their time there. The Brotherhood simply adds the photographs to files that could destroy these men if they choose to go against them. Therefore, these men become loyal servants of The Brotherhood, thereby becoming loyal servants to the devil himself."

"I just can't believe something like this goes on and nobody knows about it."

"Oh, people know about it. Once the cremation of care ceremony was caught on tape and broadcast around the world; however, most of the media whitewashed it. Anyone who was outraged became labeled a Christian fanatic. It doesn't take a fanatic to be outraged, the entire display makes the truth very clear."

"What's the truth?"

"The truth is that some of the biggest decisions affecting our country, and the world, are made at the same compound where they are making sacrifices, be them mock or real, to a demon. What does this tell you about the evil nature of their plans? Why then, would anyone believe that these plans are anything but wicked? The New World Order is nothing new; it's not just an internet conspiracy. It's something that our leaders and government have been preparing us for. It has been in the works since this nation was founded. Our leaders have been laying the groundwork for years, and we just haven't been paying attention. The signs are everywhere--literally. Look at our dollar bills. Not only do they have the pyramid, the all-seeing eye, and the phrase 'New World Order in Latin, but if you look closely with a magnifying glass you'll see the demon Molech sitting right there on the top right corner of the dollar bill," Mitch said. He pointed to the area on the dollar bill where Molech was hidden.

*****

Jacinda was glad to be finished recording her voice-over and standup for the BARAchip story. Even though she was trying to convince herself it was the right thing to do, there was something about it that made her extremely uncomfortable. She learned a lot about the BARAchip while reading her voice-overs. She learned that the implants could be placed in the right hand or forehead, depending on where the parent chooses. She didn't know why she felt uneasy, but she most definitely did. She walked to her desk, closed her eyes, and began to silently pray. She may have felt mad at God, but she desperately needed to feel close to Him. She prayed for guidance. She prayed for strength. Most of all, she prayed for Kyler.

Her heart ached for Kyler, and she needed to talk to someone who could relate. She needed to feel like she wasn't the only person in the world who was going through this kind of grief, and wanted to ask others how they were coping. She wanted to call Susie. She wanted to ask Susie if she had found anything to ease the pain. She needed to share her emotions, but she wanted it to be with someone who would truly understand. *Well, this might get me in trouble, but here I go*, she thought to herself as she picked up the phone. Susie answered on the third ring.

"Hello."

"Hi, Susie. It's Jacinda Kilmeade."

"Oh hello, Mrs. Kilmeade. How are you?"

"I'm doing well Susie, thank you. And please—call me Jacinda."

There was an awkward pause, before Jacinda broke the silence; "I was wondering if you wanted to meet for a late lunch today. I know it's short notice, but I wanted to talk to you about the BARAchip and hear your feelings on the topic. Your dad is sold on the chip, but I wanted to get another mother's perspective. Plus, it might be nice to, you know, just talk."

Susie thought for a moment and then responded, "Sure, I guess that would be okay. Where do you want to meet? Are you at the office?"

"Yes. Are you anywhere close?"

"As a matter of fact, I am. I'm right up the road; I just left a meeting. You called at a great time. How about I pick you up in about an hour? I have a few stops to make, but I'll make them quick."

"Great, I'll be standing outside the building by the double glass doors. So, about three? How will I recognize you?"

"Don't you worry about that, I'll recognize you. You're only one of the most recognizable women in the country." Jacinda was flattered, but a little embarrassed by her comment. "Great. I'll see you soon," she said, before disconnecting the call. She couldn't help but feel a little excited about the lunch. She hadn't found a close friend since moving to town. She missed going to lunch with the girls to chitchat about their lives. She wondered if she was a bit too eager.

After an hour on the internet, Jacinda logged off her computer and headed downstairs. She wasn't outside three minutes before a grey SUV pulled up. A woman in her mid-thirties sat in the driver's seat. She was smiling and waving at Jacinda. She looked very professional, but Jacinda didn't care for her bright red lipstick. Her red hair was tied a little too tightly atop her head, making her eyebrows look like they were being pulled upwards. Jacinda got into the SUV and immediately started talking. "It's so nice to meet you. I'm so glad you agreed to meet me for lunch."

"Oh, the pleasure's all mine," Susie responded. "I know just where we should go eat. There's a swanky new café a few blocks away. Does that sound okay?"

"Sounds great," Jacinda said. "I'm starving."

The women walked into the café and made their way to a corner table. Jacinda fumbled with the menu before saying, "Any suggestions?"

"I haven't eaten here, but I hear everything is superb," Susie assured her. A tall, thin waiter approached the table. "Well well, Mrs. Jacinda Kilmeade—it must be my lucky day."

Jacinda's face blushed as it always did when she was recognized.

"Can I tell you about our specials?"

"No need," Jacinda said, as she smiled politely. "I think we know what we want," she said, while trying to read Susie's face for confirmation

"Yes," Susie agreed, "I think we're ready." Both women ordered their food and began talking.

"So, how much do you know about the BARAchip?" Jacinda asked, hoping it wasn't too soon to dive into the subject.

"I know enough to know that it's the answer to

every parent's prayers. It's the real deal, Cinda, and let me tell you something else—it's easy. In fact, nothing has ever been easier, so why the heck not?"

No one had called her *Cinda* since college. Maybe she would find a friend in this town, after all.

The waiter returned and placed the food on the table. He looked at Jacinda and gave her a shy little smile. Upon seeing this, Susie snapped at him. "Okay, Romeo—switch the food. I didn't order the cheese pasta. And what is a vegetarian going to do with my beef filled ravioli?"

After he switched the plates, she apologized for the incompetence of the waiter, before biting into her fork-full of food. Jacinda was embarrassed for the waiter. The whole scene made her uncomfortable. She felt bad for him, and upon further thinking, what bothered her more was how Susie knew she was a vegetarian. She didn't remember telling Susie she didn't eat meat. In fact, it was something very few people knew. Susie, however, didn't skip a beat. Her painted smile was back in full force, as she was talking about all the wonderful things the BARAchip could accomplish. But something didn't feel right to Jacinda. Something felt forced.

Susie was clearly picking up on Jacinda's discomfort. She knew how her aggression tended to put people off. She decided to put Jacinda at ease. "Look Cinda—I *can* call you Cinda, right?"

"Oh, of course. It's just been so long since anyone has called me that."

"Well, they should. Cinda fits you beautifully. Anyway, I've just had the most horrible day, and it's just....it's just..." Susie began to dab at the corner of her eyes with her napkin. "It's just that he's all I've thought about today."

Jacinda leaned in and touched her hand. "You mean your son, Ethan?"

"Yes, of course. Well, he's all I think about most days, but today has been harder than usual for some reason. Well, not just any reason--it's his eleventh birthday today, and can you believe I actually thought I heard him last night?"

"You heard him? Where?"

"I was waking up from a dream and I could have sworn I heard him come through the front door saying, 'I'm home mom.'"

Jacinda began fighting back her own tears. "I know how you feel. Sometimes I wake up and hear Kyler crying. Sometimes I wake up and could swear he is lying right beside me."

"Well, my husband thinks I'm absolutely insane. He says things like 'Suze, it's time you start popping your anti-crazy pills.'"

"How is your husband handling this? Maybe it's all

just too much for him."

"Oh Jonathan, he's from the old school of grin and bear it. Life is fabulous. Blah, blah, blah. Plus, he has two kids from a previous marriage, so he spends a lot of time focusing on them."

Jacinda realized that beneath her hardened, feisty exterior, Susie must be one of the loneliest women in the world. "I'm always here if you need to talk, Susie, and I mean that. Twenty-four hours a day, seven days a week; I'm here for you."

The two sat in silence for what seemed like an eternity. Neither one had much of an appetite, but Jacinda felt comforted to have a friend who could sympathize with what she was going through. With one gesture from Susie, the waiter brought the check within seconds. Susie removed a credit card from her wallet and said, "This is my treat Jacinda. I hope this is the first of many lunches together."

*****

Jacinda hugged her new friend, before stepping out of the SUV in front of the news station. Susie would have happily dropped her off at home, but Jacinda didn't want to put her out. Jacinda decided to call it a day. With her story already completed and the emotions that surfaced during lunch, she decided there wasn't much use in returning to the office. She was emotionally exhausted, and it was taking a toll on her physically. She felt the D.C.

heat searing her skin, while her ankles wobbled over her high heels. She simply didn't have the endurance to deal with the subway today. She raised her delicate hand to hail a taxi. Despite her new friend, she felt lonely. She missed her baby more today than she did yesterday, and she never thought that was possible. Each day, when she should be missing him less, she missed him more. She was growing uncharacteristically irritated that a taxi had yet to stop for her. Her feet throbbed, and her neck was racked with tension. She sat her briefcase on the pavement, while holding up her hand to signal a taxi. She rolled her head from one shoulder to the other, trying to release some of the tension, fearing it would turn into a migraine. She rolled her shoulders backwards and leaned her head forward, kneading her neck with her fingers. When a taxi finally rolled to a stop, she reached down to grab her briefcase. It had fallen on its side, and papers were scattering in the wind. This was what finally moved her to tears. Tears rolled down her cheeks, and dripped off her chin. She swallowed hard, but the saltiness of her tears stung her already parched throat. She took a deep breath, bent down, and began collecting the flyaway papers. She shoved them into her briefcase with no regard for neatness.

After feeling sure she had collected every last paper, she stepped off the curb to enter the cab. Jacinda looked back to see a toddler waving a piece of paper. The smiling toddler had chubby, marker-stained hands. He handed the paper to Jacinda, and proudly stated, "I helpud, I helpud." Without even looking at Jacinda, a young woman scooped the toddler into her arms, sprinkled kisses on his cherubic cheeks, and said "Mommy's helper got a little too close to the street. You scared mommy!" The toddler didn't seem to notice he was being reprimanded, and happily giggled. Jacinda smiled at the mother and child, turned, and fell into the waiting taxi.

CHAPTER 10

Lyla placed a picnic basket on a blanket, under the watchful eye of her guardian. He was one of many guardians assigned to her and the child. Rarely did more than one accompany the two of them on outings, but Lyla would have preferred privacy to security. Privacy has been in short supply, since she was an infant. Born to a father who was active in the Illuminati, she was always being watched. As far back as she could remember, she'd always security assigned to her for protection. Although her father hired men to protect her from his enemies, he wouldn't allow them to protect her from himself. As is the case with many abused children, she retreated into herself. She was raised to believe that Lucifer would be the savior of mankind, but questioned those beliefs. Her questions caused guilt, and eventually she turned her thoughts from religion altogether.

She was handpicked by Lucio to be the chosen child's maidservant. Being selected for such an important position made her feel valued for the first time in her life. While she knew her father's position as Lucio's assistant probably influenced his decision, she still felt important. She had no intention of falling in love with the child, but two years of mothering the precious baby left her no choice. She had never been so sure of anything in her life.

She had to save him.

*****

Keith strained his eyes to see the tiny owl on the top, right corner of the dollar bill. "It's hard to see without a magnifying glass," Mitch said. "But it's there, nestled next to the 1. The Illuminati speak in symbols, and you'll see evidence of that all over this city."

"I see it!" Keith said, excitedly. "I mean, it's tiny, but I see it. That's cool." He held the dollar bill up to the sun. "What else is hidden on here?" His mind was reeling. While he was still confused as to how this had any relevance to, well, anything, he was fascinated nonetheless.

"I'm not proud of the things I've done Keith, but I've asked the Lord for forgiveness. My relationship with the Lord didn't even start until I met my Linda, years after I got involved with The Brotherhood. When I met Linda, I knew it was love. I got tongue-tied, butterflies—the whole nine. There wasn't anything I wouldn't do for her. I initially visited her church, just to please her. She went every Sunday, and her Faith never failed to amaze me. She had Faith like nobody I've ever known. She led her life by example, and always practiced what she preached. Don't get me wrong, Keith. She wasn't perfect—none of us are. She wasn't perfect, but she was amazing. She didn't force my relationship with Christ, but she definitely led me to Him. Of course, I believe Christ led me to her, so you could go back and forth with the chicken or the egg argument.

"The bottom line is there wasn't room for both Christ and The Brotherhood in my life. It was one or the other, and I would pick my glorious Savior again and again. I've never regretted choosing to walk with Christ over The Brotherhood, but it did change my life significantly. You see, I wasn't a card-carrying member of the Illuminati. Few people are. I was simply one of their pawns. They kept me in line with money and fear. I grew dependent on the financial perks for voting to pass their legislation. I grew greedy for the lifestyle they afforded me. I even tried to convince myself that it was for some greater good. that somehow I was being a patriot by letting their grand design decide my votes. After all, they let it be known that the very founding fathers of our country were part of The Brotherhood. How could I be patriotic if I *didn't* vote with them?

"Did you know that the Illuminati means 'the illuminated ones'? Illuminated. My world was never so dark as when I was consorting with the illuminated ones. Darkness, I tell you. Thankfully, Christ opened my eyes. He gave me hope. I changed my ways. Linda prayed with me, and I've never cried so hard in my life. I wasn't crying because I was sad. It was pure emotional release. I hate to sound cliché', but I felt as if this whole wicked world was being lifted from my shoulders. I was a changed man, and I wanted everyone to feel that sense of peace that I never knew existed before I was saved. When she was killed…"

"Killed?" Keith repeated, obviously shocked.

"Yes, killed," Mitch replied, as he sank deeper into his chair, and bowed his head. "What better way to punish a member they felt had betrayed them? Of course, I could never prove they had anything to do with her death, but I know."

117

"That's terrible."

Mitch nodded. "Linda told me the Lord forgave me for all of my sins, but there was one thing I couldn't forgive myself for, and that was Livingston."

"Livingston?"

"Yes, he was just a young reporter when I brought him in. Very few reporters are allowed into Rhapsody Grove, but you can see how reporters have their place in the plan. The Brotherhood needs tentacles in all major professions, but the media really shapes public opinion. They need their pawns in the media as badly as they do in government. The American public doesn't like to go against the norm, which is why The Brotherhood has to slowly but surely introduce their plan into the culture. What better way to do that than through the media?

"Livingston was sharp. He was an up-and-coming reporter. I saw that hunger in his eyes; he would do anything to succeed. His beat was Capitol Hill, and I was one of his favorite sources. I was one of his favorite sources because I was always happy to talk to him. He was delighted when I invited him to Rhapsody Grove. I could tell in his eyes that he really thought he had *made it*. I really thought I had his number, but I was wrong about him."

Keith was confused. "You were? How?"

"Well, he got caught up in the events at Rhapsody

Grove, but as soon as we came back to D.C., he changed. You could tell that he was consumed with regret, and he distanced himself from me. Of course, he enjoyed the fast track his career took by having all the right sources, and all the right connections, but I think he struggled a lot with his conscience. By the time I found Christ, Livingston was already working for *Your Nation Now,* and was far removed from his Capitol Hill beat. He had no real reason to have direct dealings with me, and I think he preferred it that way.

"Of course, once I found Christ I knew I needed to talk to him. I needed to somehow help him break free from The Brotherhood. At first, he was receptive to me. In fact, he told me a lot of things that I didn't know. His research led him to what he believed were the true plans of The Brotherhood. He was one of the reporters tasked with breaking stories that would prepare the public for end times and the Mark of the Beast. Of course, they didn't tell him that directly, but he was sharp. Like any good journalist, he did his research. He saw how his stories were shaping public opinion, and how influential the mainstream media had become. He seemed relieved that he could finally talk to someone about his fears and his regrets. He even agreed to help bring the conspiracy to the public's attention, but I could tell he was having second thoughts. I could tell he was scared, and eventually he cut contact with me all together."

Mitch looked down at his watch. "We've been here hours longer than I anticipated. I need to get going, but we'll do this again. I couldn't possibly expect you to process everything there is to know during one meeting."

*****

Jacinda walked up to her front door, happy to be home a little early. She was emotionally exhausted and the heat wasn't helping her pending migraine. She dropped her briefcase in the entryway, and tossed her key on the coffee table. She kicked off her ridiculously priced shoes and fell into the sofa, once again cursing herself for not wearing tennis shoes. She knew she should take an aspirin, but felt too tired to walk to the medicine cabinet.

She missed Kyler. She missed him with her whole heart. She wondered if he was being cared for. She worried that he was hungry, sick, or in pain. She wondered if he had parents who loved him, or if he was being neglected. Her mind raced as she wondered about a million things, but she never wondered if he was alive. She knew he was alive; she felt it in her entire being.

A ringing phone distracted her from her thoughts. She looked down at the screen, hoping it would be Gregory. Glancing at the caller ID, she saw it was Jill. While it wasn't Gregory, Jill was just about the next best thing. As much as she loved Jill, she didn't feel like talking to anybody. Jacinda met Jill at church camp when she was ten years old, and the two had remained friends ever since. They were like sisters, but life pulled them in separate directions. After college, Jill married a pastor and moved to California, while Jacinda put most of her energy into her marriage and career. Jill was always by her side during the dark days following Kyler's abduction and her husband's tragic death.. Jacinda even lived with Jill and her husband Rick for a short time after the tragedies. She usually called Jill for inspiration or comfort, but had been too busy since moving to D.C.

Feeling guilty about not answering the phone, Jacinda returned her call. Jill picked up on the first ring and said, "I was just leaving you a message, I figured it'd be days before you got back to me."

"Come on, am I really that bad?" Jacinda asked, feeling a little guilty.

"Yes, my dear. You are."

"Sorry, things have just been so busy around here."

"Well that's what I called to talk about. Tell me everything! How's the new job? How's Gregory? How is it to not be able to go to dinner with your husband without getting your picture taken by the paparazzi? You know, I was at the supermarket just today and saw your picture on Live magazine with the caption *America's New Jackie O*! Can you believe it, Jacinda?! They are comparing you to

Jackie O! All you're missing are the big sunglasses and fabulous hats. We must go shopping for hats. Hats to match every outfit. Okay, I'm rambling—tell me everything."

"Well, D.C. is good. The job is good and…" Jacinda suddenly remembered BARAchip and wanted to get Jill's take on the technology. Jacinda spilled everything she knew about BARAchip, and how missing children would become a thing of the past. Becoming so overwhelmed by her own confused feelings, she stumbled on her words. "I'll be introducing it on the show, but—I don't know. Something about it… Something just doesn't feel right. I know I should be overjoyed, but…"

Jacinda waited for Jill to respond, but she was met with only silence. "Jill?"

"Yes, hon. I'm still here. I'm just thinking. Have you noticed the similarities between this BARAchip you're talking about and the Mark of the Beast?"

"Well, at first the thought did cross my mind, but I was just being paranoid. I mean, I was being paranoid, right?"

Jill didn't seem to register Jacinda's last question. She had too many questions of her own. "Who's marketing this chip? Is it being marketed for the sole purpose of locating children? Will every parent be forced to allow their baby to get the chip, or will it be the parents' choice?"

Jacinda wanted to respond, but she really didn't know the answers. She was so excited by the idea, that she didn't ask too many questions. "To be honest, I don't know a lot of the details."

"Well, Jacinda, you'll find in life that the devil is in the details."

"That's what they say, but what does that even mean? Do you really know what that figure of speech means, or is it just a snazzy little saying?"

Jill giggled at the turn in the conversation. "Snazzy, Jacinda. Really? Snazzy? Snazzy will be the fabulous hat I'm going to send you for your Jackie O, 2.0 wardrobe. The next Jackie O! How great is that?"

*****

Lyla snuggled up to the child, while reading him his favorite story. She twirled his curls with her finger and decided baby shampoo might be the most Intoxicating scent in the world. He giggled and grasped the pages of the book with his chubby little hands, making it difficult for her to turn the pages. Rather than work against him, she simply read the same page over and over. He didn't seem to mind every time the same bear broke the same bed on the same page. He giggled as though it was the first time he'd heard it.

She had been instructed not to give the child a name. Lucio had arranged this as a way for Lyla to avoid attachment. Lucio underestimated human nature if he thought you couldn't apply love to something you hadn't named. In addition to not naming the child, she was told not to give the child a name by which to call her. That too was a ridiculous request, she decided. And as the experiment continued, the child began addressing Lyla simply as "Me." "Come to me," she'd say. "Bring Bumbly Bear to me," she'd tell him. She soon learned that a child can say, "me" with the same love and adoration as one can say "mommy."

She kissed his tiny nose and tucked him into his bed. His heavy eyes shut and he draped his tiny arm over his Bumbly Bear. "G'nite little one," she whispered as she closed his door. As she walked to her bedroom, she grabbed her purse from the hall table. She pulled out what cash she had in her wallet and stuck it in an old coat pocket in the back of her closet. The deposits she made into the coat pocket were small, but they added up. She now felt she had enough to throw her plan into action. She knew her plan would almost definitely get her killed, but she had to try. If she didn't make a move soon, the child she's grown to love would be sacrificed on the altar before the week's end.

*****

Keith's alarm clock sounded at 5 a.m.. He set his clock radio because he'd left his phone on the table after his meeting with Mitch. Thankfully, Mitch sent him an email saying he picked the phone up, and would return it when they met today. He was surprised to get an email from Mitch, knowing how paranoid he was about electronic communication. Despite his distaste for email, Keith slipped Mitch his address during their casual goodbye, the night before. Keith was used to losing his phone, but it didn't irritate him any less. His sleep was restless, because he couldn't stop his mind from racing. Mitch had given him so much information, but in the end, he was unsure of how it would all play out. His mind was racing. *Even if I believe everything Mitch said, why would The Brotherhood permit Mitch to live and share his knowledge? Wouldn't they have whacked him or something? Sure most people would just write him off as crazy or disgruntled, but what if proof does exist, and what if Livingston has it?* His mind reeled with possibilities. He had far more questions than answers, but that was the nature of journalism. His grogginess was erased with a sudden jolt of excitement. He wasn't sure how he'd use any of this information, but it was the most exciting information he's heard this side of an action/adventure novel. Sure it was scary, but that fear was temporarily overridden with journalistic enthusiasm.

On the way to the station, Keith saw D.C. in a sinister new light. He began to see the symbols in the architecture, and wondered if the monument really did measure 666 inches on each side. Fascinated by this new information, he was eager to use it in a way that would advance him as a journalist. Riding the subway with the other subway zombies, he dreaded going to work. His lack of enthusiasm was mainly due to his monkey tasks and Big Bertha. He was, however, looking forward to seeing Rob Livingston. He knew he would view him in an entirely different light.

He looked forward to meeting Mitch later that afternoon. Mitch was full of information, and Keith was an eager student. He didn't want to share this information with anybody until he found just the right way to blow the roof off with the most dramatic, timely story of any journalist's career. Maybe that made him greedy, but didn't it also make him ambitious? The newsroom will be pretty much empty today, with the National News Awards taking place in D.C. tonight. The show was selected for awards in several categories, as were most of the star reporters. Livingston was selected for one of the top awards of the year, *Most Influential News Story*. It had something to do with fluoride being put into the drinking water, but Mitch said that was just a distraction for The Brotherhood's purposes. Mitch said fluoride was added to most cities drinking water, but not at the toxic levels that Livingston suggested. Surprise, surprise--D.C. tested high that week, which made every other city in the country require fluoride level tests of their water supply. In short, nothing out of the ordinary was found, but it did have the internet ablaze with speculation, as well as protests, letters to congressmen, and all out paranoia for about a week, until everything could be settled. *If you ask me*, Keith thought, *the only thing Livingston influenced was the sale of bottled drinking water. I bet the clever guy bought stock in every bottled water company he could find.*

Keith walked in to find the newsroom empty, as expected. He made his way to the break room to find Jerry pouring himself a cup of coffee.

Keith smiled at Jerry, "You're the first person I've seen here. This place is dead! I mean, I expected there wouldn't be a lot going on, but this is ridiculous."

"Oh I'm here man," replied Jerry. "I'm always here man. I live back there in the editing room. It's my little corner of the world, tucked away from the madness. I only pop out to use the facilities and get some coffee."

Keith looked at him a little confused. "You *live* here?"

"Well, no, I don't really live here." He said with a chuckle, "You intern types got no sense of humor, man."

Keith blushed, a little embarrassed that he didn't catch that it was just a figure of speech. The truth was, he wasn't all that into what Jerry was saying, anyway. With no bosses around, he wondered if he could sneak out unnoticed. After all, he had no idea what monkey tasks he would do without one of the monkey masters around.

Jerry grabbed some packets of sugar and put them in his pocket. "Never know when you might need these, man."

Keith gave him a polite smile, deciding the man had clearly indulged too much in the 60s. "So, is it like this every year on awards day? You know--empty?"

"Oh this man, no. I mean there's not a lot going on, but all the head honchos are in a powwow right now. Somethin's got their feathers all ruffled or somethin', man. I don't ask questions. I just stay in my little corner back there. Yes sir, my little corner of the world away from the madness."

Keith smiled, amused at what a character Jerry seemed to be. "I never got your name."

"Oh right, man. The name is Jack, but everybody calls me Jerry. You can call me Jerry."

Keith instantly got the connection between him and the Grateful Dead singer. "Right. Of course. It's nice to meet you. I'm Keith. I'm the resident monkey this summer."

Jerry chuckled, "Resident monkey, I like that. I hadn't heard that one. Well, you're one of several resident monkeys this summer. I get 'em wandering into my editing bay all the time. There's one really cute one, too. I think her name is Sarah or Lacey or something. You should take her a cup of coffee or something. Tell her Jerry sent you."

Keith just smiled and started to walk away before saying "I'll catch you later, Jerry." *Great* Keith thought. *He's even got me talking like him now.*

Keith walked to his computer, deciding to play on the internet. He enjoyed the silence, and didn't miss Big Bertha's booming voice telling him to get to work. He wasn't a slacker, by any means. He simply didn't know what else to do with his time. He pulled out a chair, and scooted up to his workstation computer. He hadn't even had the chance to log in when he heard the hollow clank of high heels coming down the hallway. Looking up, he saw Jacinda walk through the door, slowly scanning the room with her eyes. "Where is everyone?" she asked Keith, looking a little confused.

"Jerry said they are in the meeting room, but I haven't seen anyone since I've been here."

"Jerry? You mean Jerry, my-name-is-Jack-but-you-can-call-me-Jerry Jerry?" she asked with a teasing smile.

"Yup, that's the Jerry/Jack I'm referring to."

"That guy's a riot I like him a lot. So, I still haven't gotten your name. I'm Jacinda Kilmeade, by the way."

Keith looked a little nervous as he rose and extended his hand. "I'm Keith Ludwig. I'm interning here for the summer."

"Oh, an intern. We've all been there. It gets better, I promise. So Keith, where do you go to school?"

"The University of Texas."

"Oh no way! That's where I went! I love Austin."

"Yea, it's okay. I'd trade it for D.C. any day, though."

Jacinda recognized the ambitious twinkle in his eyes. "Don't be in such a hurry to get out."

"Oh, I'm ready," Keith said with a smile. He never expected Jacinda to be so nice. "So the awards show is tonight?"

"Oh, yes. Nails at noon, hair at two, and makeup at four. I'll be cover-girl ready by six."

Keith nodded, "sounds like a lot of work. I hate getting my nails done."

Jacinda winked at him. "Come on, we all know how much you UT boys like a good manicure."

"Hey watch it," Keith said. He liked Jacinda. He'd never dreamed someone as successful and beautiful would be so down-to-earth and sweet. He absolutely knew what Gregory Kilmeade saw in her. The truth is, it took him this long to notice what anyone saw in her except a pretty face.

Angela Caldwell

CHAPTER 11

Lyla packed neatly folded clothes into the suitcase she was preparing for the toddler and herself. She talked Lucio into letting her take the child to the country this weekend, insisting he needed to breathe fresh air. She knew just where she wanted to go—a beautiful farmhouse owned by her family for generations.

Of course, she wouldn't be going alone. She was never allowed to do anything, or go anywhere, without the watchful eye of at least one security guard. Getting clearance for such a trip had been difficult, because the child was to be sacrificed a week later. In the end, she convinced Lucio that the happier the child is at the time of his sacrifice, the happier it will make their Lord Maitreya. She knew it was a ridiculous argument but it worked nonetheless.

She opened her bathroom drawer, and fished out a travel sewing kit she had stashed away. She picked up the child's beloved Bumble Bear, and cut a small slit in the stitching. She neatly folded the two thousand dollars she had been saving in her old coat pocket, and tucked it into the bear. Sewing the bear back up, she felt confident the money was safe.

*****

Keith waited at the meeting place he and Mitch decided upon. He liked meeting Mitch at the coffee shop, but understood that maybe they should avoid being seen in one place too often. He chose a bench in the shade, although the shade offered little relief from the sweltering D.C. heat. He checked his watch, realizing Mitch was thirty minutes late. Keith absentmindedly reached for his phone to call him, but remembered he'd left it behind the night before.

Keith second-guessed himself, fearing that he wasn't at the correct meeting place. He became angry with Mitch for always insisting they meet in public. *He's so paranoid*, thought Keith. Maybe the heat was making him irritable. Maybe he was getting swept up in some delusional guy's fantasy. Maybe he would feel better when he had his phone back in his hands, but he knew one thing for sure, it was now six o'clock, and Mitch still wasn't there.

*****

Jacinda walked into the awards banquet, feeling like a princess. All the time spent primping for this event paid off; she had never felt so lovely. Her stylist couldn't have picked a prettier gown for the event. It was both glamorous and sexy, but simple and understated. She rarely wore black, and was hesitant when she first saw it, but after trying it on, she was sold. It was floor-length with iridescent strands of thread which reflected the light, making her twinkle like the night's sky. She hadn't even felt this beautiful at her wedding to Gregory, although it was close. Her mood was especially high, even though she wasn't nominated for an award. She may not have been personally nominated, but the show she now worked for was nominated for four awards. She took pride in knowing she was now part of something so successful.

Not only was she proud of her career; she was beaming with pride over her husband. He looked so handsome, and she loved to see him work a room. She watched him turn on that Gregory charm that made him so loved by the masses. The banquet room looked elegant. The candle flames danced, and the smell of fresh roses filled the air with a sweetness she wished she could bottle. She closed her eyes and hoped she'd remember this moment exactly as it was. It was the first time in a really long time that she truly let herself feel happy. Well, as happy as she could feel with a black cloud of grief hanging over her head.

After mingling for about forty-five minutes, Gregory and Jacinda decided to find their seats. Gregory leaned down to kiss her shoulder. "Where did they stick us, darling?" he asked, as he scanned the tables for their nameplates. Jacinda found her name on the table closest to the stage. "Wow, front row seats. They must have known I'd be bringing a very distinguished guest," she teased.

"I'd be flattered, if I didn't recognize everybody at that table as being from *Your Nation Now,*" Gregory said with a wink. As they made their way to the table, George stood to greet them. "Gregory," he said, as he placed a firm hand on Gregory's shoulder. "How have you been, buddy? How's the old man?"

Gregory glanced over at Jacinda, seemingly embarrassed for once again stealing the spotlight. "Dad's good, George. How 'bout yourself?"

"Oh, you know me. Keeping busy. The show's nominated for four awards, you know."

"I've heard. Congratulations." George beamed with pride, as if he had single-handedly been responsible for all the award nominations. The three took their seats next to a petite blonde woman who looked a little awkward and self-conscious. George must have noticed her discomfort, because he turned the focus to her. "I'd like you to meet my lovely date, Brenda. Brenda, this is Senator Kilmeade and his beautiful wife

Jacinda. Jacinda is the newest reporter at the station."

"Yes, I know," said Brenda with a genuinely kind smile. "It's so nice to meet the both of you." The corners of her delicate mouth turned down slightly as she teasingly scolded George, "We've been in a relationship for two years, and he still introduces me as his *date*."

Jacinda found Brenda adorable. In fact, she never would have guessed the two were a couple. She had no idea George was seeing anybody, but of course there wasn't much she did know about George. She now knew he had a daughter, and that his grandson had been kidnapped. Aside from that, the man was still somewhat of a mystery. She did take comfort in knowing he had such a sweetheart for a girlfriend. *A man who has been through losing a grandchild needs happiness in his life. We all do,* she thought.

"Well," Brenda said, while standing up, "I have to go to the little girl's room. Would you like to join me Jacinda?" George threw up his hands. "Why do women always need to go to the restroom in packs. What is it that goes on in there that can't be done alone?"

Gregory chuckled and said, "You can be sure I'll never invite you to the restroom, George Count on that."

Jacinda collected her purse, and accompanied Brenda to the restroom. She welcomed the opportunity to get to know her a little better. She wondered how her socially awkward, workaholic boss could be dating such an adorable creature. "Do you have any idea where the restrooms even are?" Jacinda asked.

"Well no." Brenda replied. "But I'm just happy to be standing up and moving around. We've been sitting at that table for an hour. George isn't much for mingling."

"Well I wouldn't have thought so either, but he was quite talkative back there."

"Oh, that's just because it was Gregory. He's known Gregory since he was a boy. Oh look, there's the restroom." The two walked toward the door, and Jacinda's curiosity got the best of her. "So two years, huh? I didn't know George was seeing anyone. Of course, I didn't even know he had a daughter until a few days ago. I actually met her for lunch."

"Oh Susie? Yes. Can you believe in the two years I've been with George, I've only seen her once? She came down to visit Christmas before last. Of course, George and I were pretty new back then. But she's in town, you say? I wonder why George didn't mention that."

Jacinda was confused. "What do you mean she

came down to visit? Doesn't she work here in the city? You'd think she could find her way to her dad more than every couple of years. Plus, I'm sure she's needed her dad quite a bit since her son was taken."

"No dear," Brenda said with a smile. "You must be thinking of somebody else. Susie teaches English in Thailand, and she's never had any children."

"No, I had lunch with her the other day—red hair, mid-thirties."

Brenda slowly shook her head. "No, Susie is a little brunette, and I believe she's only about twenty-two. George had her late in life. They aren't really all that close, but George blames his ex-wife for that. He says his ex was bitter after the divorce, and poisoned Susie against him. I don't know I try not to get involved. He doesn't talk about her much, but I thought she was a lovely girl."

Jacinda felt her stomach tying into a knot. For some reason, she didn't feel the need to question Brenda any further. She knew Brenda wasn't mistaken, and that the woman she met couldn't have been George's daughter, regardless of what she had been told. Something never felt right about the entire situation, but she never could put her finger on it.

Why? Why would they lie to me about that?

CHAPTER 12

Lyla and the child sat in the back seat of the black SUV, as they headed towards her family's farmhouse. Both the driver, and the man sitting in the passenger seat were armed guards, working for Lucio. She knew there would be heavy security accompanying her. In fact, it wouldn't surprise her if there were more armed men waiting at the farmhouse. She had the feeling Lucio was starting to distrust her. She wasn't surprised at all when security checked all her belongings before the trip, and was relieved she had the forethought to hide the cash. She never would have been able to explain the substantial amount of money.

She started to recognize the scenery. Anxiety set in, and she began twirling her hair around her finger. Looking over at the precious child, she noticed he'd asleep with a cracker in his chubby, little hand. She didn't know how anyone could fall asleep while strapped in a car seat, but it didn't seem to bother him at all. His slow, deep breathing indicated he would probably sleep until they reached the farmhouse. She wondered how looking at him could bring her so much joy, and so much sorrow at the same time. She knows she doesn't have the means to provide for the child without Lucio. The only money she has in the world is the two-thousand dollars she sewed into the baby's stuffed animal. She was given credit cards to use during her two-year stint as maidservant, but knew they would be worthless once she put her plan into action.

She was overwhelmed with memories, as they pulled onto the farmhouse property. They passed a rickety, whitewashed gate. It was a rustic look that was very much intended by the designer. The air was still scented with the sweet smell of magnolias. Magnolias have always been her favorite. When she was little, she sat under those magnolia trees for hours, while playing with her dolls. Sometimes her dolls were the only emotional escape she had. The farmhouse was just a summer home, but she remembers wishing they could live there year round. Her father insisted they spent time at the summer home so that he could spend weeks with them without being noticed. He never married her mother. In fact, her mother was his mistress. He managed to keep two families, simply because her mother was devoted to not only him, but the luciferian church. Her mother allowed both she and her daughter to be stashed away from the public— stashed away from the truth. It's almost as if she was excited by the challenge of keeping such a damning secret.

It was easier for her to escape her father here than at their condo. Here, she could get lost for hours among the magnolia trees. Here, she could avoid a cold mother who viewed her as nothing more than a trophy of her own sins.

She was pulled away from her thoughts, when the

child started twisting in his car seat. He was stretching as he awoke from his nap. Lyla leaned over and kissed his soft head. "We're here my angel," she whispered. A quick shudder went through her heart like a volt of electricity. Suddenly, her plan was in action, and she hoped she could pull it off. Anxiety overwhelmed her and her hands began to sweat. She had come too far to back out of the plan now. Besides, she knew backing out wasn't an option. If she backs out, the child will be sacrificed within the week.

*****

Keith sat on the tattered couch in his tiny, efficiency apartment. It wasn't much, but there weren't many places in town that would give him a three month lease. He flipped through the television channels in an attempt to take his mind off of Mitch. It had been over twenty-four hours since he's spoken to Mitch and he was getting frustrated. He was frustrated with Mitch for not meeting him when he was supposed to return his phone. He was frustrated with himself for being drawn into Mitch's stories, when he was clearly a flake who couldn't even be counted on to show up when he was supposed to.

Keith mindlessly channel surfed, letting his nervous energy escape through his fingers, as they punched at the buttons on the remote control. He felt too anxious to actually watch a television program, but there was something about the television just being on that made him feel a little less anxious. His mind raced with all of the information Mitch had given him. *Could there really be an ancient secret society that had so much influence and power?* He sank into the couch, and threw his head back onto the cushions. He closed his eyes, and tried to talk himself out of his anxiety. He even tried a breathing exercise that his mother had once shown him to help combat stress. Nothing seemed to be helping the tightness of his back and shoulders, which is where he carried his tension. He couldn't get past the unsettling feeling that something bad was about to happen. He likened his premonitions to those an animal might have when sensing a storm. He didn't know what would happen or who it would happen to, but he felt unsettled, and full of restless energy.

Unable to find a comfortable position on the couch, he moved to his computer desk. Sometimes surfing the internet helped him relax. He logged onto his favorite news site, and there, buried under three other headlines, read: **Former U.S. senator, Mitch Tatum, found dead in his apartment of an apparent suicide**. Keith read the headline over and over, unable to believe what he was seeing. A wave of nausea ripped through him. He reluctantly clicked on the headline, so that he could read the accompanying information.

Former U.S. senator, Mitch Tatum, was found dead early this morning with what appeared to

be a self-inflicted gunshot wound to the head. Those who knew the Senator told our reporters that Mitch wasn't the same after his beloved wife, Linda, was killed in a tragic hit and run. It was only months later that the senator resigned, after being allegedly involved in a drug scandal from which his reputation never recovered. Friends say Tatum became reclusive after his resignation, and most say it's been years since they've had contact with him.

Keith fought back the vomit rising in his throat. It wasn't right. He knew the story was wrong. Maybe Mitch had died. That much he could accept. However, no part of him accepted that the death was a suicide. His religious beliefs alone were too strong for him to commit suicide. Suicide wasn't an option for Mitch. Mitch was determined to bring evil to light. Mitch was a one-man army against the evil agenda of The Brotherhood. He had taken it upon himself to educate and protect the public when the time was right. Mitch Tatum, a man of God, would never kill himself. Now more than ever, Keith believed Mitch was telling the truth. Keith felt hot tears run down his cheeks. He had only known Mitch a few days, but he suddenly missed him in a way he wouldn't have expected. Of course, loss of a human life is always devastating, but this seemed even more tragic.

*****

The ride home from the awards banquette was

spent in silence. With one hand on the steering wheel, Gregory placed the other one on his wife's hand. Even though *Your Nation Now* won two of the four awards it was nominated for, Jacinda appeared distant and disinterested.

"What's wrong, my love?" Gregory asked her in his most charming voice.

"Nothing," she replied.

"Oh come-on, beautiful, you can't tell me that nothing is bothering you."

Jacinda looked at her husband with eyes that were more confused than hurt. "Did you ever meet George's daughter, Susie?"

Gregory thought for a moment and responded, "George has a daughter? You don't say? Dad never mentioned him having a daughter."

"Well, what *did* your dad mention about George?"

"What's all this interest in George?"

Jacinda shifted in her seat, so she could face her husband. "It's just that I had lunch with a woman who claimed to be his daughter. She didn't just claim to be his daughter; George confirmed it. Now, I find out that his daughter lives in Thailand and doesn't fit the description of the woman that I met at all."

"Well, maybe he's got more than one daughter."

"Both named Susie?"

"Where did you hear that Susie lived in Tahiti?"

"Thailand."

"Thailand. Who told you she lived in Thailand?"

"George's girlfriend, Brenda."

"Well my love, she was obviously confused."

"No—no, I don't think she was."

"So then what *do* you think?"

"I don't know yet." She responded, as she turned to look out the passenger window.

"Well, don't think too much about it. After all, who cares where his daughter lives?"

"I care. I had lunch with her. She told me that her son was taken while he was outside riding his bike."

"How terrible for her."

"Yes, only thing is—Brenda said that Susie doesn't have any children. She said that she's *never* had any children."

"Well, clearly Brenda is mistaken."

"Will you stop saying that?"

"What do you think, Jacinda? Do you think George

is playing games with you for his own sick amusement? It doesn't make any sense. What seems much more logical is that Brenda simply doesn't know what she's talking about. Besides, I've never even heard of Brenda. If they were serious enough that she knew all the details of his life, I probably would have heard of her by now."

"You would have heard he had a girlfriend but not a daughter?"

Frustrated, Gregory put his free hand back on the steering wheel. "Love, let's not waste any more energy talking about George. I leave for California tomorrow, and I really wanted to spend a pleasant evening with my stunning wife."

"Will you be gone five days or six?"

"Five. The retreat lasts for three weeks, but I'm not staying the whole time this year. I think my father will be staying the entire retreat, so maybe we could visit my mother while he's away. I know she'd like it if we visited."

Talk of Chandra Kilmeade made Jacinda completely forget about George. She dreaded visiting her mother-in-law, but couldn't politely refuse. "Of course we can visit your mom, but check the dress code first, will you?"

*****

Lyla sat in bed next to the sleeping child. She

peered out the open window at the SUV sitting in the driveway. The house was not equipped with air conditioning, and the hot, sticky night provided little sleep. She planned their escape for the following night, but the heat made her restless. *What if they suspect me?* She worried. *What if they take the child earlier than planned, to prepare for his sacrifice?* Her mind raced with *what ifs,* and she felt the same sense of panic that she felt in the car. To panic, you must care, and she hadn't cared in a very long time, not until she was blessed with the child. Until now, her plans were carried out in a calm, detached manner. As is the case with many victims of prolonged childhood abuse, she learned to detach herself from stressful situations. She took the necessary steps to get here, but it's almost as if she were taking them for somebody else. Tonight was different. Tonight, she was all too aware that if she made one misstep, the baby she had come to love would die.

She stood up and slipped her jeans on beneath her nightgown. She looked down and saw Bumble Bear's neck rested in the crook of the sleeping child's arm. Gently prying the stuffed animal from the child, she hugged the bear tight against her chest and stood to pace the room. No matter what, she had to remember to grab Bumble Bear when she made her escape. Inside the innocent looking stuffed animal, was all the money she had in the world. A nervous energy settled across her, and she couldn't stay still. *The time is now,* she decided.

It was time to go downstairs, and look for the keys to the SUV. She walked slowly across the bedroom, in an effort to not awake the sleeping guards. At least she hoped they were asleep. Her body froze, as she stepped on a board, causing it to loudly creak. Her muscles tightened, as she slowly turned to see if she disturbed the sleeping child. When she saw the toddler hadn't stirred, she continued forward. The board creaked again, as she shifted her weight. Although the two guards were in bedrooms down the hall, she worried that such a noise would rouse them.

She took a deep breath, and listened for any signs of life in the house. Much to her relief, she heard only silence. She never realized how loud the hum of silence could be. It sent a nervous shutter through her body. They would be here only three nights, and if she wanted to escape with the baby, she needed to act now. She didn't have the luxury of time. She continued to creep towards the closed bedroom door. She took the cold doorknob in her hand and slowly twisted it. Quietly and cautiously, she slowly opened the door.

With no hallway windows, the hall was pitch black. Before she could reach the staircase at the end of the hall, she first had to pass the two sleeping guards. She hoped their bedroom doors were closed, but the darkness made it impossible to tell. She ran her fingers down the wall, as she walked toward the staircase. She could follow the wall to the staircase and quietly descend to the first floor. The stairs were old and creaked in pain with each step she took. She rose to the tips of her toes, hoping to avoid the creaking. Her efforts were futile, each stair squeaked as loudly as the one before.

Finally, she reached the bottom of the stairs. She ran her trembling hand over the wall, looking for a light switch. She flipped the switch, and illuminated the entryway. She searched the table for the keys, but there was nothing more than a few soda cans. She quickly moved from room to room, searching for the keys, but realized her efforts were in vain. It was clear one of the guards had taken them upstairs. She knew there was no way she could enter the guard's bedroom unnoticed. Besides, she didn't even know which guard's bedroom the keys were in. Defeated, she threw herself onto the couch. She silently sobbed into her hands, and wondered if she had come all this way for nothing. In the beginning, the country home seemed like the perfect place to make her escape. She knew that her every move would not be monitored by video surveillance, and she felt confident she could sneak past the guards. *The keys,* she thought to herself, *how am I supposed to do this without the keys?*

She stood to walk back upstairs. Tonight was a failure, but tomorrow would present new opportunities. Tomorrow she could devise a plan.

Tonight, however, she had to sleep. Escaping would require her to be alert. *It is time to sleep,* she decided, as she switched off each light behind her, before heading to the stairs. With her foot on the first stair, and her hand on the light switch, she saw them. She saw the keys hanging on the wall leading upstairs. The darkness prevented her from seeing them earlier, but there they were, hanging on a hook. Her heart skipped a beat, and she straightened her posture. A smile involuntarily sprang from her unsuspecting lips. She reached for the keys and lifted them off the hook.

A loud creak invaded the hum of silence, and her body jumped with surprise. "Going somewhere?" ask a voice from atop the stairs.

*****

Jacinda laid next to Gregory in the darkness of their bedroom. Her mind was reeling from the events of the night. *Why the fake daughter?* She asked herself, as she tried to wrap her brain around the situation. Gregory seemed restless, too. While he hadn't spoken in an hour, he was tossing and turning every couple of minutes, before finally sitting up in the darkness.

"Gregory," Jacinda said, reaching to touch his arm.

"I thought you were asleep," he said, placing his hand over hers.

"No, I haven't been able to drift off," she replied.

"Me either."

"Are you anxious about your trip tomorrow?"

"No, not anxious really. I just haven't been able to sleep. Do you know how much I love you?"

"I love you too."

"No, I mean I've never loved anything as much as I love you. The thing is—the more I love you, the harder it gets."

"The harder what gets?"

"Watching you suffer."

"Suffer?"

"I mean, watching you miss Kyler. Whenever we see a baby at dinner or on television, I always see you change."

"Change?"

"You zone out and tear up. You always smile, but it's not the same smile you have when you're happy. It's like you smile to distract people from looking at your eyes."

"You notice stuff like that?"

"Of course I do. You do that when there's a baby, but sometimes you just zone out, and I know what you're thinking, because you tear up and get that look."

Jacinda wrapped her arm around her husband's waist to pull him back down. She snuggled up to him, letting her tears fall onto his shoulder. "It's never going to go away, Gregory. Until I find him, this feeling is never going to go away."

Feeling absolutely helpless, he held her while she sobbed. Collecting herself, she wiped her face with the palm of her hand, grateful for the darkness, which hid her tears. "I'll find him Gregory—I will. I have to. I don't know how I know I'll find him, but I just have a feeling. I don't want you to always see the sadness, because I know there's nothing you can do, and I know that you'd do anything to find him."

"Yes anything," he whispered, followed by a long silence. She didn't know if it was the way he said it, or the silence that followed, that bothered her the most.

****

The guard walked down the dark staircase, eventually stepping into the light of the entry hall. "What?" asked Lyla, in a voice she hoped didn't mirror her surprise.

"I asked if you were going somewhere."

"Well," Lyla responded, her mind searching for an answer. "Yes, I need something."

"What?"

"The child," she said, pointing upstairs. "The child is coughing, and I can't find his medicine. I was going to check and see if I left it in the car."

The guard eyed her suspiciously. "The child, huh?" he asked, while scanning the length of her body with is eyes. He was one of Lucio's favorites. He was ruthless, and frequently called upon to do Lucio's dirty work. He was a short man with red, receding hair. His stocky build was not intimidating, but it was strong. She knew there was no way she could overpower him, even on her best day.

She now had no choice but to continue her lie. "Now that you're awake, maybe you can help me find his medicine." The guard slowly came downstairs and took the keys from her hand.

"I will go look," he told her. "You stay inside with the child." He headed to the front door, as she sat on the bottom stair. She buried her face in her hands. *Does he believe me?* She tried to convince herself that he did, but knew deep down she was fooling herself. *You're being paranoid,* she thought to herself. *He doesn't suspect a thing.* But she knew he did. Her body felt weak, and it seemed she had been sitting on that bottom step forever. Her thoughts turned back to the sleeping child. She watched enough television after the abduction to know the baby's name was Kyler. She also knew that Jacinda Kilmeade was his mother. In fact, she knew a lot about Jacinda. Enough to know that her baby was chosen for three simple reasons: she was a reporter, a woman of God, and she was pregnant. It was as simple as that.

They needed the child to be born during the transit of Venus, but they also needed a mother who was in the public eye. Jacinda happened to be far enough along in her pregnancy that inducing the labor, by spiking her food, wouldn't hurt the child. She also happened to be likable. People trusted her reports, and that's just the kind of woman they needed to push their agenda. They could have chosen any God-loving, pregnant reporter in the country, but Jacinda won the lottery of doom. Lyla felt connected to Jacinda, despite the fact they'd never met. She felt connected through the baby that she'd come to see as her own. She could only imagine the unbearable pain Jacinda must be feeling, and tried to erase it from her mind. She thought The Brotherhood's killing of her husband was especially cruel, so soon after taking the baby. She originally thought a hit-and-run would be too suspicious, but knew The Brotherhood could make anything look possible.

Becoming the child's maidservant began as an honor—a duty. Her sense of obligation came from the twisted loyalties she had for her wicked father. However, in the past two years, her loyalties had shifted to the innocent child she had come to love and adore.

The door opened, and the guard stepped back inside. "I checked everywhere, it's not out there. Are you sure it's not upstairs?"

"I'll look again," she said, as she stood and headed up the stairs. As she walked upstairs, she heard the guard's footsteps moving away from the stairs. She stopped and continued to listen. When she could no longer hear his footsteps, she turned, and headed back downstairs to find him sitting on the couch. "I'm sorry I woke you up," she said. She wanted to determine how much longer he would be awake. She hoped he would return to bed soon, so that she could continue with her plan. "Hopefully I'll find the medicine upstairs when I dump out the suitcase." The guard studied her, squinting his already beady eyes.

"Goodnight," he said dismissing her.

"Goodnight," she replied, as she turned to head upstairs. "I guess we can go back to bed."

"I am in bed," he responded.

She turned her head to find him gazing at her with a look that told her everything. He was suspicious, after all. He planted his stocky body between the only two exits to the house. He was an equal distance between both the front and back door. Escaping would now be impossible.

*****

Jacinda awoke to the cruel squealing of the alarm clock. While she's always hated waking up, today was especially hard. She rolled over to hold her husband and found only an empty bed. Sitting up, she looked to where his suitcase had been the night before—it was gone. "Gregory," she said, as she stood up, but she was answered with only silence. She walked down the hall, looking into the study, but he still didn't answer. "Honey," she said in a louder voice, as she made her way to the living room. The apartment was empty, and Gregory was gone. Her heart sank as she let herself fall onto the couch.

MARKED I

CHAPTER 13

Lyla woke up with a warm, tiny hand cupping her nose. She opened her eyes to see the child's face inches from her own. She took his hand and kissed it several times. The little boy giggled and moved his hand back to her nose. His big, blue eyes sparkled in the morning sunlight that was streaming through the windows. A warm breeze blew through the room, bringing with it the scent of the night blooming jasmines that were growing beneath the bedroom window. "Up," said the child between giggles. "Up? Up?" she said, as she playfully tickled him. "I'll wake up and TICKLE you! You just woke up the tickle monster!" The little boy roared with laughter as she tickled his ribs. When she stopped tickling him, she leaned down to kiss his nose. He grabbed her face, looked her in the eyes and said, "ticko moner."

"Tickle monster?" she teased. "You want a tickle monster? I'll show you tickle monster." Once again, she tickled his ribs as he giggled wildly.

She stopped tickling the child and sat up on the bed. She looked out the window, noticing how beautiful the trees looked bathed in the early morning sunlight. *This would be heaven to some people* she thought. But to her, it was a prison. And the men downstairs were her wardens. The child moved, straddled her lap, took her face is in his hands, looked her in the eyes, and said, "ticko moner." He began laughing even before she swung him to the mattress and began tickling him.

She stood and put her jeans on beneath her nightgown. She then dug into her suitcase and found a clean shirt. She turned her back to him and slipped it on. She scooped the toddler into her arms, sprinkled his face with kisses, and headed downstairs. She could hear that both men were up, before she even reached the bottom of the stairs. As she stepped onto the first floor, their conversation abruptly ended. She walked into the kitchen, and found both of them sitting at the breakfast table. Both men made her extremely uncomfortable, but she tried to seem at ease. "Good morning," she said, as she walked to the teapot. "Would you like some tea?"

"Only if it's iced," replied the guard who had discovered her downstairs the night before.

"Sure, I could do that. There were people up here just last month. Hopefully they left us some tea." She opened the pantry door and found a box of tea bags. "Here we go, we'll have iced tea in no time." She spun on her heel, and headed back towards the teapot. She was unnerved by their silence. Finally, the stalky, balding guard broke the silence.

"I was telling Ben here about last night."

"Yea, I hear you were going for a midnight drive," said the much younger, much better looking guard. He held the keys up and jiggled them, before putting them in his pocket.

"I was looking for the child's medicine."

"Of course you were," he said in the most sarcastic tone she's ever heard.

"With the baby being sick, Lucio has decided to cut our little vacation short."

No! She thought, *we can't leave!* "He's not sick," she protested. "He just has a cough. It's nothing serious. I just thought he'd sleep better if he had cough syrup. But the coughing died down this morning." She picked up the toddler and cradled him close to her, as if holding him tightly would keep them from taking him. *How could I do that, how could I tell them he was sick? How could I say something so careless?* "We can't leave today; I promised him we'd play outside. Can't we stay for just one more night?"

"We are staying for one more night," the short, balding guard answered. "Lucio doesn't want him back until tomorrow. He leaves for California tomorrow night." He then turned his attention to the toddler. "You are a lucky little guy," he cooed to the child. "You get to go to California to fulfill your glorious purpose. Yes you do," he said in a playful, high-pitched voice that made the child giggle with glee.

Lyla suddenly felt sick. She wanted to run. She wanted to scream that it wasn't a glorious purpose. She wanted to scream that they couldn't have him; they'd have to find another child. She knew protesting would do more harm than good. She lowered the child to place him on the ground. She fought back the nausea that was now overwhelming her, and braced herself against the counter. Her sickly state did not go unnoticed by the guards. "Does that bother you, Maidservant?" asked the short, balding guard, continuing to bait her.

"You're not upset that the little rug rat here is going to be snuffed out in a few days, are you Maidservant?" he asked in a taunting manner. *How can he be so cruel*? She wondered. She wanted to throw the teapot at him. She wanted to scream at him until she felt better. She knew that would only be playing into their hands. She drew in a deep breath, forcing herself to be reasonable. She realized that when they looked at him, they didn't see a child, but a sacrifice. To them, he was nothing more than a vessel that held the sacred blood needed to bless the earth, before their lord is born. It was not the baby they found precious, but his life, and his blood. In mere days, that life would be ended and his blood would be spilled. Only one thing made his blood precious, and that was the unfortunate time of his birth. He was born during the transit of Venus.

There were a million thoughts a minute racing through Lyla's head. She was panicking on the inside, but knew she couldn't let it show. She collected herself and tried to act cheerful. "Well, if we only have until tomorrow, let's make the most of today," she said. She headed to the back door with the toddler wrapped securely in her arms. "We're going to sit outside for a little while, and get some fresh air; it's already getting stuffy in here," she explained, as she walked towards the front porch. She knew she couldn't hold back her tears for another second. Once her back was turned to them, tears welled up in her eyes. The door she was walking towards blurred into nothingness. She blinked hard, trying to squeeze the tears from her eyes. She opened the door and stepped outside. She sat down on the porch swing, and tried to clear her head. She knew she needed a plan, and had to pull herself together. The baby was delighted to be outside in the sunshine. He headed straight for the jasmine bush, and stuck out his little hand. "Bower," he squealed, as he grabbed a hand-full, and yanked it off the bush. He opened his hand, and picked through the flowers to find something that interested him. He found a tiny berry, and popped it in his mouth. "NO!" Lyla shouted, as she raced over to him and plucked the berry from his mouth. "Those berries will kill you!" She paused as she considered the weight of her words. The jasmine flower is one of her favorites. Not only do they smell divine, they are beautiful. She spent many summer nights falling asleep to the sweet aroma of the jasmines that grew beneath her window. She simply loved the flowers, but was well aware of their darker side. She knew the toxicity of the jasmine berry was enough to cause violent illness --even death. How could something so beautiful be so dangerous?

Ben, the younger guard opened the door and stepped onto the porch. "You can't be out here all alone," he said. Lyla rolled her eyes, hoping he didn't see her. She wasn't alone; she had the baby. Of course, that was the problem. It was obvious that they weren't going to take the chance of her snatching him. Her emotional attachment had apparently not gone unnoticed by Lucio either, because that is most definitely where they got their orders.

He started to walk inside, but turned and said, "Hey, how about that iced tea you promised?" Lyla's eyes grew wide, as she considered the possibilities. "Iced tea," she responded. "Of course. I'll make some right now. Just give me a few minutes for the baby to look at the flowers. He loves flowers."

"Okay, but make it quick," he said, before going inside. Lyla's heart was racing. It was now or never. Now that they were suspicious of her, nothing else could work. She looked down at the baby who peered back up with so much love in his eyes, that she felt a tinge of pain. Never had she loved so much that it actually hurt. She looked into his loving, trusting eyes, knowing she would do whatever it took to protect him. She turned and quickly gathered as many berries as she could fit into the pocket of her jeans. Suddenly, she remembered the oleander shrubs beside the house. The oleander, she's been told, is extremely toxic. She studied these flowers in detail, when trying to determine the death of her dog one summer.

She and the child walked around the house, picking several oleander blooms. She stuffed as many as she could into her pockets, then looked down at the child. It was clear the child wanted to play. "Ticko moner," he squealed as he threw his arms around her knees. "Oh, you're going to get the tickle monster, little man. Just you wait." The child giggled, completely oblivious to the plan he was watching unfold. *It's now or never,* she thought to herself again. *I have to. I have no choice.* She then smiled at the toddler and thought to herself, *it's time to go brew some tea.*

*****

Still feeling abandoned, Jacinda made her way to the kitchen to retrieve her cell phone from her purse. She was sure Gregory had a reason for not saying goodbye, but couldn't imagine what that reason might be. It was then that she saw the note sitting on the counter. Fear shot from her heart to her feet, like a volt of electricity. She didn't understand why she felt so irrational and scared. Had Gregory decided her pain was simply too much to deal with? Was Gregory leaving her? She knows that grief can be burdensome, but has done her best to cover her sorrow whenever possible.

Picking up the paper, with shaking hands, she read the note. It simply said: *I LOVE YOU*. The note was penned in Gregory's messy handwriting. She always said he had the penmanship of a doctor. Grabbing her purse, she clumsily dug for her cell phone. She retrieved it from her purse, and scrolled to Gregory's number. Frantically calling his phone, she prayed he would answer. His phone went straight to voicemail, causing her to squeeze her own phone in frustration.

She had to know—had to understand why he left without saying goodbye. Maybe he wanted her to sleep. After all, he was very considerate; maybe he was just thinking of her. While she wanted to believe his reasoning was as simple as that, he's never left for a trip without saying goodbye. Her mind raced with possibilities, until she felt like she might explode with nervous energy. Scrolling down her list of contacts, she found her friend Jill's name. She knew it was early, but hoped Jill wouldn't mind the phone call. After all, she had always been there for Jill whenever Jill needed someone to listen.

Jill answered the phone in a groggy voice, "Hello."

"Hey, it's Jacinda. I know it's early, but I really need to talk."

"What's wrong?" Jill asked, sounding panicked.

"No, don't worry. It's nothing really. I mean—well, I don't know what I mean."

"Are you okay? What happened?"

"I don't know. I mean; yes, I'm okay. I'm okay, there's just something going on."

"With what?"

"I don't know. Maybe I'm just being paranoid, but it's just all been so strange. First of all, my boss told me that his grandchild had been kidnapped, and then gave me the number of his daughter to use as a source."

"That's terrible," Jill said, clearly saddened.

"But that's not the weird part. I found out later that the woman he said was his daughter, wasn't his daughter."

"Huh?"

Yea, it's weird. Not only that, but…" Jacinda was

about to tell Jill about how the story was handled, but decided not to breach professional confidences.

"Wait. Why did he give you a fake daughter?"

"I don't know. I didn't want to ask. It was just weird, and now I don't want to even face him. Not only that, but Gregory left for California this morning without even saying bye."

"That doesn't sound like him. Everybody knows he's the perfect husband. I mean, that's something that my goofball husband would do—not yours."

"I know! He wasn't even supposed to leave the house until later this morning."

"Are you sure he didn't run to the store or something? He might not even be gone, Jacinda. He probably just ran out to get something for his trip."

"No, his suitcase is gone. I tried to call him but his phone went straight to voicemail."

"Maybe he caught an earlier flight. If he's flying, he would have to turn off his phone. Why are you so worried? Did you guys have a fight last night or something?"

"No, it doesn't make any sense. I got really emotional about Kyler, but I don't think that's it."

"Don't you dare blame yourself for that—not for a second. I'm sure there is a logical explanation.

Just don't over-analyze. You need something to distract you. Do you work today?"

"Yea, Jarrod Kabul is stopping by the studio. He's taking time out of his campaign schedule to give us an interview. I doubt I'll be interviewing him, but for some reason my boss wanted all the reporters there anyway. It's kind of weird since the other presidential nominee came by last week, and nobody cared."

"Jarrod Kabul," squealed Jill, like a teenager. "I swear that man is the most beautiful creature on the planet."

"Yea, but you've got to admit he's kind of creepy."

"Creepy?"

"Yea, I don't know what it is about him. Gregory knows him really well, but I've only met him once at a party. He just does this creepy stare thing when he talks to people. It doesn't seem to bother anybody but me, though. I just felt like he was trying to look through me, or something. Like— literally.

"You're crazy," Jill said, laughing.

"I don't know, he just made me uncomfortable."

Jill sighed. "He's still handsome. The hubby isn't a big fan though. He says his policies are downright un-Christian. He claims he's going to lead this

170

country straight to hell in a hand basket. I couldn't tell you, I stopped paying attention to politics a long time ago."

"How can you not pay attention to politics?" Jacinda asked, sounding more like a statement than a question. Glancing at the kitchen clock, Jacinda realized she needed to get going. "Well, hey—I better get ready for work. Call you later?"

"Yea, call me soon. Hey, how are you holding up aside from the weirdness?"

Jacinda considered the question for a moment. She knew she didn't have time to get into her pain, and decided not to burden her friend like she had her husband. "I'm okay," she said half-convincingly. "I'm fine."

CHAPTER 14

Both men were still sitting at the kitchen table when Lyla and baby Kyler entered the house. Lyla glanced in their general direction and was surprised to see the keys lying on the table. She wanted nothing more than to swipe them and drive the toddler and herself to safety, but knew that was impossible. Not only would she have to physically get past the two guards, they would surely call Lucio, as soon as she drove off the property. She wouldn't get ten miles before Lucio would have the local police searching for the stolen SUV. She knew a few of the officers personally. Sometimes, on the nights that her father was in town, her parents would entertain them, along with other members of The Brotherhood. There was no profession that exceeded The Brotherhood's grasp. She couldn't just wait for the guards backs to be turned; she had to be calculating. She couldn't risk them picking up their phones, and making the call that would seal her and Kyler's fate.

Lyla learned a lot of things from her part-time father, including the art of charm and deception. She wasn't born with his natural charisma, but what she lacked in that department, she made up for in beauty. Beautiful women don't need brains or charisma, her mother would often tell her; beauty is its own power. She believed this was true. She was able to see how envious her mother was of her beauty. Her mother wasn't beautiful, nor was she charismatic. Her mother had her own power in that she was discreet. Her only strength was her weakness, which Lyla now found ironic. Her father knew he could continue a double life with his mistress and daughter, because of her blind loyalty and discretion. Her mother believed in two things, and only two things—Lyla's father, and the mission of the luciferian church. Apparently, those two beliefs weren't enough to sustain her, because she took her own life when Lyla was nineteen.

Lyla wondered how she could have ever come from a woman who was so completely different than her. In fact, the mother/child bond seemed to be severed at birth; there was no attachment on either end. Neither seemed to feel much for the other, and it was a very lonely existence for both of them. Her mother seemed to live for her father's visits, the same visits Lyla dreaded. She feared her father, but was raised to respect his authority completely. He repeatedly subjected her to ritualistic abuse at the hands of both The Brotherhood and himself. Her mother offered no protection. In fact, her mother seemed jealous.

Entering the kitchen, Lyla saw both guards sitting on the couch in the living room. She could see the back of their heads as well as the television they were watching. They were watching one of the daytime court shows that Lyla despised. Both men laughed, as the loud judge reprimanded the plaintiff in a fashion clearly done for ratings. She glanced at the table where she was relieved to see the keys. *This is it, I could take them right now and run,* she thought to herself, before coming to her senses. She knew she wouldn't even make it out of the driveway. She locked her eyes on the guards, making sure they weren't paying attention. When she realized they were fully engaged, she removed a cup from the cabinet. Removing the berries and oleander leaves from her pocket, she placed the toxic handful in the cup. Using a spoon to smash it into a poisonous paste, she added it to the tea in the strainer.

Adding plenty of sugar to offset the bitterness of the berries, she poured two large servings over ice. Her hands shook, as she made her way to the living room to serve the guards.

"It's about time," Ben said, as he reached for one of the glasses. "I was beginning to think I would never get my tea."

"It took a minute to cook and cool," she said, as she handed the other guard his glass.

*****

Keith didn't think twice about attending Mitch's funeral. Although he barely knew the man, he felt a genuine connection. He felt honored that Mitch would trust him with such dangerous secrets. Now, more than ever, he was convinced there was something to all the craziness.

The morning was off to a rough start. After missing the first metro, he had trouble finding the church. He wished he had his phone's navigation, but he didn't. He was on his own. He worried about arriving late to the service. Running the last half-mile, he had a hard time catching his breath as he reached the tiny church. As he reached for the door handle, he felt a sudden sense of panic. *What if someone asks me how I know Mitch? What if Mitch really was murdered? Will the murderer be here?* He knew his imagination was turning his life into a ridiculous suspense novel, but was unable to curb his dramatic tendencies.

Standing frozen in front of the church doors, he closed his eyes and felt a wave of nausea. He wiped a layer of sweat from his face and wondered if he should turn around and leave. The clanking of high heels walking up the stairs snapped him out of his deliberations. He looked back, and saw a well-dressed, middle-aged woman. He felt grateful he wouldn't be walking in alone. After opening the door for the woman, he followed her inside. The cold church air felt good against his damp skin. It was a welcomed sensation, in contrast to the hot, summer morning.

The church was small and smelled of lemon soap. Three rows of wooden pews left little room for the small sanctuary stage. Over the stage, was a beautiful stained glass window. It's intricacy seemed out of place in its simple surroundings. Keith noticed the all-but-empty pews and felt a little surprised. He expected the church to be packed. After all, disgraced or not, he was an ex-senator. Truth be told, he expected a 21-gun salute, and a military jet flyover. With such high expectations, he was a little surprised there were only fourteen people in attendance. He wondered if he was at the right funeral. He wasn't an expert on funerals, having only attended three in his entire life. However, all three funerals he attended had large pictures of the deceased by the casket; here, there were none. How was he supposed to know if he was at the right funeral? It was a question he never thought he'd have to ask himself.

He could turn around and leave, but he would feel ridiculous. He had no choice but to sit in the back, and hope for the best. After all, Mitch or not—this person needed mourners. He looked up to see a man walking on stage with a tripod and picture. It was a picture of Mitch. While the image was clearly the same man Keith had known, he looked two lifetimes younger. He looked like a U.S. senator, not the man whose very posture revealed the weight of the secrets he carried.

Keith's emotions wrestled for position—one just as powerful as the next. He was saddened to see the casket, because that meant it was real. Mitch was dead. The lack of flowers and mourners not only saddened him, it angered him. It just didn't feel like a proper sendoff for a man who served his country, a man with integrity and strength.

Organ music filled the church's sanctuary, as did a few sobs from the front row. Keith shifted in his seat, hoping to not draw any attention to himself. He heard the door open behind him and was silently grateful he hadn't been the last to arrive. Maybe more mourners were coming; maybe Mitch would get the memorial service he deserved. A tall man who looked to be in his sixties entered the church. He never took his eyes off the casket as he made his way to Keith's pew. *Great,* Keith thought, *couldn't he have sat somewhere else? Practically all the pews are empty.* The man shot Keith an awkward smile. Keith returned the gesture, with a simple nod.

Ten minutes passed, and there was still no sign of a preacher. The front row guests began chatting among themselves. Keith checked his watch. "What is it? About ten-thirty now?" the man next to Keith asked, in what appeared to be an attempt at conversation.

"Yeah, wasn't it supposed to start thirty minutes ago?"

"That it was," he said, with his voice trailing off. "That it was." The man nervously smoothed both sides of his gray mustache with his forefinger and thumb. It was clear Keith wasn't the only one who felt uncomfortable at funerals.

Keith looked away; he wasn't in the mood to chat. He felt awkward being here in the first place. After all, he only knew Mitch from their secret meetings. What would he say if someone asked him how he knew the deceased?

Keith felt his pew mate staring at him, and turned to meet his gaze. The man looked at Keith through narrow, tired eyes, and fumbled with his tie. "My name is Andy. Andy Barlow."

"Keith Ludwig," he said, reaching out his hand. The man's eyes danced with recognition as he shook Keith's hand.

"Well you don't say," said Andy. "The hotshot reporter Mitch told me about."

"No, sir. Not a hotshot. Not even really a reporter," he said, attempting to sound humble. "I'm still an intern—well, technically." Keith wished he could stop rambling, but the recognition made him extremely uncomfortable. *After all, what did Mitch tell Andy? How much does Andy know? Is it possible that Andy had something to do with Mitch's murder?* All of these questions swirled around Keith's head, making him feel dizzy. He suddenly wished he had gone with an alias; after all, AJ Lovely wasn't *that* bad of a name.

Andy saw the panic in his eyes and placed a friendly hand on Keith's shoulder. "I was actually a very good friend of Mitch's," Andy explained. "He was like a brother to me." Keith didn't know if Andy was being truthful, but he sounded sincere enough. Andy sighed, and gritted his teeth. He looked at Keith through tortured eyes and shook his head. "You know, I was just hoping more people would come to see Mitch off, that's all. He may have lived like a hermit these last few years, but there was still an entire network of people that should have come."

Keith thought *network* was an interesting choice of words, but didn't comment. "Why didn't they come?"

Andy just shook his head and sighed again. "Mitch's hermit lifestyle forced a lot of his friends and family out of his life. I think he wanted to protect them. The ones who are still around must just be scared."

"Scared?"

Andy realized he said too much, "I can't really get

into it here, but let's just say Mitch had some enemies. He didn't sugarcoat his beliefs. In fact, he wrote a book. Of course, nobody was interested in publishing it."

"A book? Really? Was it about symbols?" Keith replayed the question in his head. *Was it about symbols? Dumb, dumb, dumb!*

"Oh sure, he covered the symbols. Of course,, there was a lot more than that."

Keith didn't feel so dumb anymore. He was glad that the symbols didn't come out of left field. "So you've read it?" he asked enthusiastically.

"Oh yea, of course I read it. It's very interesting— enlightening really. It was a little too enlightening, which is why nobody wanted to publish it. All the literary agencies said it came off as too fanatical. They said there wasn't a big market for Christian conspiracy theories."

"I figure there would be a market for that kind of thing."

"You'd be surprised. His theories—our theories— aren't too popular, but the truth never is. He definitely ruffled some feathers, though. He started to get scared towards the end. He had a feeling it was only a matter of time. I thought he was just being paranoid, but he seemed to know his days were numbered."

"He did?"

"He did, indeed. In fact, the last conversation I had with him was the night—well, you know, the night they say he committed suicide."

"So you don't believe that either?"

"You listen here, Keith," Andy said with authority. "I knew Mitch well. I've been through thick and thin with that man, and he would never, and I mean never, take his own life."

"I figured that much," Keith said with an apologetic smile.

"He never came right out and said he was scared. It wasn't his style. But I could tell." Andy seemed to be uncomfortable with the direction the conversation was taking. Even though they were talking in hushed tones, he wondered if maybe the conversation was too risky. "So, *Your Nation Now*, huh? That's pretty impressive."

"It's alright," Keith replied, doing his best to appear modest.

A preacher finally arrived, and the service passed quickly. He spent the entire time lost in his own head. He wondered if he would ever figure out what Mitch was trying to tell him. He wished Mitch had gotten to the point. He felt a sense of duty, but more than that, he felt driven by ambition. He desperately wanted to solve the mystery of Mitch's death. What could Mitch have known? How could that information be so threatening to world leaders, and men of power? How could it, as Mitch once said, change the world? Keith was certain there was a story to tell and he wanted to be the one to tell it.

CHAPTER 15

Lyla sat upstairs rocking the precious toddler she'd grown to love more than anything. She watched as the child's eyelids became so heavy that he had no choice but to close them. Touching her lips to his forehead, she closed her own eyes to collect herself. *This is it,* she told herself, before laying Kyler on the bed. Hearing a loud crash echo throughout the house, she clinched her hands into a fist. She began walking down the hall, willing herself to take each step. Never had she felt such unbridled fear. As much evil as she had been exposed to, she never feared for herself the way she feared for Kyler. She knew if she didn't make her move at exactly the right time, the child would be sacrificed in a matter of days.

Standing at the top of the stairs, she could hear someone vomiting. The sound was loud and unmistakable. She had no doubt the poisoned tea worked. Her body went numb and she felt paralyzed. Fear consumed her as she desperately tried to hold back the vomit rising in her throat. Her knees felt weak. *Where is the other guard? Why is he being so quiet?* She stood frozen at the top of the stairs listening for any signs of life, but she couldn't even hear the television.

She surprised herself when she darted downstairs. It was if her body were on cruise control. A cold volt of fear shot through the veins in her hands when she saw the television on the floor. One of the guards had clearly stumbled into it, knocking it off the stand. Her eyes darted around the empty living room. Her eyes focused on a pair of legs sprawled out from behind the couch. Her heart was beating so loudly that she could actually hear it echo inside her head.

She raced by the bathroom, to find the other guard lying motionless by the toilet. *Get the keys,* she told herself, before running for the kitchen table. Such relief and intense panic had never coexisted inside her at the same time. She grasped the keys for dear life and headed back up the stairs. She hoped against hope the men would not gain consciousness before she had time to get the baby.

Running upstairs and into the bedroom, she scooped the sleeping baby into her arms. She slung her purse and baby bag over her shoulder and headed for the door. Remembering the bear, she turned on her heel, making her way back toward the bed. With the baby's head on her shoulder and her arm securely under his bottom, she used her free hand to snatch the bear from the mattress.

With her arms now full, she ran downstairs and out
the door without so much as looking back. Running
towards the vehicle, she slipped on the gravel. Her
hands were full, so she was unable to catch herself.
She took a nasty spill, but managed to hold on to
the toddler. She stood up, and made her way to
the SUV, then secured the baby into his car seat.
She opened the other door and flung herself into
the driver seat. She dropped the keys twice before
they made it to the ignition. Her hands trembled as
she threw the car into reverse. The car swerved
from one side of the road to the other as she
recklessly drove backwards the entire length of the
driveway.

Taking a deep, stabilizing breath, she checked her
speedometer. She didn't want to risk being pulled
over for something as careless as speeding. *The
tracking device*, she thought to herself. *How could I
not think of the tracking device?* In all her planning,
she failed to realize the SUV would probably have a
tracking chip. Panic overcame her again, and she
was unable to think clearly.

Her eyes darted to the speedometer, realizing her
foot had become heavy during her panic attack.
Looking back up to focus on the road, she saw a
car coming from the opposite direction. Her heart
sank. It was such a secluded area that she rarely
saw traffic on this road. Her fingers tightened
around the steering wheel and she began talking to
herself. "Look natural," she repeated over and

over. "Look natural."

As the car got closer, she strained her eyes to see if she recognized the driver. She was still talking to herself. *"Did they call for backup? Please no—no!"* The car was within feet of her own when she saw him. Even at fifty miles an hour, she recognized the driver. She would recognize him anywhere; it was her half-brother—her father's son. "NO!" she gasped. Her hands began sweating and she realized she was holding her breath. "Breathe," she willed herself. "Just breathe."

*****

Jacinda made her way to the newsroom and was sitting at her desk. Her eyes were on the computer, but her mind was on her husband. *Why did Gregory leave for California without saying goodbye? Did I upset him?* The sound of her phone ringing snapped her back to reality, and she rolled her eyes when she saw it was Chandra. She had too much on her mind to deal with her mother-in-law's hatefulness. Hoping Chandra had heard from Gregory, she answered her phone.

"Hello."

"Hello, Jacinda daahling," Chandra cooed. "Is Gregory with you, dear?"

"No, he went to California for that retreat this morning. How are you holding up without Nicholas?" Jacinda didn't really care about her mother-in-law's current state of loneliness. She was just making polite conversation.

"Well that's why I'm calling, dear."

Heaven forbid she call just to see how I'm doing. She never calls just to talk. Of course, Jacinda had to count her blessings for that one. After all, Jacinda had absolutely no desire to chitchat with her mother-in-law. Maybe this would be short and sweet. Okay, with Chandra it was rarely sweet, but she was still holding out hope for short.

"You see, Jacinda. Gregory and Nicholas had the same flight to California, but Gregory never showed up to the airport. Nicholas tried to reach him by telephone several times, but his phone went straight to voicemail."

"Yea, that's what happened when I tried to call him. Maybe he just took an earlier flight."

"Well Jacinda, that is just ridiculous," said Chandra. "Why would he take an earlier flight without notifying his father? Did he say anything this morning?" She wouldn't stop asking questions long enough for Jacinda to reply. "What time did he leave the apartment?"

Jacinda didn't know which question to answer first. "He left this morning before I woke up."

"Before you woke up, dear? Did he say anything about taking an earlier flight?"

"No, I mean—well, no. I don't know where he is. I'll have him call you as soon as I hear from him though. If you hear from him first, please tell him to call me," she said, trying to end the conversation.

"That's it? You aren't at all worried? What if he's in the hospital, Jacinda? What if something has happened?"

Jacinda paused. Suddenly she *did* feel worried! She never thought to call the hospitals. "Oh my gosh, Chandra, you're right," she said, in one forced breath. I'm going to call them right now; I'll call you later." Without waiting for Chandra to respond, she hung up the phone. She knew she would pay for her lack of phone etiquette later, but for now only one thing mattered—making sure Gregory was safe.

Jacinda pulled up local hospitals on her computer. One by one, she called each hospital, checking each one off her list. She could imagine the gossip chain she probably just put in motion. After all, it's not every day that someone calls hospital admissions looking for a famous senator. Now that she knew he hadn't been admitted to the hospital, she wondered if she had over-reacted.

Jacinda tried Gregory's cell phone again. Straight to voicemail. *It's just so irresponsible. It's so unlike him,* she thought. She tried to distract herself from thinking the worst.

George walked past her desk and looked genuinely surprised to see her. "Today is your day off, Jacinda. Why in the world would you come to this place on your day off? Were all the malls closed?"

Jacinda felt a tad bit insulted by the insinuation that she'd have nothing better to do on her day off than shop. I mean, really, who did he think she was? Chandra?

"I got a memo saying that everybody needed to be here when Jarrod Kabul shows up for his interview. I know it's not for another hour, but I wanted to be here in plenty of time."

"Too late," George said in a matter of fact tone. He had to come in early—something about schedule conflicts. I guess he wanted to catch an earlier flight to the west coast."

"Oh," Jacinda said, trying to hide her relief. Kabul gave her the creeps, and she really didn't feel like making small talk when she had so much on her mind. She doubted he'd single her out for too much conversation, but he would probably consider it insulting to Gregory if he didn't at least say hello to his wife. "So, did the interview go well? Who ended up doing it? Livingston?"

"No, Livingston left for California last night. I'm headed there myself in a few hours, when I get all this wrapped up," he said, lifting the stack of paperwork in his hands. I'm ready for a break. I can't get out of here soon enough." George was uncharacteristically chatty, but Jacinda had no interest in talking. She especially had no interest in talking to George, now that she knew he pawned a fake daughter off on her. She still couldn't imagine what he was up to, or why.

"Why don't you go ahead and get out of here," George said with a dismissive wave.

"Yea, that sounds like a good idea. I didn't get much sleep last night." Jacinda wondered if George could tell she didn't want to talk to him. She wondered if he could sense the suspicion. Maybe she should just ask him. *Maybe it's just a misunderstanding.* She didn't know how, but she knew better. Something inside told her that George couldn't be trusted. She didn't know what he was up to, but she knew he wasn't the victim of miscommunication. He was a liar.

*****

Keith was walking into the newsroom as Jacinda was walking out. Keith waved and flashed Jacinda a polite smile, not knowing if she remembered him. Jacinda smiled back, but clearly looked distracted. He was looking forward to today. He knew Jarrod Kabul would be gracing the studio. Keith had little doubt that Kabul will be the next President of the United States. For once, he wouldn't mind fetching coffee or soda. In fact, he'd volunteer. He didn't care if he came off as desperate—he was star-struck.

For someone who attended a funeral less than three hours earlier, Keith was in relatively high spirits. He was happy the studio's big wigs were all going to California and he wished Big Bertha would follow. According to Mitch, this was the same retreat where the world leaders come together to drink, do drugs, and burn human effigies to Mollech. While it all sounded far-fetched, he *did* watch the video that the Austin reporter posted on the internet. He wouldn't have believed Mitch if he hadn't seen it with his own eyes. Rhapsody Grove did freak him out, to say the least.

He wondered if the men would be leaving for the retreat right after Kabul left the studio. He hoped so. Making his way to the intern cubicle, he wondered if Kabul would look as tall in person. He heard that most celebrities look much shorter than they appear on television. He had to admit, the man was dripping with charisma. Even before he got to his seat, he could see Sarah, the other intern, already claimed the comfortable chair. He didn't mind. After all, Sarah was beautiful, and beautiful women had a way of making Keith feel very forgiving.

"Hi Sarah," said Keith, as he literally tripped over his own foot. He managed to catch himself before he hit the floor. Sarah just smiled. "Hi Keith!" she said very enthusiastically, which caught Keith a little off guard. *I can't believe I just tripped,* Keith thought to himself, horrified. *Idiot, Idiot, Idiot!* He had to think of something to say, something charming.

"Wow, you're in a good mood today," he said, trying to act unfazed by his clumsiness.

"Heck yeah! Kabul came by for his interview this morning, and I got to get him a bottle of water!" she bragged. Keith look deflated.

"I thought his interview wasn't for another hour. I got here in plenty of time. Is he still here?"

"No, he had some schedule conflict or something and had to do it early. That man is GOR-GEOUS," she said, breaking the word into two syllables. She continued her giddy rant, but Keith couldn't hear anything coming out of her mouth. He couldn't hear her over his beating heart, because sitting there on the desk, was his cell phone. The same cell phone that Mitch was supposed to return the night he died. He recognized it right away because of the huge scratch across the face. The phone was a victim of both his clumsiness and the outside curb.

Keith yanked the phone from the desk. "Do you know how this got here? Who put it here?" he asked, clearly panicking.

"I don't know, I think it's been there all morning. I figured someone just forgot it. Is it yours?" Keith began scrolling through the numbers, making sure that it was, in fact, his phone. It was his phone all right, but how did it get here? Who could have taken his phone from a dead man's house, and set it on the desk like nothing happened? Keith probably should have felt grateful, but he was confused, and truthfully, a little nervous.

Sarah pulled him out of his trance. "Hey, I don't know how the phone got there, but Edna at the front desk asked me if I'd give you this," she said, holding up a package. "I guess she saw my intern badge and figured we all knew each other."

"We do all know each other. There are only five of us," he reminded her.

Sarah handed him the brown box sealed with silver duct tape. "You know, you're lucky they didn't call the bomb squad," she sassed. "That thing looks pretty shady."

"Yea, so does the desk lady…"

Sarah interrupted him midsentence. "Edna—her name is Edna."

"Sorry," Keith said. "You're a little sensitive about the desk lady—I mean Edna. Is she a friend of yours or something?"

"No, I just think everyone deserves to be called by their name, not their occupation. How would you like to be called water boy?"

"I do more around here than get water." Keith smiled, realizing how ridiculous this argument had become. "I also get phone numbers, check emails, and on occasion remove dead skin from Big Bertha's feet," he said with a grin.

"Ew! That's disgusting," Sarah laughed.

"Okay, well everything except the feet part," Keith admitted.

"I'm sooo telling her that you call her Big Bertha!"

"You wouldn't dare! Besides, if you do, I'll just tell her what you really do over here all day. I see you playing on the computer from the time you get here until the time you leave."

Sarah smiled a guilty smile. "I also give you shady packages from time to time as well."

"I will give you that," Keith agreed. "Okay fine, I won't tell her you don't work."

"Good. Then I won't tell her that you call her Big Bertha."

"Deal," Keith said with a smile.

Keith got so caught up in flirting that he almost forgot to open the package. The strange looking package had no formal address and no return address. It looked as if it had been hand delivered without the assistance of the postal service. It simply had a small hand-written note that read:

Please give this to Keith the intern. Thanks, Andy.

Upon seeing the name Andy, Keith's curiosity was piqued. *He works fast,* Keith thought. *I just saw him about three hours ago.* He opened the desk drawer to look for a letter opener.

"What are you looking for?" Sarah asked him.

"You certainly are nosey," Keith said with a flirtatious smile.

Sarah's cheeks turned red. She looked back at her computer screen, hoping he wouldn't notice the change in her complexion. Keith didn't know if she was blushing because of his flirtation, or because he called her nosey. "I was just looking for a letter opener," he said, trying to relieve the sudden awkwardness. "I want to open the package."

"Sarah laughed. "Nobody uses letter openers anymore. Besides, a letter opener would never get through all that tape. Whoever wrapped that thing meant business. Here, use these," she said, handing him scissors.

Thanking her, he took the scissors. His curiosity got the best of him and he began opening the package.

"What do you think it is?" Sarah asked him, now looking every bit as curious as Keith. He looked up to see her staring at the package with anticipation, and thought better of opening it in front of her.

"Who knows," Keith said, suddenly sounding disinterested. He was trying to diffuse some of the excitement surrounding the package. He stood up with the package and scissors in hand. "So thanks for delivering this to me. If you decide against journalism, you can always work for the postal service," Keith said with a wink. He hoped his flirtation would distract her from her curiosity—and it did. Her cheeks turned an even brighter shade of red and she shifted her gaze to the floor. "I'll see you later," Keith said, before walking away. Sarah just waved with her fingers and returned to her computer. He was proud of himself for acting so smooth in front of a girl he found so attractive. It was very out of his character, but many things were about to change for him. He was becoming a new man.

Keith made his way to the break room, relieved to find it empty. He felt high from the fear and curiosity. On one hand, the return of his phone was frightening, because of what it meant, but on the other hand, it thrilled him. He was also thrilled and intrigued by the package he was now holding in his hands. He sat the box on the counter and used the scissors to rip through the tape. Inside was a stack of papers with a cover sheet that read *True Signs of Evil, By Mitch Tatum.* Handwritten beneath the title was Andy's name and telephone number.

Jerry's voice echoed from the doorway. "Hey, man! It's the resident monkey. How ya doin', brother?"

Keith didn't feel like having a conversation, but couldn't bring himself to be rude. "Good. I'm just— " His phone rang and he grabbed it to look at the caller ID. It was his mother. He wondered how many of her calls he had missed while his phone was missing. He pushed ignore and focused his attention back to Jerry. "I just got this thing back. It's been lost for days. I can't even imagine how many voice messages I have."

"Yea man, sometimes I wish mine would get lost. I miss the good old days where people couldn't track you down. The Man always has to know where you are, man—it's spooky." He pulled his own station-issued phone out of his pocket. "I feel like I'm walking around with a homing device in my pocket man. They got me on a leash. What are you gonna do, though. Bills have to get paid."

"Huh?" Keith knew Jerry was a little *out there*, but he totally lost track of the conversation.

"They have a chip in all the phones. They say it's only active when the phone is on, but how stupid do they think we are?"

"How do you know? I mean, how do you know they have a tracking device in them?"

"Oh everybody knows man. It's not a secret. They were really proud when they first got 'em. They acted like they were way ahead of the technology curve, but if you ask me, man, it's just another form of control. Corporations run everything man. They're taking over the world."

Keith nodded in agreement, but he was getting lost in his own thoughts again. Since he got the package, he hadn't thought much about his phone. Whoever returned the phone had to be familiar with both Mitch, and the show. He was narrating the thrilling twist of events in his head. He could already picture the movie his life would inspire. His body began to tingle as fear and excitement settled into his bones. *They returned my phone as a warning. They want me to know they know.*

MARKED I

CHAPTER 16

Lyla felt somehow relieved when she hit the Westport city limits. It wasn't a guarantee of safety, but it did mean there was distance between her and the house she worked so hard to escape. "I hungee," said a small voice from the back seat. Lyla tilted the rearview mirror to get Kyler in view.

"You're hungry?" Lyla said, as a smile tugged at her lips. She knew a smile was inappropriate at this point, but couldn't help brighten at the sound of his little voice. "How was your nap?" she asked, her eyes darting between the road and the rearview mirror.

"I hungee," he repeated, not one to be distracted.

Eating was just one more thing on the long list of

things she hadn't planned in advance. She hit her forehead with the palm of her hand, realizing she failed to prepare for the obvious. "Oh sweetie," she said in an apologetic tone, "I didn't bring anything." She knew she had to feed the toddler, but focused on ditching the vehicle. She was sure it had a tracking chip, and didn't know if Lucio had already been alerted to her escape. The guards were unconscious when she left, but had no idea if they had since regained consciousness. She wanted to think that she just put them to sleep, because the thought of killing someone horrified her. She wasn't a killer. Of course, she would do anything to protect the baby, but she hoped it hadn't come to that.

"There's a mall," she said. She hadn't intended to speak the thought out loud, but found herself voicing everything in her head. "We can leave the car there. There's got to be a pay phone I can use to call a cab. We'll take the cab to the bus station, and get the heck out of here."

"Heck ow da here," the child repeated, driving his tiny fists into his car seat. Lyla just smiled. "You wanna get out of here?"

"Ow da here," he smiled, feeling the verbal exchange had become a game.

Lyla pulled the vehicle into a parking space, and reached for the bumble bear. She split the seams with her fingers and removed the money she had stashed inside. Tucking it into her purse, she got out of the car and opened the back door. "Ugh, the car seat. I totally forgot about the car seat." She hadn't figured the car seat into her escape plan, but knew she needed to bring it. She couldn't have a two year-old in a cab, or on a bus, without a car seat.

She put the baby on her hip and realized she needed a free hand. "Here take Bumble Bear, sweetie," she said, handing the bear to the child.

"It boken!" he exclaimed, after noticing the split seam.

"It's broken, but I'll fix it soon. I promise," she assured him, lifting the car seat and shutting the door. "We'll grab something to eat in here. You can eat while we wait for the cab."

On a normal day, Lyla would have felt ridiculous toting a car seat through the food court of the mall, but today was different. Today she didn't feel anything but focused on the child's protection. Her own safety was also at stake, because if The Brotherhood caught her, they would surely kill her too.

After ordering chicken nuggets and fries for the toddler, she made her way to a pay phone and called a taxi. "We're in the food court now, but we can be outside the mall as soon as I hang up. I think there is a sign that says food court, we'll be right there." After a brief silence, Lyla said, "Sure, my name is Jessica. Jessica Hadley."

Lyla hung up the phone, feeling proud of how quickly she managed to think of an alias. "Common kiddo, we're going to go ride in a taxi, and then a bus. You'll like the bus. Buses are fun."

"Bun?" the child repeated as best he could.

"Yes, fun. We're going on an adventure."

*****

Jacinda was happy to be home early, but the empty apartment made her feel lonely. She noticed Gregory's laptop sitting by the couch, and wondered why she didn't notice it earlier. Lighting a few scented candles, she settled onto the couch and closed her eyes. Trying to relax was pointless; she had too much nervous energy.

Grabbing her cell phone from her purse, she found Sgt. Allen's number in her list of contacts. Sgt. Allen was in charge of the recovery efforts, after Kylar was kidnapped. While he was no longer heading the recovery efforts, she felt comfortable talking to him and knew he would know if there were any new developments. Jacinda knew he'd call her if anything had changed, but she called him once a week, regardless. He picked up on the second ring.

"This is Sgt. Allen."

"Hi Sgt. Allen. This is Jacinda Kilmeade. How are you?"

"Fine, Jacinda. Just fine. How are things out in D.C.?"

Jacinda appreciated Sgt. Allen's attempt at normal conversation, but needed to get right to the point. "Well, I miss Texas, but I knew I would. I don't suppose anything has changed?"

"No, I'm sorry. You know I'd call you as soon as I heard something, but there's nothing new to report."

"I didn't figure there was, I was just hoping. Just call me as soon as anything changes, okay?"

"You got it, Jacinda," he said, knowing he would be hearing from her the next week, and every week after that, until her child was found.

Jacinda put down the phone and picked up Gregory's laptop from the floor. She logged onto her email, and waited for the page to load. After deleting a few spam messages and answering a few emails, it occurred to her—maybe there would be something in Gregory's email that would explain why he left so suddenly. She knew it was a long shot, but would try anything to gain perspective, at this point.

She clicked on the mail icon, prompting Gregory's inbox to appear on the screen. *I can't believe it's not password protected,* she thought, pleased by her husband's carelessness. She felt a twinge of guilt settle over her as she began reading subject lines. She's never been the type of wife to snoop-- she'd never had a reason. Gregory always seemed so devoted and forthcoming. She scanned the subject lines, until one in particular stood out: *BARAchip Unveiled.*

She opened the message and began reading the text. The BARAchip technology excited her to the core. If only BARAchip would have been in existence two years ago. If only they'd implanted the chip while doing other routine birth procedures like cutting the cord. Shedding her guilty conscience about snooping, she continued reading the message.

We would like to extend our gratitude for the hard work and dedication you all put towards the creation and unveiling of BARAchip. We are closer than ever to making the technology a reality. The television news magazine, Your Nation Now, will be introducing the chip to the country this Thursday 9 P.M. Eastern Time. We hope you'll share in our pride, because without the hard work of everyone involved, this would not be possible.

Jacinda felt a rush of excitement, knowing the email was referencing her story. She felt proud of her self and proud of her husband. BARAchip truly was a noble cause. Gregory clearly loved her; why else would he put so much effort into something so near and dear to her heart? She clicked on *search mail*box, typed in BARAchip, and hit the enter button. She wanted to read about the progress made in the six months Gregory had been working on the legislation. Sure, this could be viewed as an invasion of privacy, but somehow it seemed harmless.

The search box displayed at least seventy-five emails on the results page. The earliest email was dated three years ago—more than a year before they met. Her heart dropped into her stomach; he claimed he wasn't approached about BARAchip until six months ago. *Why would he lie?*

*****

The long subway ride afforded Keith time to think about the day's events. By the time he reached his apartment, he already lost control of his imagination. He wondered if the phone really did have a chip, or if Jerry had done too many drugs. Or both.

Keith pulled Mitch's book out of his backpack and threw himself onto the bed. He kicked off his shoes and peeled the sweat-drenched socks off his feet. The temperature outside was suffocating and he felt exhausted from the heat. No amount of exhaustion was going to keep him from reading Mitch's book. He was hungry to learn what was inside.

Mitch spent a lot of time talking about symbols, but never explained the reason behind them. Keith was fascinated to learn that The Illuminati communicated with symbols. He learned we had become desensitized to symbols that still speak very loudly to Illuminati members. He thought about the language of corporate logos: the owl, the pyramid, and the all-seeing eye, just to name a few. Symbols were the most basic, primitive form of communication. After all, symbols were the same in every language—there were no barriers.

Keith's eyes began to ache, as he pushed himself well past his bedtime. He wondered why Mitch spent so much time on symbols, when there was clearly so much more at hand. Before reading Mitch's book, he never stopped to think about how technology was stripping us of our privacy. He devoured every page, each making more sense than the one before. *Of course*, he thought. *How did I not see it?* America is becoming a cashless society, as predicted. With the use of debit and credit cards, he rarely ever used cash. He never thought about the possibility of someone keeping track of his spending; the very thought made him uncomfortable.

He also never thought much about his social security number. He never used his name at school—just his social. He figured writing his social security number, in lieu of his name, was just the breaks for attending such a large university. It always did make him feel a bit like cattle, but he never viewed it as sinister.

He did sometimes fear identity theft, but never dreamed it was a government creation. He never had a reason to, until he put it in perspective with the chip; the chip was an entirely different chapter. His mother has always liked to talk about the Mark of the Beast. He could tell she was both fascinated and frightened by it. He always promised her he would never accept a chip in his head or hand, but he never really thought he'd be faced with the choice. Whenever she talked about "the chip," it always sounded like science fiction. But now, the thought didn't appear so unlikely; it seemed like the next logical step.

With everyone fearing identity theft, who wouldn't want to secure their own with a chip? The convenience of swiping your hand instead of entering a pin number would seem like an added level of security. The ideas in the book seemed so rational—so logical. He wondered why he hadn't thought of this before. He was never a government conspiracy kind of guy, but he also wasn't an idiot. The government and banks clearly have control of both the people and their money. Just after he quieted his fears by rationalizing the banking system and government were separate entities, he remembered the government bailout. The government had given banks billions of dollars, but refused when the banks tried to return the money.

The government agreed to the bailout for economic stability. However, they refused to accept the money back, thereby keeping control of many financial institutions. Keith's muscles tightened when he made the connection. *The government is taking control of the banks. The symbols, the agenda, the mark--Mitch wasn't crazy, he was right.*

*****

Sitting on the bus, Lyla felt relieved to be leaving the SUV behind. She bought tickets to Oklahoma City, simply because it was the first bus to depart. Oklahoma was far from Lucio, but she knew it didn't exceed his grasp. She didn't know if she would stay in Oklahoma. She hadn't planned that far in advance. She just knew she had to put distance between where The Brotherhood thought she was and where she would actually be. Two thousand dollars wouldn't get her far; she knew she had to spend her money wisely.

Why didn't I bring a change of clothes? She asked herself, after noticing the ketchup stain on the child's shirt. She hadn't given him the ketchup. He simply fished it out of the fast food bag and opened it himself. "Oh baby, you're a mess," she said, while wiping at the stain with a napkin.

"I mess!" the child proudly stated. He smiled in delight and stuck his chubby hand back in the sack. He pulled out a French fry, and popped it into his mouth.

"Aren't you finished with those?" Lyla asked, while continuing to dab at the stain.

"Not binshed," Kyler insisted, before reaching back into the bag. "I hungy."

"You're not hungry. You just ate all your chicken nuggets."

"Uh-huh. I hungy," he repeated, clearly sticking to his story. Lyla's heart ached when she thought about this precious child being sacrificed in a matter of days. He was so carefree and innocent. "Doy," he squealed, as he pulled a small toy from the bag.

Lyla was so involved with Kyler, she hadn't noticed they caught the attention of the lady across the aisle. "You have a toy," the lady said, clearly admiring the child. Lyla didn't want to draw any attention, but with Kyler, she had little choice. Kyler ignored the lady, so she repeated herself. "Do you have a toy?" she asked, speaking a little louder this time.

"Doy," he said proudly, while holding up his hand.

"Well that's a very neat toy," she responded.

"My doy."

"Yes, that's your toy. What's your name?" she asked in a gentle tone that was probably an octave or two higher than her regular speaking voice.

Not understanding her question, Kyler smiled and lifted his toy. After all, if she truly understood the magnificence of the toy, she wouldn't need to waste her time with silly questions.

"You're name, sweetie. What's your name?"

Lyla's heart began beating, and her face became flushed. She hadn't thought of this scenario. She had never given him a proper name. In fact, Lucio forbid her to name the child. The lady's eyes met Lyla's flustered gaze. Her face looked cheerful, but wrinkled well beyond her years. Her blush was orange and streaky and her lips were painted pink. "What's his name, sweetheart?" she asked, with a kindness that was alien to Lyla. Lyla panicked. She hadn't picked out a name. She knew his name was Kyler, but that word had long been forbidden.

"Kyle," she blurted out, before thinking it through. His name is Kyle."

"He certainly is a beautiful -child," she said, looking back towards the toddler. "Those are the prettiest blue eyes I've ever seen."

"Thank you," Lyla said, in a tone that was polite, but indicated she was done with the conversation. The lady seemed to respond to her tone, as she returned her attention to the book in her lap.

Lyla hated being unfriendly, but didn't feel like answering questions. There were so many unknowns. Mostly she felt a sense of guilt. He wasn't Kyle; he was Kyler, and he belonged to someone else. She knew the right thing to do was to return him to his rightful mother, she just didn't know how. Jacinda was surrounded by danger, and the last thing Lyla wanted to do was expose the child to danger.

CHAPTER 17

Jacinda arrived for work an hour late. She didn't really see the point of being on time. She hadn't been assigned a story since the BARAchip piece, and even then she didn't do any of the work herself. Work had become a place to simply show up, and nothing more. She spent her days surfing the internet and waiting for somebody—anybody—to give her an assignment.

Gregory's disappearance weighed heavily on Jacinda. Worse than his absence, was the suspicion she now felt about her husband. He had clearly lied. She couldn't shake the feeling that he was deceiving her about more than just BARAchip.

She looked across the room and saw Keith on the

telephone. She smiled, knowing he was put on phone duty. She was so relieved her intern days were behind her. Although, in her current position, she would probably feel more useful as an intern. At least interns had assignments, even if they were answering the phones.

Jacinda's cell phone rang. Her father-in-law's name flashed across the screen. Her heart sped, and her hands shook as she reached for the phone. Maybe he had information about Gregory. "Hello, Nicholas. I'm so glad to hear from you. Have you heard anything about Gregory?"

"Hi Jacinda. No, I haven't heard anything; I was hoping he had contacted you by now."

"No, I haven't heard anything. I'm getting really worried. This isn't like Gregory. Are you in California?"

"No, I came back home when I realized Gregory was missing."

The word *missing* made Jacinda's heart drop. She knew his whereabouts were unknown, but she never really thought of him as *missing*.

Nicholas continued. "Jacinda, I really think it's better if you stay with us for a while—just until we get this figured out."

"What do you mean? Do you think I'm in danger? Do you think Gregory is in danger?" Jacinda felt consumed by panic. Her head began to ache and her breathing became shallow. "I've got to call the police. I know Gregory will probably be furious, since he's probably fine, but I can't just sit around and do nothing anymore.

"Jacinda, calm down.; I've already called the police. It's already been taken care of. I just think that you need to be with family right now. I've talked to George, and he said he had no problem giving you the time off until we get to the bottom of all this."

"You talked to my boss?" Jacinda suddenly felt a little irritated. She felt like a schoolgirl whose father spoke to her principal.

"Well, yes. Of course, he's worried about Gregory too. He and I go way back, as you probably know. To be honest, Jacinda, Gregory is a target—he's a politician. You know as well as I do that someone in his position is going to have enemies. I'm not saying that his disappearance has anything to do with foul play, but I just want to be on the safe side. You're like my daughter, Jacinda, and I just want to make sure you're protected."

Nicholas' comment warmed Jacinda's heart. It's been so long since she'd had a father figure, and to know someone loved her and wanted to protect her made her feel so safe—so cherished. However, spending time with her in-laws didn't appeal to her in the least. She loved Nicholas, but spending that much time with Chandra wasn't even an option. "I appreciate it, Nicholas, but I'll just stay at the apartment. I'll make sure the doors are locked."

"Jacinda, I'd just feel so much better if you were here. Please reconsider. I'll give you some time to think about it. I can be there in an hour to pick you up, if that's what you decide. Please Jacinda, think about your safety.

"I'll think about it, but I really don't think that I'm in any danger. I miss Gregory like crazy, but my gut feeling tells me he's not in any danger either. I have no idea what's going on, but I'm sure there's a good reason he hasn't called."

Jacinda hung up the phone and closed her eyes tightly. Her head throbbed and she massaged her temples in an effort to relieve the pressure. Opening her eyes, she reached for her purse. *I know I have to have an aspirin in here somewhere,* she thought. Jacinda dug through her purse, but couldn't find anything that would relieve her headache. She looked up at Keith, noticing he was off the phone. She walked over to his desk and he looked up to greet her with a smile. "Hi Jacinda; what's wrong? You don't look right."

"Hi, Keith. I just have a splitting headache. Do you have any aspirin?"

"No, but there is a ton of aspirin in the break room. Sit down. I'll go get you some."

"Thanks, but I'll go get it."

"Don't be ridiculous. I'm an intern; It's my job to get coffee and aspirin," he said with a smile. "Besides, it will get me off phone duty for a few minutes. I'll be right back."

Keith walked into the break room to find Jerry sitting with a cup of coffee. "Hey, it's the resident monkey! How's it goin', brother?"

"It's good, just getting Jacinda some aspirin. Hey, you've been here for a while, right?"

"I've been here longer than that; you sound like you need some inside information."

"I was just wondering, I mean, do we have security cameras here?"

"Why? Are you thinking about breaking into the place?"

"No--nothing like that. I don't even know how to say this in a way that will make sense, but yesterday something appeared on my desk, and I don't know how it got there."

Jerry looked at him with amusement in his eyes. "That happens to me all the time, brother, but I did a lot of drugs in the sixties."

"No, it was something important. I was just wondering if we have cameras, that's all."

"Sure we do, but the tapes reset every week. You'll only be able to review the past seven days. What day are you talking about?"

"Yesterday. Hey, you promise you won't say anything to anyone? I don't want anyone to think I'm crazy or paranoid."

Jerry just smiled. "Not a word man. I won't say a word."

Keith smiled a grateful smile. "Hey, I have to go give these to Jacinda. Will you be here in two minutes?"

"Sure, brother. Hey, I don't have any packages to edit until Rob brings me his tapes. Do you want me to go pull the security tape from yesterday so you can take a look at it?"

Keith looked surprised. "You'd really do that?"

"Sure, I've got nothing else to do, brother. Just meet me at editing bay three in about five minutes."

Keith started to walk out, before turning on his heel. "Hey, isn't Rob at that retreat in California?"

"No, man. He stayed back this year."

Keith's mind flashed back to the picture of him standing with Senator Kilmeade in Mitch's email. He knew Rob Livingston was up to his eyeballs in the Rhapsody Grove garbage. After all, if he said Mitch was crazy, he was guilty as sin. Walking to Jacinda's desk, he couldn't stop wondering why Rob wasn't at the retreat. He handed Jacinda the aspirin. "I hope this helps your headache."

"Thanks, Keith," Jacinda said with a forced smile. She had too much on her mind and was in entirely too much pain to flash a genuine smile.

"Well, if you ever need more, they are in a box by the coffee creamer."

This time, Jacinda's smile was genuine. "Only in a news room, huh?"

Keith smiled and walked away. He couldn't get to the editing bay fast enough. He couldn't wait to see who placed his phone on his desk. After all, the last place it had been was Mitch's apartment the night Mitch allegedly killed himself.

Keith walked into the editing room to find Jerry staring at his computer screen. Jerry's screen displayed what looked like endless rows of numbers. Jerry turned to Keith and smiled, "So, when did the item mysteriously appear on your desk?"

Keith knew Jerry was making fun of him, but was too focused to care. "Yesterday. I left the evening before last, and when I got back yesterday afternoon, it was on my desk."

"I don't get out there much. Where is your desk?"

"The interns sit at the desk closest to Bertha's office."

"Gotcha," he said, as he began highlighting a series of numbers. "What time did you leave the office the night before?"

"About five, I guess. Can we just watch everything from about five that evening until yesterday afternoon?"

"Sure," Jerry said, as he continued to highlight numbers. "Once I highlight the timeframe…" Keith tuned him out. He really didn't care about the process. He just wanted Jerry to hurry up and show him what the cameras captured. Jerry clicked his mouse, and Keith's desk appeared on the screen. Actually, several desks appeared on the screen. The wide shot captured the intern desks, along with the offices of Bertha and George. The time marker said five o'clock; nothing out of the ordinary was happening on screen.

Jerry became impatient. "We can speed this up, man. We'll just fast forward until we see someone near the desk, okay?"

That sounded fine to Keith. He didn't really have an extra twenty-one hours to watch the video in real time. Jerry began to fast forward as Keith watched the time stamp reach eleven p.m. and everyone clear out for the night. Jerry turned to Keith. "Well, nothing that night. Do you want me to skip to yesterday morning?"

Keith couldn't explain why, but that sounded like a

horrible idea. He wanted to continue watching through the night. "No, Jerry; just keep fast forwarding at this pace. I want to see everything."

"Whatever you say, monkey boy," Jerry said, as he continued to fast forward.

Jerry and Keith stared intently at the computer screen until a figure walked across the screen. "There," Keith said, pointing to the screen. Both men watched as the man on screen placed a small object on Keith's desk. Keith leaned closer to the screen. "Who is it?"

"Well, I can't say for sure," Jerry replied. "But from here it looks like—"

"Livingston!" Keith exclaimed, as the man's face came into view. "It's Rob Livingston!"

"Well, I'll be," said Jerry. "Why would he be in the office at three a.m..?" They watched as Livingston began to move towards George's office. Jerry moved his face closr until it was three inches from the screen. "He has a key!" Keith said. "He's going into George's office."

Jerry began to shift his weight in the chair. "I just don't feel comfortable watching this anymore, man. I don't know—something just doesn't feel right."

Keith continued watching the screen, mesmerized. "What is he doing?" Keith asked in little more than a whisper. Jerry stood up and headed towards the door. "This isn't my thing man. I didn't expect to catch anyone doing something they shouldn't be doin', man. I'm going to go get some coffee. When you're through watching that, just ex out of it. Click the X on the top of the screen to exit. Hurry up though, man. This just feels wrong."

Keith nodded, but stayed focused on the computer monitor. Due to George never closing his office blinds, the entire office was in view of the camera. After Livingston entered George's office, he began shuffling around George's desk. It was hard to read Livingston's facial expression from the angle of the camera, but Keith could sense the tension in his movements. Livingston was clearly searching for something; he was digging through George's drawers. Keith felt sheer terror and excitement coarse through his veins. *What does it all mean? Was it Livingston who killed Mitch?*

"So, they've resorted to having interns review security cameras?" Keith froze when he heard the voice behind him. He spun in the chair to see Rob Livingston standing behind him. Keith's heart skipped a beat and his face felt hot. Rob's eyes bored into him, daring him to speak. Keith couldn't speak if he wanted to—he was literally paralyzed by fear.

*****

Lyla stepped off the bus, carrying Kyler on her hip. *Oklahoma City*, she thought to herself. *I can't believe I'm in Oklahoma City.* Kyler stretched his little arms and arched his body away from her. "You want down?" she asked the child. "Dow," Kyler repeated. Lyla lowered Kyler to the ground and readjusted the shoulder strap of the bag. "Don't take off, baby. Stay by me."

"I hungy," Kyler said, as he looked around the unfamiliar city. Lyla had no idea where to go from here. She was starving and exhausted. She'd sort out the details later. For now, she just needed food and a motel. The journey was long, and they both needed rest. She cringed while thinking of the seedy place she and Kyler would have to spend the night. They would have to rent a room that charged by the hour. Any reputable hotel would make her put a credit card on file, and she didn't want The Brotherhood to trace her to Oklahoma City. There was a line of waiting cabs by the bus station, and Lyla wasted no time securing one.

She opened the back door of a parked taxi. "Can you take us to a motel?" she asked the driver. The woman sitting behind the steering wheel looked up from her book. She appeared to be in her forties, with beautiful black skin and kind, brown eyes. Lyla secured Kyler in his car seat, before clicking her own seat belt. The woman smiled at Kyler before turning her attention back to Lyla. "What hotel are you headed to, sweetheart?" she asked, as she turned to face the steering wheel. Lyla didn't really know what to say. She couldn't very well tell her to head to a motel that didn't request credit cards, because she was on the run with a stolen child—a twice-abducted child, actually. "Well, I don't really have a lot of money, so one that doesn't cost a lot. Plus, I only want to rest a couple of hours before hitting the road again. Do you know anywhere that will prorate for four hours or so?"

The woman turned to face Lyla, with knowing eyes, and then focused her attention on Kyler. Kyler waved at the woman and smiled. "I hungy," Kyler informed the driver. The woman didn't answer, she simply stared, shifting her eyes from Kyler to Lyla, then back again. Lyla began feeling anxious. She immediately regretted the hourly prorate comment. Though her eyes were now fixed on Lyla, her mind was clearly somewhere else. Lyla grew so unnerved by the awkward silence, that she attempted to strike up a conversation. "So, I don't mean to be intrusive, but what were you reading? I love books."

"I'm reading the Bible," the woman said with a warm smile. "I don't go anywhere without it. I read it every chance I get--saved my life. The name is Marlene." Lyla instantly felt at ease. "I'm Loren," she lied.

"It's nice to meet you Loren." Marlene drove out of the bus station parking lot, nearly hitting another car as she turned right onto the main road. The other driver honked his horn and shot Marlene an obscene gesture with his hand. "The eyes aren't what they used to be," Marlene said, seemingly unfazed by the driver's display of rage. "So Loren, you just need to rest a few hours, then you're headed out?"

"Yes, that's right. I just need a place for a few hours."

"The boy said he's hungry. Don't you need something to eat?"

"Well, I just thought I'd order a pizza once I got to the motel."

"Loren, you and the boy really don't belong in a place that charges by the hour. There's a lot of questionable characters at those types of establishments."

Lyla felt both annoyed by her bossiness and warmed by her concern. "It's just that I don't have a lot of money, and we won't be here for long."

"Where ya headed after here?"

Lyla's tongue felt tied, as she searched for an answer. She opened her mouth to speak, but Marlene began speaking, saving her from having to tell another lie. "Have you ever felt something strongly in your gut, but had no logical reason to feel it?" she asked without turning around. Not waiting for a response, she continued. "Some people call it women's intuition, or a sixth sense, but I'm a woman of Faith. I believe that feeling is

God talking to us. Some people think God has to speak in a voice like you or me, but I don't think so. I think He puts things on our hearts. God puts things on me sometimes, and I believe He is putting something on me right now."

Lyla was speechless. Ordinarily, she would have thought she had chosen a cab driven by a crazy woman, but for some reason, it didn't feel crazy. She knew nothing about the Christian God this woman was speaking about, but she felt at ease. She didn't know if it was the kindness in her voice, or a supernatural calm, but she didn't feel threatened. She didn't respond—she couldn't.

"You're on the run, aren't you?" Marlene inquired, looking at her through the rearview mirror. "I know it's none of my business —abusive boyfriend? Husband? I just feel that God put it on me to help you;. I know that sounds crazy. I can't just drop you and your baby off at a seedy motel." Lyla felt relieved Marlene thought she was running from an abusive husband and not The Brotherhood. For now, her identity was safe. Lyla knew she should feel uncomfortable, but didn't. She felt calm—a calm she had never experienced. The sense of peace was foreign, but delightful. The feeling was also overwhelming, and she began to tear up, but didn't know why. Feeling ashamed, she wiped the tears from her cheeks, but they kept flowing.

Marlene gave her privacy by averting her eyes from the rearview mirror. Lyla's tears confirmed

Marlene's suspicions. Marlene continued to drive. "I was in your position about twenty-five years ago. It takes a lot of guts to leave, you know. I left when my son was three weeks old. I never felt like I deserved any better, but when my Tommy was born—well, let's just say I knew he deserved better. I wasn't going to let him hurt my baby

Marlene's words hit Lyla especially hard. She never escaped The Brotherhood's abuse to save herself; she escaped to protect Kyler. Marlene finally looked into the mirror to meet Lyla's gaze. "Loren, you're going to think I'm crazy, but I think God wants me to help you."

Lyla felt confused. "Help me?"

"Yes, I couldn't sleep tonight if I just dropped you and your boy off at an hourly motel, and hoped you survived. We all need a little help sometimes, and God sent someone special to me when I was in your shoes. All day, I've felt like God has put something on my heart, and now I think I know what He wants. I've never felt anything stronger in my life. I know you don't know me and for all you know I could be an axe murderer, but how 'bout you crash at my place for a while? You know, just till you get on your feet."

Once again, Lyla was speechless. She had no idea why this woman's eagerness to help her didn't make her feel uneasy. The truth was, in that instant, she felt like she had known Marlene her entire life. She felt safe. She also struggled with guilt. She wondered why she wasn't fearing for Kyler's safety by entertaining the idea of saying yes, but she felt such peace. Lyla smoothed the area under her eyes, trying in vain to erase the tears. "I just don't want to put you out. It's not fair," Lyla finally answered.

In the rearview mirror, Lyla could see Marlene's lips curve into the kindest smile she had ever seen. "Sweetheart, you wouldn't be puttin' me out. I'd welcome the company. Besides, when God talks— I listen. My place isn't much, but I have a roof over my head and a fridge full of leftover spaghetti." She then glanced at Kyler. "You like spaghetti little fella?"

"Sgetti," Kyler squealed, while pumping his tiny fists in the air. Lyla smiled and reached out to hold Kyler's hand. "I guess it's settled then," Lyla said, not fully believing she was agreeing to such a proposal.

*****

Keith's muscles tightened, as his eyes focused on Rob's face through the dimly lit editing room. He realized that he was sitting no more than six feet from a man who could have very well been a cold-blooded killer. His palms began to sweat, but he managed to turn on the outward confidence that earned him the internship in the first place. He didn't get such a prestigious internship by allowing others to see him sweat. Keith's mouth opened, and what spilled out was just as much a surprise to him as it was to Livingston. "Yea, I wondered who returned my phone, so I was just investigating." Rob eyed him suspiciously. "Investigation is something this internship usually doesn't encourage. Phone duty must really have you pulling your hair out with boredom, if you're investigating the return of a lost phone."

Keith felt fairly confident he could pull off his ruse, by way of naivety. His mom used to call it playing dumb, but let's face it--only the smart actually *play* dumb. "Yea, I couldn't remember where I left it. Thanks for returning it." Livingston still didn't look convinced, so Keith continued, "You work harder than anyone I know, it looks like George even has you doing his work. I never talk to George; he doesn't deal with us lowly interns." There, Keith gave Livingston an out for the breaking and entering caught on the tape. If he thought Keith didn't talk to George, maybe the whole issue would be swept under the rug. Well, at least until Keith could get the evidence he needed to win a Pulitzer Prize for his investigative reporting. After all, The Brotherhood story is sure to rock the nation. When Keith exposed this ancient, sinister plot, Livingston would be in prison and Keith would have his job.

On the surface, Livingston seemed satisfied, almost relieved by Keith's reaction. He slowly handed a tape to Keith. "Here's the footage Jerry needs, I also wrote the in and out points for my standup. Can you make sure he gets it?" Keith felt relieved, and his panic transformed into a feeling of triumph. "Sure, I'll make sure he gets it. Thanks again for returning my phone."

Livingston forced a smile. "Sure, kid. Be more careful next time."

As soon as the Livingston turned to leave, Keith turned to face the computer monitor. He was staring at his screen, but he wasn't processing anything. His mind was too preoccupied with the events that just transpired. Pride swept through him, and he felt ten feet tall. He just talked his way out of the toughest situation he has yet to face in his young life. Of all the sticky situations he had managed to talk his way out of, this was his crowning achievement. He could pull off anything. He was brilliant.

The residual adrenalin forced him out of his chair and down the hall. He couldn't sit still. Walking into the break room, he saw Jerry talking to Jacinda. "Hey Jerry, Livingston just dropped by the editing room and left his tape and notes. I left them on the desk." Jacinda looked confused, "I thought Livingston was at the retreat."

"He had something going on here--a wedding or a family emergency; I don't really remember, man. He was put back on the schedule at the last minute."

Jacinda's cell began to ring and she glanced at the caller ID. It was Jill. Looking up at Keith and Jerry, she said, "I need to catch this." Walking into the hall, she answered the phone. "Hi, Jill." Jacinda continued walking towards the bathroom. Maybe she could get enough privacy in there to update Jill without the entire office eavesdropping. Swinging the bathroom door open, she was relieved to find it was empty. "Oh my gosh, Jill. I still haven't heard from Gregory. I'm scared to death. I'm a nervous wreck."

"It's been too long for you not to have heard anything. Have you called the police?"

"No, I was afraid to because I didn't want it to make headlines. But my father-in-law called them. I'm sure he told them to keep it out of the press, but I don't know if demands like that ever work. I don't know what to do Jill."

"You're not at work are you?"

Jacinda paused, then replied, "I don't know where else to be."

Jacinda began breathing heavily, as tears began to flow. "I can't lose him too, Jill. I just can't. At first, I thought there was nothing wrong--that he just took a different flight But Nicholas came home from the retreat. Nicolas is worried enough that he cancelled his plans. Now, I'm scared to death. What am I supposed to do?"

Jill didn't let a moment of silence pass, before saying, "I'm online now getting a plane ticket. I'm coming up there."

"Really, Jill? You'd do that?"

"Of course I'd do that; in fact, I'm booking it as we speak."

Jacinda felt grateful. Ordinarily she wouldn't hear of Jill flying across the country to babysit her, but right now, she truly needed her friend. "Okay, Jill. I've got the next couple of days off; you have no idea how much this means. Don't even think about buying your ticket, though. I'm going to buy it. Just tell me what day and time you are coming, and I'll take care of your flight."

Jill sighed, sounding almost insulted. "Look moneybags, I appreciate it, but I can buy my own airline ticket. In fact, I just did. I'll be there at eleven o'clock tonight. I have a long layover in Chicago, of all places. I need to get off the phone and start packing if I'm going to make it in time. Can you be there to pick me up?"

Jacinda didn't skip a beat, "Of course I'll be there! Dulles, right?"

"That's the one."

"Eleven o'clock. See you then."

Jacinda continued standing in the bathroom, not yet

ready to face anyone in the office. She felt so blessed to have a friend like Jill who would drop everything and come to be with her in her time of need. At the moment, Gregory couldn't be found, but Jacinda didn't feel he was in any danger. Sure it was strange and out of his character, but he was acting strange the night before he left. Unlike Kyler, Gregory was a grown man. She didn't worry about Kyler and Gregory in the same capacity. She thought there was no more room in her heart for grief, but she was wrong. Clearly, the heart's capacity for love and grief is endless. She couldn't even begin to let herself think Gregory might be in danger. She would be letting Kyler down if she let even a tiny bit of fear distract her from the heartbreak she felt for her baby every minute of every day.

Jacinda composed herself, before walking out of the bathroom. She headed back down the hall towards the break room. Keith and Jerry had already left, but Rob Livingston was now pouring himself a cup of coffee. When he heard the clanking of Jacinda's high heels, he turned to greet her. "Hi Jacinda. I haven't seen you in a while. It's weird that we can all work in the same office and not run into each other more often." Jacinda forced a smile. "Yeah, well—you always seem to be out on assignment".

Livingston nodded, "Story of my life. How about you? What story have you been working on?"

Jacinda was almost embarrassed to answer. "I haven't really been working on anything since the BARAchip story. Hopefully things will pick back up when George gets back. So, you decided not to go to California?"

"Yeah, there are some things I needed to get done around here. I'm working on something, but can't really talk about it."

Jacinda gave him an intrigued look. "Oh, top secret, huh?"

"Yeah, something like that," Livingston said with a dismissive wink.

"Well, it was good seeing you again, I'm taking a few days off, but I'll see you when I get back. Good luck on your top-secret story." With that, Jacinda turned and walked to Bertha's desk. Bertha was nowhere to be found, so Jacinda picked up a pink post it note, and wrote, **George approved a few days off; I'll be back next week. Jacinda Kilmeade.**

CHAPTER 18

Lyla looked out of the taxicab's windows as they drove through Oklahoma City. It was nothing like New York. The tall buildings she was used to were replaced with strip centers and chain stores. She could see downtown in the distance, but there weren't many high rises. Marlene turned the taxi into an old apartment complex, before turning to face Lyla. "Home, sweet home. It's not much, but it's where I hang my hat, so to speak." Lyla didn't see outdated harvest gold paint, or fences that clearly needed repairs. She simply saw safety. "It's lovely," Lyla said with a smile. Marlene chuckled. "Well, that's sweet of you to say, dear. I'm punching out for the day. What do you say we go get your little fella fed, and the two of you settled in?"

"That sounds perfect," Lyla said, reaching over to touch Kyler's hand. The Brotherhood would never think to look for her here. The child was due to be sacrificed in two days, and if she could just hide out until then, she felt Kyler would be safe. Sure, she'll still be put to death for her dissent, but at least she can save the child she has come to love as her own.

As Lyla unloaded Kyler from his car seat, Marlene grabbed Lyla's bag and locked up the cab. "Well, let's get to it," Marlene said, flashing that kind smile that put Lyla at such ease. Lyla put Kyler on her hip and followed Marlene up the stairs. Marlene unlocked her apartment door, and Lyla welcomed the cold rush of air that came pouring out of the apartment as the door swung open. "This is lovely," Lyla said politely. Marlene just smiled. She walked into a bedroom and set the baby bag on a bed. This is my room, but I want you and the baby to take it. I'll sleep on the couch." Without even thinking, Lyla shook her head, resisting the offer. "Oh no, we could never take your room. We'll sleep on the couch. I just wouldn't feel right about taking your bed."

Marlene waved her hand dismissively. "Don't be silly Loren. You and the kiddo stay in here. I sleep on the couch most nights anyways. I can't sleep without the television on, and as you can see, there is no TV in this room.

"Well, if you're sure," Lyla said while lowering Kyler to the ground. Marlene looked at Kyler and smiled. "You want to know the best part little fella? My grandbaby is your age, and I have a whole basket of toys in the closet."

"Doys!" Kyler repeated with delight.

Marlene smiled and walked towards the kitchen. "First things first though. What do you say we eat some of that spaghetti I told you about earlier?" Kyler's little legs moved as fast as they would carry him to catch up to Marlene. He reached up and grabbed her hand, walking side by side with the kind woman. "He likes you," Jacinda said with a smile.

"Oh, darlin'. All kids like me. Especially after I bribe them with spaghetti and toys."

Marlene pointed to the small kitchen table. "Why don't you and the little man take a load off, and I'll warm you up something to eat."

Lyla sat down, feeling the chair wobble beneath her as she pulled Kyler to her lap. "So, you have a grandchild Kyler's age?"

"So Kyler is his name, huh? I never got his name. I thought I'd have to call him little fella forever." Lyla felt rude for not volunteering that information. She also felt foolish for giving Kyler's real name. She worried she had said too much. But something about this woman put Lyla at ease. Lyla studied the small kitchen. She looked around to see the walls adorned with crosses and scripture. She put Kyler down, stood up, and moved closer to a small frame. Inside the frame was a prayer, which she read out loud "God grant me the serenity to accept the things I cannot change; courage to change the things I can; and wisdom to know the difference.

"Wow, I like that, did you write that yourself?"

"You've never heard that sweetheart? That's the serenity prayer. I recite it every day. It's helped me through some tough times."

Lyla continued her tour around Marlene's apartment. Scripture was everywhere. She continued to read each aloud. "Rise up; this matter is in your hands. We will support you, so take courage and do it. Ezra 10:4."

Lyla absentmindedly touched the quote with her finger and traced the word *we*. Marlene turned from her task of putting the spaghetti in the microwave. "I put that one up just this morning. I don't know why, but God put it on me to hang it up. Do you know that scripture?"

Lyla turned to face Marlene. "I'm afraid I don't know any scriptures. I wasn't raised in the Christian church, I've never so much as touched a Bible."

Marlene looked at her, kind smile intact, "Oh baby doll, you're missing out. The Bible saved my life. I was lost until I found Christ. The day I was saved was the day I really started living."

Lyla looked confused. "Saved?"

"Yes, doll. You know, the day I let Jesus into my heart. He saved me that day. The day I began to walk with Christ was the single most important day of my life."

Lyla looked skeptically at Marlene, "How exactly do you become saved?"

"You invite Jesus Christ into your heart. You accept Jesus as your personal Savior."

"What do you mean accept?" Lyla asked, looking a little confused.

"Well, I've always thought it meant that you truly

believe He died on the cross for our sins. My God is a good God." Marlene eyed Lyla compassionately. "So, you grew up without religion?"

"Well, I wouldn't say that I grew up without religion, but not Christianity."

Marlene turned to continue preparing their meal, but she continued talking. "So, Muslim, Judaism, Hinduism. Did you study any of those religions?"

Lyla didn't really want to continue the conversation. She was embarrassed of her luciferian roots. She couldn't possibly tell such a good woman that she grew up believing Lucifer was Lord. Of course, she never really believed it. She never studied the doctrine or understood too many of the details. Her exposure to the cult was simply through the abuse she endured and the rituals she witnessed. In her heart, however, it never felt right. It always felt wicked. Desperate to change the subject, she turned her attention to Kyler. "Your food is almost ready. Are you hungry?" Kyler walked to Marlene, who was standing by the microwave and wrapped his arms around her legs. "I hungry. I bant doys!"

"Wow," Layla said. "He really has taken to you, hasn't he?"

"Oh sweetie, all kids love me. I'm a grandma. Plus, I'm a grandma with toys," she said, before lifting Kyler into her arms. She kissed the top of his head and lowered him back to the ground. Pulling the spaghetti out of the microwave, she scooped a generous portion onto a plate and had Kyler follow her to the table. "This one is for you little fella," she said, as she set it on the table. She then stuck her finger into the spaghetti to test its temperature. Realizing what she had done, she shot Lyla an apologetic smile. "Sorry, I know that's gross. It's just a habit. I do that for my grandbaby."

"I do the same thing," Lyla assured her.

Marlene retrieved a booster seat from under her cabinet and placed it on the Kyler's chair. "There, now you're all set to go." Kyler climbed into the booster chair and began shoveling the noodles into his mouth. "Maybe I should have cut them up," Marlene added, as an afterthought.

"No," Lyla responded. "He's fine."

Marlene began scooping spaghetti into another plate for Lyla. How much you want doll? Are you pretty hungry?" Lyla smiled. "Starving!"

"Well, we can't have that. You just eat until your belly is full and your worries are gone."

Lyla thought that was a strange statement; after all, food was good, but it would hardly erase her worries. The three sat at the table eating their meal. Kyler entertained them with his unique method of eating noodles. After becoming frustrated with the fork, he began picking up each individual noodle with his thumb and forefinger, before slurping it into his mouth. Lyla was convinced he managed to get more sauce on his face than in his stomach. She loved seeing him so happy. Most of all, she loved seeing him so safe, if only for this moment.

Marlene stood and began clearing the table. Lyla jumped up to help. Once the dishes were clean, Kyler reminded Marlene of her earlier promise. "Doys," he said, while tugging on Marlene's jeans. "Oh right, toys. I did promise you toys, didn't I, little fella?" Marlene walked to the hall closet and pulled out a laundry basket filled with toys. Kyler's eyes got huge and he began pulling out each toy, one at a time. Within seconds, all the toys were on the floor. "Honey," Lyla corrected him, "we don't want to make a mess. Just play with one toy at a time. Put the rest of the toys back in the basket until you are ready to play with the next one." Kyler didn't even look up at Lyla while saying "I blay wit awe da doys."

Marlene shot Lyla a smile that calmed her. It was clear Marlene was unfazed by the mess. "Oh sweetheart, let him have some fun. My grandbaby does the same thing."

Lyla felt rude for not inquiring about her family earlier. "What is your grandbaby's name?" Marlene's face lit up with pride. "His name is Thomas Charles, after his father. But we call him Tommy. Tommy turns three next month. He's growing in leaps and bounds, that one."

Lyla felt warmed by the love radiating from Marlene when she spoke of her grandchild.

"Oh, you'd love Tommy," Marlene continued. "He's the sweetest kid in the world. Well, I guess he isn't a kid anymore, but you know what I mean." Lyla wanted to know everything about this woman. She was hungry to learn what made her so kind—so loving. "You haven't mentioned a husband, were you ever married?"

"Oh, I thought I did. I was married to Tommy's father. He's the one that beat the tar out of me. He lived at the bottom of a bottle. That man drank from sunup till sundown. One morning when Tommy was a few weeks old, he woke up cryin'— you know how babies do. Anyway, I guess Tommy's crying didn't agree with my ex-husband's hangover, 'cause he walked right over to my baby's crib and slapped him. That was it; that was all it took. I waited until he passed out drunk, packed a bag, got my baby, and we hit the road. I did call my ex-husband from a bus stop somewhere in Kansas, I don't know why, I just did. You know what he said? He said if he ever found me he'd kill me for leaving with his baby. He said he'd kill us both. Needless to say, I never called him back."

Lyla sat quietly, processing the story Marlene just shared with her. "Where did you go? Did you have any family?"

"Oh no, all I ever had was a father. The state took me away from him when I was twelve. I was a ward of the state for the next six years, bouncing from foster home to foster home. I left my last foster home the day I turned eighteen, and met my ex-husband almost immediately. We were married two months later. Less than a year after that, Tommy was born. When I left my ex, it was just me and my boy. He was the only family I needed."

Lyla knew the feeling. Kyler was all she needed, but unlike Marlene and Tommy, Kyler wasn't hers. She often wondered how much pain Jacinda felt on a daily basis, having lost her son. Lyla knew her own story wouldn't have a happy ending, but would do anything in her power to ensure that Kyler's did.

*****

Lucio sat in the back seat of a limousine, screaming into his cell phone. "What do you mean the maidservant and child are gone? Where could they be?" He anxiously tapped his fingers on his knee, as he waited for a response. "Both guards? Are you sure? How? How did this happen? How far could they have gotten? What about the tracking device in the car: Have you morons even thought to try to find the car?"

Lucio wiped the sweat beading up on his forehead and waited for the man on the other end of the phone to finish. "Then search the entire mall! If the car is in a mall parking lot, I assume she and the child are in there! I want everyone on this. The child is to be sacrificed in two days. How long have you been sitting on this information? When were you going to tell me? I will say this—and you better be listening—if the child is not found by tomorrow, you will not live to see another day. I will see to it that you and every member of your family is killed. You put out a bulletin to all of our brothers across the land. I want everyone looking for those two. Have you checked credit card records? Use all your resources; they must be found!"

Lucio sat in silence, as he listened to the man on the other end of the phone. Growing impatient, he cut him off and began yelling. "It was *your* country home they escaped from. It was *your* daughter that escaped with the chosen child! It is *you* that will be held completely responsible if the child is not returned by tomorrow. The child's blood *must* be spilled to consecrate the ground for the birth of our lord. What does the media know about the deaths at your country home?" After a long pause, Lucio looked outraged, "No an alternate child will not suffice! I don't care if they *were* born on the same day. The prophecies are very clear that the mother of the sacrificed child must introduce The Mark to the world! I am on my way to the airport, and if that child is not at the grove in time for the sacrifice, your entire family will be killed." Clicking the phone shut, Lucio threw it to the ground. He continued wiping sweat from his brow, and pulled out a cigarette to calm his nerves.

CHAPTER 19

Jacinda felt relieved to be going home. She picked up a newspaper and headed towards the subway. Although a headache was beginning to build, she felt excitement about seeing Jill in a matter of hours. Maybe Jill could help her make sense of the madness. Hopefully, Jill could help ease the pain and anxiety. After finding a seat on the subway, her mind turned to Gregory and Kyler. Both were her two greatest loves, and both were missing.

While reading the headline of the paper, pain pierced her heart. **Child Abducted From Local Park**. Tears clouded her vision, as she continued to read the article. **Billy Morrison was taken from his mother at gunpoint days before his second birthday. The abduction happened early this morning. Police say a masked man entered the home through a window, abducting the child, as his mother stood helpless against the armed intruder.** Feeling as if a hand had a vice grip on her heart, Jacinda wiped her tears. The child had just celebrated his second birthday. In fact, he was the exact same age as her Kyler—to the day.

Jacinda's heart ached for the parents. Her heart hurt for little Billy Morrison, whom she knew must be confused and frightened. She began to pray. She prayed for his safe return. She prayed for his parents. She prayed for Gregory, Kyler, and everyone else who had ever lost anyone. She prayed through tears, she prayed through pain, she prayed until it was time to get off the subway.

Walking to her apartment, she was overcome with grief and helplessness. She felt a strong desire to go the police department to talk to the authorities. Maybe they had a lead, maybe she could offer a bit of information that would speed the case along. She walked to the street and hailed a taxi. As she climbed into the cab, the cab driver noticed her tear stained face. "Hey, I recognize you. You're Jacinda Kilmeade." Jacinda couldn't even speak; she simply nodded her head. Finding her voice, she managed speak. "Will you please take me to the police station?"

The taxi driver eyed her with concern. "Are you okay? Did someone hurt you?"

Jacinda didn't avert her eyes from her lap "I'm fine, thank you. Please just take me to the station." The cab driver nodded and started the meter. The distance was short, but traffic made the journey seem impossibly long. Upon pulling into the police station, Jacinda pulled a hundred dollar bill out of her purse, and said, "Keep the change." It wasn't that she was feeling incredibly generous. She simply didn't want to wait for the change.

Jacinda charged into the station. She approached the first person in uniform that she could find. "Can you please direct me to the person in charge of the Gregory Kilmeade investigation?" The handsome young officer looked extremely confused. "Senator

Gregory Kilmeade?" Jacinda simply nodded and said, "Yes." The officer excused himself and walked into a nearby office. After a few minutes, the officer emerged, followed by an older man. The older officer approached Jacinda with an outstretched hand. Jacinda placed her hand in his. "Hello Mrs. Kilmeade, I'm Chief Brown." Jacinda shook his hand and introduced herself out of habit, although he clearly knew who she was.

"Ma'am, can you please step into my office?" Jacinda followed him into his office. "Have a seat ma'am." Jacinda sat down and nervously shifted in her seat. "So you say Senator Kilmeade has disappeared?" Jacinda nodded. "Yes, my father-in-law filed the missing person report. I can't be sure exactly when, but he said it's already been taken care of." Chief Brown eyed her suspiciously. "Ma'am, I assure you that if a United States senator had gone missing, not only would I have heard about it, but the feds would be involved as well. No such report has been made."

Jacinda shook her head in disbelief. "I'm sure it's been filed. My husband has been gone for two days now. Nobody has heard from him. My father-in-law, Nicholas Kilmeade, made a missing persons report. Could you have overlooked it?" Chief Brown seemed lost for words. "Ma'am, I doubt I've overlooked it, but I can make a few calls." Chief Brown picked up the phone and began dialing. "Yes, can you please connect me to Agent Asher.

Yes, I'll hold." Chief Brown looked up at Jacinda, nodding as if assuring her this matter would be resolved. "Yes, Agent Asher—Chief Brown. I have Jacinda Kilmeade in my office. She says her husband, Senator Kilmeade, has been missing for over twenty-four hours, and that there has been a report filed to that effect. No, sir, this isn't a joke. Are you sure? Of course, how soon can you be here? Okay, I'll see you then."

Chief Brown hung up the phone and looked up to meet Jacinda's gaze. "Ma'am, I just got off the phone with Agent Asher of the FBI, and he assured me that no such report has been made. If a senator has gone missing, every agent on the force would be on the case. Nobody has heard a word about it. Are you sure your father-in-law filed the report?"

Jacinda looked annoyed. "Yes, he said he's already spoken to the police."

"Well, Agent Asher is on his way over here to speak to you. Do you have time?"

Jacinda wondered who wouldn't have time to speak to a federal agent about their missing husband. What could be so pressing that someone couldn't find the have time? "Yes, of course I have time." Chief Brown stood from his chair, "Can I get you something to drink? Agent Asher should be here shortly."

"No thanks, I'm fine," Jacinda said, realizing how absurd her statement had been. She wasn't *fine;* she was a mess. She didn't know who or what to believe. Had Nicholas been lying about filing a report? What reason would he have to lie about something as basic as filing a missing persons report? Chief Brown began walking towards the door. "Alright, well, I'm going to go get a refill," he said, holding his empty coffee mug up as if she needed proof it was empty.

Jacinda sat in the Chief's office—minutes feeling like hours. What could be taking him so long? Glancing at the clock on the wall, she realized she had been waiting for forty-five minutes. *This is ridiculous!* Jacinda's phone began to ring inside her purse and she answered it without taking the time to check the caller ID. "Jacinda!" said a frantic voice at the other end of the phone. It was her mother-in-law, Chandra. "What have you done? Our phone has been ringing off the hook for the past twenty minutes. The press wants to know my thoughts on my missing son! Who have you spoken with? This matter was to be handled privately. Nicolas told you he had everything under control!"

Jacinda was stunned. First of all, she's been at the police station less than an hour. If the media had been alerted, it wasn't by her. Secondly, shouldn't Chandra use any resource available to find Gregory, even if that meant media involvement? "I haven't talked to the media," Jacinda said, in little more than a whisper. She didn't want curious ears in nearby offices to overhear her conversation.

"You are the media, dear heart," Chanda retorted in a condescending tone.

"I haven't spoken to anyone about Gregory except the police chief, and they said that Nicholas hasn't filed a report."

"Well of course Nicolas didn't file a report with the D.C. police department. A missing U.S. senator is not handled in the same way that a missing vagrant would be, Jacinda! Why don't you think before you act? Nicholas knows what he's doing. He's already spoken to the FBI." Jacinda knew Chandra was lying. After all, Agent Asher knew nothing about Gregory's disappearance. Jacinda's head felt foggy. Her pending migraine was worsening, and she tried her best to will it away. She didn't have the strength to deal with Chandra—not now. "Chandra, I hate to be rude, but I'm getting another call." Jacinda hung up the phone and pressed her fingers to her temples. Massaging her temples, she wondered what it was about Gregory's disappearance that was so top secret. Neither Chandra nor Nicholas seemed too concerned with their missing son, except for their need to keep the situation out of the press. Saying it was strange was an understatement. As the mother of a missing child, she would do anything to recover her son.

Why were her in-laws more concerned with keeping the news under wraps than finding Gregory? Did they know something she didn't? Jacinda sank deeper and deeper into a migraine. The light coming through the blinds began hurting her eyes. She felt nauseous and longed for the comfort of her own bed. She didn't have time for a migraine. She had too much to do—too much to figure out. Jill would be here in a matter of hours, and she still hadn't talked to Agent Asher.

Her mind wondered back to Chief Brown. *How long does it take to get a cup of coffee?*

*****

Keith sat on the couch in his apartment, letting the feeling of cheating death settle into his bones. Could Livingston really believe that he was so naïve? Keith picked the copy of Mitch's book up off his nightstand. He opened it up, and found Andy Barlow's number. After all, Andy probably wouldn't have included his number if he didn't want further contact. Something told Keith not to call; he didn't know why, but he felt the urge to try to find Andy's address online.

He found People Search on his computer, and typed in *Andy Barlow*. There were two listings for Andy Barlow in the D.C. area. Keith picked up his cell phone and called a taxi service.

"Hi, I need a taxi. How soon can you pick me up?"

After giving the dispatcher his name and address, Keith waited outside for the cab to arrive. He didn't really have a game plan. What would he say to Andy? What would be his excuse for not calling first?. He didn't know what drove him to hire a taxi and show up at Andy's. Any sane person would have just called. Keith, however, was not sane— not when he was on a mission. That's exactly what he considered this to be—his own private investigation. He should have been terrified, but he felt exhilarated. He was anxious, but completely pumped.

When the taxi driver pulled up to the curb at Keith's apartment, Keith opened the door and asked, "Are you here for Keith?" The taxi driver shot him a disinterested glance. "Yeah, you Keith?" Keith scooted into the cab and shut the door. He handed him an address and said, "You know the place?" The taxi driver eyed Keith, looking completely annoyed, before running his fingers through his shoulder length greasy hair. "I don't, but my GPS will." He punched the address into the system, and started the meter. "It's about a twenty-minute drive with traffic."

Keith got the feeling the cab driver wasn't much for conversation, so he sat quietly in the backseat. Looking around with fresh eyes, he noticed all the symbols Mitch discussed in his book. There was an eye clinic with an owl on the sign. Keith wondered if this was a sign of Mason ownership.

Sure, not all Masons were part of the Illuminati, but the conspiracy excited him nonetheless.

His mind wandered back to Mitch's book. Mitch pointed to natural disasters and the trend towards a cashless society. The book also alluded to the removal of national borders, which has not yet been implemented, but has been discussed. So much of Mitch's book made sense. To someone who hasn't researched the book as thoroughly as Keith, it might seem a bit paranoid, but most of Mitch's observations seemed spot on.

What he hadn't yet pieced together was Livingston's role in the conspiracy. Obviously, Livingston recovered Keith's cell phone from Mitch's house. Did that mean Livingston killed Mitch? Would Livingston also become suspicious of Keith? Keith had all these questions and a million emotions coursing through him, but fear was suspiciously absent. He just wanted the story. He wanted to break the story to the world.

The taxi driver strained his neck backwards. "We're here. Forty-two dollars even." *Highway robbery,* Keith thought to himself, as he handed him his debit card. He exited the cab and placed his feet on the lush, green lawn of the apartment complex. Glancing down at the address, he noted he was looking for apartment 202. As he walked to the apartment, he ran a million scenarios thought his mind. Would he say he was *just in the neighborhood?* Nothing really seemed adequate.

Would he be honest with Andy, and tell him about the returned cell phone. After all, Andy was a friend of Mitch. Wouldn't he want to know if Keith had a suspect?

Keith walked to the door. His body froze, before his finger could ring the doorbell. *Maybe I should have just called.* Before he had time to think it through, his finger rang the bell, and within seconds Andy was at the door. Andy looked confused, "Keith, right?" Keith smiled and nodded his head. "Keith Ludwig. I read the book you sent me, and just had a few questions." Andy shot a glance behind him and then back at Keith. "Now might not be the best time."

Keith heard a man call from the other room, "Is it Larry?" Andy shot back, "No, it's someone—" Before he had a chance to finish his sentence, Rob Livingston appeared at the door, standing behind Andy. That was all Keith needed to feel the fear he should have been feeling in the taxi. His body felt numb. "Uh. Hi, Mr. Livingston." Livingston looked like a deer caught in headlights. "What are you doing here?" Keith might have asked Livingston the same question, but his mouth wouldn't move, despite his best efforts. "So you know my friend Andy, huh?" Livingston asked, in his most nonchalant tone. Keith paused, searching for just the right answer. "We've met." *Is that all you've got Keith,* he thought to himself in total disgust. *I'm showing up to the apartment of a man I just met?*

Keith's head felt light. Livingston put his hand on Keith's shoulder and said, "You might as well come on in." Keith's feet felt cemented to the welcome mat. He couldn't move forward. Andy shot Livingston a look, wondering if Livingston had lost his mind. He looked at Andy. "The kid thinks I killed Mitch. It's better he know the truth, especially since we have so little time. Besides, the kid is impressive. He keeps a poker face even in the most dangerous of situations. He wants to be the first to bring the world a story. We could use a kid like this.

Keith still couldn't move. What if this was a dirty trick to get Keith into the apartment to finish him off?

CHAPTER 20

Lyla tucked Kyler into bed and kissed his forehead goodnight. "I'll just be in the next room talking to the nice lady. If you need anything, I'm only a few feet away." Kyler reached his chubby palm to touch Lyla's beautiful, tired face and said, "Go seep." Lyla smiled at the precious child. "Trust me angel, I'm going to sleep before long. I'll come crawl in bed right beside you, and we'll have the sweetest dreams we've ever had."

Her answer seemed to appease Kyler. "I yike seet deems."

"I know you do, kiddo. We all do. Just close those pretty little eyes and when you open them, I will be lying right next to you, okay?" Kyler closed his eyes hard, then opened them, before saying, "Hi." Lyla smiled. "You little stinker. You know what I meant," she said, as she tickled his ribs. "Just go to sleep my love."

Kyler closed his eyes, and Lyla slipped back into the living room. Marlene was in the kitchen. "I'm making myself some tea, you want some?" Lyla smiled and tried to rub the sleepiness from her eyes. She couldn't help but remember the last time she brewed tea. "Um. No thanks. I don't really drink tea. Maybe some warm milk?"

"Ask and you shall receive," Marlene said in her southern drawl. Marlene was now in sweat pants and a black t-shirt. She had let her hair down, and looked like a totally different woman than Lyla met in the cab. Lyla was still in awe of her kindness. "Listen, I can't thank you enough for being so good to us. I still don't know why you're being so nice. Marlene smiled with her kind eyes, "Do unto others as you would have them do unto you. Luke 6:31." Lyla looked at her in confusion. "Is that another Bible verse?"

Marlene poured Lyla's milk into an oversized coffee cup, "Yes darlin'. One of many. So you say you've never read the Bible?" Lyla looked down, almost embarrassed. "No, I was never given the chance. Let's just say my upbringing was pretty far from Christian."

Marlene put the mug of milk into the microwave. "Well, if you don't mind me asking, what was your upbringing?" Lyla felt uncomfortable. "You wouldn't believe me if I told you." She desperately wanted to share everything with this kind woman. Marlene was everything she dreamed a mother should be. She wanted to spill her heart out, and have Marlene hug and comfort her. As much as she desired the acceptance, she felt the truth would work against her and strike fear in her new friend.

"How about you?" Lyla retorted. "What was your upbringing like?" Marlene watched the seconds tick away on the microwave until the buzzer sounded. She opened the door, lifted Lyla's drink, and walked toward the living room. Handing Lyla her milk, she secured a place for herself on the recliner. "That's a big can of worms. Are you sure you want to hear about my upbringing?" Lyla smiled, and welcomed the distraction from having to talk about herself. "Yes, I'm sure. I'd love to hear about you."

Marlene sat down and focused her eyes on a framed scripture sitting on her small coffee table. "You see that scripture?" Lyla looked. "Yes, why?" Marlene focused her eyes on the scripture, but it was clear she knew it by heart, "Isaiah 41:10. Fear not; for I am with you. Be not dismayed; for I am your God. I will strengthen you; yea, I will help you; yea, I will uphold you with the right hand of My righteousness." I read that every night as a child. It got me though a lot of hard times. My birth father was a drunk. And I'm not talking about one of those nice drunks that drank and passed out. No ma'am, he was a mean son of a gun. He used to beat the tar out of me.

He called himself a man of God—in church every Sunday. Not everyone who calls himself a Christian walks with the Lord. Sure, God still loves them, but he had a lot of demons. Lyla looked confused, "You think God loves everyone? Even the sinners?" Marlene smiled, but her eyes were a million miles away, seemingly staring into her childhood. "God loves all his children, darlin'. The mean ones, the murderers, the sinners, the liars; he loves them all. God doesn't give up on men, it's men who give up on themselves. I'm not saying their sin doesn't go without punishment, but I've always thought of God as loving us like we love our children. There's nothing our children could do to make us stop loving them. We just hope they'll change."

A feeling of hope overwhelmed Lyla. "The liars?" Marlene met Lyla's gaze. "Yes, dear heart, the liars too. Why, do you fancy yourself a liar?" Lyla looked down. "Well, I don't fancy myself anything. I just wondered. I mean, doesn't everybody lie, I mean, at one time or another?" Marlene eyed her, seemingly still deep in thought. "Well, Proverbs 19:5 says, 'A false witness will not go unpunished and he who tells lies shall perish.'" Lyla looked very distraught by that scripture. "Perish? As in die?" Marlene smiled a warm smile, "We all die, dear heart. That verse can be interpreted in many different ways. Most believe that lying is a sin and that sin shall be punished."

Lyla felt a strong urge to confess, to come clean. "My name isn't Loren. It's Lyla," she said. Tears were now streaming down her face. "I gave you the wrong name because I was scared." Marlene moved to the sofa, now sitting only a foot or so from Lyla. She put her arms around her to comfort her. "We all get scared, sweetheart. I don't think that's the kind of lie the scripture was referring to, but who really knows. I do appreciate that you trusted me enough to tell me the truth."

Lyla began sobbing. The tears wouldn't stop, as much as Lyla willed them to. "I was scared Marlene. I was scared for Kyler." Marlene lovingly stroked Lyla's hair. "Weren't you scared for yourself?" Lyla shook her head and did her best to wipe the streaming tears from her face. "No, I don't care what happens to me." Marlene continued to stroke her hair. "I used to feel the same way, you know. I didn't care what happened to me, as long as my child was safe. The more I got into the Bible though, the more I realized that God cared about what happened to me, and if I mattered to God, then I mattered to myself. It's funny how that works. God loves you, you know. If he didn't, he wouldn't have sent you to me. You may not care what happens to you, doll, but I do. And so does God."

Lyla began to feel uncomfortable with the direction the conversation was heading. "So, where is your son?" Lyla asked Marlene. She recognized Lyla's discomfort and decided to drop the subject. "Well, Tommy joined the military the day he turned eighteen. He was determined to do his part to save the world. That's my boy. I wish I saw him and my grandbaby more than I do, but he's off doing what he considers God's work." Lyla considered that for a minute. "Do you consider it God's work?" Marlene just nodded, "Securing our country's freedom—it's as noble as anything, I'd say." Lyla smiled. "You have a point." Marlene nodded again. "Well, sometimes I do, don't I? My points come in random spurts, you never know when a good one is going to hit."

"I hope you don't mind me asking, but why did you become a ward of the state at twelve?"

"Nope, don't mind at all. I was always showing up to Sunday school with a bruise here, and a bruise there. I usually always had a good excuse, but one day, I just told the truth. I told my Sunday school teacher that my daddy hauled off and punched me, and that he was the reason for my black eye."

Lyla looked at her sympathetically. "So what did they do?" Marlene closed her kind, tired eyes, like she was trying to recall an ancient event. "Well, they called child protective services. For a while, I stayed with a family from the church, but that didn't last for too long. The couple I was staying with got a divorce, and couldn't afford to keep me. I was shuffled from family to family, until I was sent to live with Lilly. I called her Grandma. Grandma Lilly was the sweetest little lady you'd ever want to meet. She's the one who really taught me about God's love and Grace. She helped me see Christianity in a whole new light. She died when I was seventeen, though, and I was sent to live with another family. That family didn't seem to take an interest in me, and I didn't really bond much with them either. I mostly kept to myself.

"Most girls who were taken away from their parents when they were young were sent to orphanages, in those days. I never had to live in an orphanage. I always felt God had his hand on my shoulder. Not that orphanages were bad, of course, but I always had a home with good people. I was blessed."

*****

It felt like an eternity before Agent Asher entered Chief Brown's office. Jacinda rose to greet the man. "No need to stand up ma'am," he said as he shook her hand. "I'm Mike Asher, FBI. I'm sorry it took so long to get here, but traffic—well, you know," he said with an apologetic grin. Jacinda couldn't smile back. "My husband—have you heard anything about my husband?" Asher shook his head. "Nothing yet ma'am. But you can bet we'll put all the resources necessary in an effort to find him. How long did you say he's been missing?"

"He's been gone a few days. I didn't want to alert the authorities, in case it was just a miscommunication."

"What do you mean a miscommunication?"

"Well, he left for a trip to California, but then I heard

from my mother-in-law that he never made it."

"I see, was your mother-in-law supposed to be joining him?"

"No, my father-in-law was supposed to accompany him. They were supposed to be on the same flight, but Gregory never showed up."

Agent Asher absentmindedly shook his head while making notes. He was a distinguished looking man. Jacinda guessed he was in his mid-thirties. His dark suit was pressed to perfection. His blue eyes looked older than his age, as if he'd seen a lot in his thirty some-odd years. His hairline was receding, but not enough to really call him *balding*. He looked kind, but in her line of work, she learned that looks were often deceptive. Agent Asher looked up to meet Jacinda's tired eyes. "I don't mean to pry, ma'am, but every detail is crucial. Did you two have an argument or a fight before he left for his trip?" Jacinda shook her head, "No, but he actually left earlier than he was supposed to."

"What do you mean, 'earlier than he was supposed to'?"

"Well, he left before I woke in the morning,. I'd say at least two hours before he was supposed to leave for the airport." Asher began making notes. Jacinda looked concerned. "Could that be significant?"

"Ma'am, you can never really know what will end up

being significant. I just like to be thorough."

The stress of the past two days, once again, caught up to Jacinda. Her hands began trembling. Tears began streaming down her face and her breathing became erratic. Agent Asher looked sympathetic. "Ma'am if you want to take a minute—maybe grab something to eat or drink?" Jacinda politely refused. "No, I'm okay. I'm just hoping there is nothing I'm leaving out." Asher nodded, and gave her a comforting smile.

"So," he continued, "this is the first report you've filed?"

"Yes, but my father-in-law said he filed a report earlier." Asher continued making notes on his pad. "You say 'said' like maybe you are a little skeptical."

Jacinda looked embarrassed. "It's not that I'm skeptical. It's just that Chief Brown said he hadn't heard of the report. He also said the feds weren't notified. I mean, I can see why my father-in-law would want to keep this out of the press, but I don't think he's the type of man to flat-out lie." Asher tried to lighten the mood. "Is this the same man that used to be a politician?" The joke hadn't been lost on Jacinda, but she was too tired and upset to smile.

Jacinda continued to fill Asher in on the days leading up to the disappearance, and Asher continued making notes. Before long, two hours had passed. Jacinda noticed the time. "I set my phone to silent," she said, while thinking out loud. She grabbed the phone from her purse. She had missed two calls from her friend Jill. Jill also sent a text saying **en route, be at Dulles at 6. Amtran Airlines. See you then!**

Jacinda turned her ringer back on and pressed her forehead into her hands. "My friend must have gotten a direct flight. She's five hours early. I have one hour to get to the airport. I hate to cut this short." Agent Asher nodded and looked pensive. "Do you have a car here?" Jacinda looked as if she was just struck another blow. "No, and I don't have time to go home and get it; I'll just get a cab." Asher grinned. "No need ma'am, I can take you to get your friend. And on the way, we can finish the interview. Besides, that will give us time to get an officer to your house for observation." Jacinda looked surprised. "Observation?"

"Nothing to be alarmed by, ma'am. It's just that when men as high profile as your husband go missing, we can't help but rule out foul play. Okay, that sounded alarming, but that's not what I meant. I simply mean we'll post a plainclothes officer on the premises for your own protection."

"Do you really think that's necessary?"

"I tend to err on the side of caution. Plus, it's protocol, and I'm not really one to part with protocol."

Jacinda and Asher walked toward his government vehicle. Asher could see Jacinda's nerves were getting the best of her and tried to make small talk. "So you have a friend coming in from out of town, huh?" Jacinda welcomed the subject change. She already told Asher everything she knew about Gregory. "Yes, she's my best friend; she couldn't have offered to come at a better time." Asher just smiled. "So is she a journalist like you?"

"No, she's not a journalist. She's a computer geek. At least, that's what she calls herself. She's a data recovery specialist."

Asher seemed familiar with the term. "I heard once that a popular novelist dropped his computer and lost his entire novel. It took a specialist months to retrieve everything he lost."

Jacinda smiled. "Well he clearly didn't take it to Jill. It would have only taken Jill a few minutes. She's a genius."

Traffic seemed endless, but Washington Dulles Airport was finally in view. Jacinda's phone rang, as Jill's name popped up on the caller ID. "Hi Jill," Jacinda said. Asher could hear a female's voice coming from the other end of the phone, but couldn't make out the words.

"What airline did you say she was traveling?" He asked.

"You're on Amtran, right?" Jacinda turned to Asher

and nodded her head. "Dulles, Terminal D," Jacinda continued without being asked. As they pulled up to the terminal, Jacinda said, "We're in a big black car." A look of recognition crossed her face as she said, "Oh, I see you. Okay. Bye." Asher immediately knew which one Jill was, as she stood on the curb waving. Asher pulled into passenger pickup and helped Jill with her luggage. Jill thanked him and attempted to give him a tip. "Not necessary ma'am." Jacinda looked embarrassed. "He's a federal agent, not a chauffeur." Jill turned red. "Sorry." Asher just grinned. "No harm, no foul, ma'am."

The ride home did little to lift Jacinda's spirits. She was happy to have her friend in town, but still scared to death for her husband. Not to mention the ever-present sadness she felt for her son. Asher decided to use the silence to retrieve more information. "So Jill—your name is Jill, right?" Jill smiled. Yes, sir." Asher continued. "I've been asking Jacinda if anything suspicious has been going on, but she can't seem to recall anything. Sometimes when people are grieving, their memories tend to be hazy. Can you think of any conversations you two might have had that sounded like anything was—I don't know—off?" Jill thought for a second before turning to Jacinda. "I can't think of anything off hand. But if Jacinda or I think of anything, we'll be sure to call you. Did you give Jacinda your number?"

Asher pulled a card out of his wallet. "Here's my card. I don't want to alarm you, but if you think of anything—and I mean anything—please make sure I'm the person you call."

Jacinda directed Agent Asher to her condo and he parked the car. Asher popped the trunk and retrieved Jill's luggage. "I hope you don't mind, but I'm going to wait here until my officer shows up to survey the place. I also want to check the inside of your condo before the two of you enter." Jill looked at Jacinda. "Just what did you get me into?" she asked in her usual sassy tone. "I wish I knew," Jacinda responded, burying her forehead into her hands.

CHAPTER 21

Keith entered Andy's small, dimly lit apartment.
The apartment smelled of cigar smoke, which made
him crinkle his nose in disgust. Six men sat on two
couches, along with a couple of kitchen chairs that
were brought in for extra seating. "Am I interrupting
something?" Keith asked, letting his nervousness
show. "That's the first time I've seen you look
nervous Keith," said Livingston. Keith was
impressed that Livingston remembered his name,
and instantly put on his confident persona. "I just
didn't mean to crash the party, that's all." Andy
eyed Livingston nervously. Livingston stood and
began pacing the room. "Keith is an intern at *Your
Nation Now*, Livingston announced to the others.
Keith caught me red-handed breaking into the
place, returning his phone, and rummaging through
George's office. When I confronted him, Keith here
didn't even break a sweat. You know who he
reminds me of? Me. Well, me twenty years ago.
Me before I began to worry about my eternal soul.
He wants a story, and he'll do whatever it takes to
get it. Am I right Keith?" Keith didn't know how to
respond. It was a backhanded compliment, which
didn't escape him.

Keith nodded his head, "Sure, I want the story. Of
course I'll do whatever I need to do in order to
break it. I'm not a bad guy, I'm not going to murder
or hurt anyone in the process, but I want the truth to

be told." Livingston interrupted his rant, "So, you are truth-seeker, you say?" Keith shot him an annoyed look, "Yes, isn't that what every great journalist is—a truth-seeker?" Livingston eyed Keith up and down. "What if I had a story so big that breaking it would make you world famous? Would you do it?" Without skipping a beat, Keith said, "In a New York second."

"Well, what if I told you that breaking that story would most likely get you killed, or at very least blackballed from the field of journalism?" Keith pondered this question, "Would it make me famous?" For a moment, Keith's question disgusted Livingston. "Yes, it would make you very famous. It would also make you hated by a lot of very powerful people." Keith began to pace the floor as well. "I don't get it, why me? Why would you trust me with such a story?" Livingston didn't hesitate, "You could have called me out for returning your phone. To you, it must have looked like I killed Mitch, but you didn't report me. You didn't report me because you wanted to get to the truth. You wanted the story even worse than you wanted to reveal Mitch's killer."

Keith should have been offended by the accusation, but after hearing it out loud, he did have to admit Livingston had a point. "I can't prove you killed Mitch," Keith offered, for reasons he wasn't even sure of. Livingston slapped his own forehead. "I didn't kill Mitch, but you didn't know that! I've been monitoring you since I saw you called Mitch from your company cellphone. I monitor all those phone calls. You have no idea how deep The Brotherhood's roots run in politics, media, and the banking system. I can't watch out for every career field, but what I can do is watch my newsroom. I wanted to know who was and wasn't involved. I saw that you were calling Mitch, and when I heard Mitch had been killed, I became concerned. We have a system that allows us to track all the station phones at any given moment. I saw your phone was located at his apartment. I simply retrieved the phone before you could be implicated."

Keith thought for a moment, then asked, "So you didn't kill Mitch?" Livingston closed his eyes, desperately searching for his lost patience. "No, I didn't kill Mitch. I'm not a killer. I liked Mitch, we all did." Keith pondered that last statement. "If you liked him so much, why wouldn't you return his emails?" Livingston stopped pacing and sat on the sofa. "Mitch was a good guy. He had a great heart. He just let his emotions get the best of him. He wasn't good with strategy. He thought truth was enough. He thought all we had to do was blow the whistle, and an ancient evil society would come crumbling down. It doesn't work like that. There are hundreds of people like me, in hundreds of occupations around the world. We are insiders. We infiltrate The Brotherhood and know the plans. We act, but not before considering the best tactics.

After this weekend, I'm probably a dead man. I have nothing to lose by telling you this. Once George realizes the BARAchip report is gone, I'm going to be implicated, because I backed out of the retreat."

Keith nodded. "Is that what you were looking for in George's office?" Livingston nodded. "I replaced the original story with dead air—blank tape. The story starts the same, but before the chip can be introduced, the tape fades to black."

Keith had to think about that for a minute. "What good would that do?" Livingston smiled, "Well, since we're spilling everything we know, we might as well tell you everything. BARAchip is the industry name. What it should be called is The Mark of the Beast. Ancient prophecies say the mother of an abducted child should be introducing The Mark to the world." Keith looked as if someone smacked him in the face. "You mean Jacinda?" Livingston nodded. "Yes, Jacinda. Her son is to be sacrificed in two days. His blood is supposed to bless the ground for the anti-Christ to be born."

Keith felt ill. You mean you're just going to let it happen? You're just going to let them kill her son? Just like that—you're not even going to try to stop it?"

Livingston look insulted, "Well a good source says the child is missing. The maidservant took the child and is on the run. The Brotherhood doesn't know where the child is, but there is chatter of there being video of her boarding a bus to Oklahoma City. That is where you are going to come in. You want to be famous? You want to make world headlines? Here's your chance. I'm a dead man, Keith. There is nothing you can do to hurt me, but I can do far more good here than I can do chasing down a child in Oklahoma City. So, there's your challenge, should you choose to accept it."

Keith felt ill, but most of all, he felt exhilarated. "Of course, I'll accept it." Livingston smiled. "Good. I was going to have Larry do it, but this is better. Besides, he still hasn't shown up. Here's a cell phone. There is no GPS, and no way to trace you. I will tell the station that you had to return home for family business." Livingston opened his wallet. "Here is five thousand dollars, which should get you there. But listen, The Brotherhood is everywhere. You are to tell nobody. You never know who is involved. I have a camera in my car; you can take that to document your journey. Once you find the Kilmeade baby, I have supporting footage of the sins that take place at the retreat. We have enough to rock The Brotherhood, but not stop it completely.

Keith felt pumped—high with excitement. "Sure, I'll do it. I'm in."

"One more thing Keith, you aren't to ever speak of anything we told you. You were never here tonight. Do you understand?" Keith shook his head. "Got it."

*****

Marlene leaned in to hug Lyla, "Well, I'm going to turn in. Morning comes early. I have to go to work at seven, but there's food in the fridge for you and Ky. If you need anything, here's my number. Just use the house phone." Lyla smiled, "I guess I'll get out of here so you can get some sleep."

Lyla made her way to the bedroom and couldn't help but feel overwhelmed with love when she saw baby Kyler sleeping peacefully. His lips curled into a smile, and she hoped her promises of sweet dreams had come true. Lyla desperately wanted a shower, but didn't want to disturb Marlene She would just take one in the morning. *There must be a God,* she thought to herself. *How else would Marlene have come into our lives?*

Lyla climbed into bed and snuggled Kyler close. She felt his chest rise and fall, as he slowly breathed. Hee was clearly in a deep sleep. She kissed his cheek and whispered, "I couldn't love you any more if you were mine." But she knew he wasn't. Somewhere out there, she knew Jacinda Kilmeade was burdened with a deep sadness for the loss of this precious child. She knew she couldn't keep him, as much as she wanted to.

Sleep came easy for Lyla. Exhausted from the trip, she closed her eyes and slipped into a deep sleep. For the first time in years, her dreams were peaceful. For the first time in her life, at least for this moment, she felt safe.

*****

After Asher was sure the apartment was clear, he allowed Jacinda and Jill to enter. "The place is secure," he assured them. Jacinda didn't know if she should be grateful for the security, or annoyed at the overkill. After all, she didn't feel that she was in any danger. Asher's phone rang. "This is Asher." From what Jacinda could tell, the officer outside was in position. "Okay ladies, we have a plainclothes officer in his car right outside. We'll have someone here around the clock until we have some idea of what's going on with Senator Kilmeaede. The officer can take you anywhere you need to go." Agent Asher pulled out a pen and paper to write down the officer's number. This is Officer Jackman's cell number. He will be here until the next shift. If you need anything, give him a call. I will call you with the name and number of the officer who has the next shift. In fact, I should be talking to you quite a bit throughout this process. Please keep my number on you. Also, can you write down the best number for me to reach you, in case I need additional information?"

"Or in case you have any information," Jacinda finished.

"Of course, ma'am."

Jacinda wrote down her cell number. "I always

have this on me. Please don't hesitate to call if you hear anything," she said in a sincere tone. "I don't care what time it is."

Agent Asher turned and headed towards the door. "I'll call you if I hear anything ma'am, and you do the same, if you don't mind." Jacinda walked him towards the door. "Of course. Thanks so much for everything. I'll be in touch." After letting Asher out of the door, she looked over at her friend Jill. Jill's eyes were begging for answers.

Jill grabbed Jacinda's forearm. "The FBI, twenty-four-hour police surveillance, I feel like I'm in the middle of a movie." Jacinda walked away from Jill's grasp. "Oh, that's a little dramatic, don't you think?" Jill made her way to the couch. Sitting down, she removed her shoes and rubbed her feet. "So, what happened while I was on the airplane, Jacinda? When did you get in contact with the FBI?" Jacinda joined her friend on the couch and removed her own shoes. "I didn't. I mean, eventually I did, but only after going to the police station. I went to see if I could help and to find out if they knew anything. I was wondering why nobody had contacted me already. Well, long story short—there was no missing persons report. The officer realized a U.S. senator was missing; he called the feds, and well, you got to meet Agent Asher.

Jacinda began dabbing tears from her eyes. "Why Jill? Why this? Why now?" Jill moved closer to her friend. Jill tried to comfort her by touching her arm, but Jacinda jumped from the couch. The sudden movement made Jill jump in response. "Good grief Jacinda. Jumpy much?" Jacinda grabbed the remote control and returned to the couch. "My BARAchip story is on soon." Jill began surfing through channels until she found her show. "Jill, you'll see. This technology might have saved Kyler." Both women watched the program and waited for Jacinda's piece about BARAchip to air. Jacinda's story was never so much as mentioned.

Jacinda picked up her phone and began scrolling through her contact numbers for Bertha. She pushed "Send" and waited for Bertha to answer. "This is Bertha. Talk quick." Bertha's harsh, rushed tone made Jacinda wish she wouldn't have bothered calling. "Hi, Bertha. It's Jacinda Kilmeade. I was just wondering why the BARAchip story didn't air today."

"Yeah, you and everybody else. We discovered during the run-through that the tape was blank. George is going to fire somebody over this one. I don't have time to talk. I'll see you soon." With that, the conversation ended. Jacinda didn't even have a chance to say goodbye. She simply hung up the phone.

Jill set the phone on the couch next to her. "That was weird. She said my tape was blank." Jill looked at Jacinda. "You know, a lot of weird stuff has happened today. Have you stopped to think that it could be less weird and more organized?"

Jacinda shot her friend a confused look. "So I'm not organized enough?" Jill smiled. "No silly. I mean, have you considered that all of today's strange events might be connected—intentional?"

Jacinda looked tired and was in no mood to play word games with Jill. Jacinda rubbed her temples. "Just say it Jill. What do you think is going on?" Jill looked almost offended. "Good grief, Grumpy. I just meant that all of this chaos might be organized chaos. Maybe someone is responsible for everything that has happened today." Jacinda thought a minute about Jill's theory. "Well, my father-in-law didn't file a missing persons report, so there's that. But I doubt he's responsible for the tape being blank."

Jill glanced at Jacinda, clearly a bit confused. "So Nicolas said he filed a report and didn't?" Jacinda continued rubbing her temples and nodded. "Yes, I don't know why. It doesn't make any sense." Jill pondered Jacinda's last statement. "No, it doesn't make any sense that he wouldn't report him missing *unless* Nicholas knows where he is." Jacinda looked at her friend suspiciously. "That's crazy. How would he know?"

Jill retorted, "This is all crazy. Let's stop trying to pretend it's not." Jill eyed the laptop sitting on the coffee table. "Is that your laptop?" she asked Jacinda, while lifting it into her lap. Jacinda glanced over. "No, it's Gregory's." Jill's face seemed to brighten as she opened it. "Jackpot!"

MARKED I

CHAPTER 22

Keith still had so many questions to ask of

Livingston and his conspirators. While he believed they had good intentions, there were so many things he needed to understand. Mitch's book talked about a one-world political system and an ancient bloodline, which conspired to rule the world. If anyone would have answers to those questions, it would be these men.

"Before I take off for Oklahoma City, I need some answers," Keith said in a matter-of-fact tone. Livingston nodded, "I'm sure you have lots of questions, and we have some of the answers you seek, but we don't have time to reveal any of that now. We will give you all the information when the time is right.

Keith eyed Livingston suspiciously, "You said you were a dead man. How do I know you will even be here to answer my questions when I return with the baby? How do I know I won't be killed?" Livingston looked at Keith for a while before he answered. He ran his long fingers through his graying hair. "I can't make any promises, Keith. To them, The Brotherhood, you will be just a reporter, not a traitor. They have given you no inside information, or trusted you with any ancient secrets. If you were to be killed after your story aired, it would lend more credibility to your story than anything else. The Brotherhood is not made of stupid men. They are going to paint you as a Christian, rightwing wacko. I can't guarantee you'll ever work in this business again, but you'll be famous. Plus, you'll be paid money to tell your story again and again. Invest that money well, and you will never have to worry about money again. If it's breaking the story of a lifetime you are after, then this is your calling. If it's a long, sustainable career in journalism you seek, then perhaps you aren't the man for the job."

Keith took Livingston's statement into consideration, before speaking. "What was Mitch talking about when he said The Brotherhood was part of an ancient bloodline?" Livingston looked at the men surrounding him and shrugged. "That's the most basic question he could have asked, do you think there would be any harm in answering him?" Andy stood and began to pace the room. "I was the closest to Mitch, before he was murdered. I probably have the most insight into what he meant by an ancient bloodline. It was just a theory. Mitch couldn't prove it was anything but a theory, and when you return safely from your journey, I will get into the bloodline theory in greater detail. In fact, I will tell you all you need to know when I see that the child is safe and reunited with his mother. That is when you and Mr. Livingston will put together one of the greatest truths ever told."

Keith picked up the phone Livingston had given him. "Aare you sure nobody can trace my whereabouts on this phone? There is no GPS, or anything else that will get me caught?" Livingston smiled. "I promise that phone is clean. In a month, A woman in Detroit will get a bill, which will have an itemized listing of who you called. But by then, the mission will either be a failure, or it will be a success. You go save the child. Document your journey and reunion with the camera I've provided for you. I will take you to the airport. You can fly to Oklahoma City and rent a car there. The Brotherhood won't be looking for you, because they have no idea you are even involved." Livingston removed keys from his pocket. "Are you ready to go to the airport?"

Keith thought a minute. "No, just give me the camera. I need to stop by my apartment first. I'll find my own way to the airport. You can trust me though. I will do everything I can. You will give me any leads if you get any, right? I mean, I won't just be wandering around will I?" Livingston gave Keith a long, pensive stare. "I don't know if you are a Godly man, but I feel assured you will hear from the maidservant before she hears from you. You won't be alone on this journey. If you have Faith in that fact, this journey will not be a difficult one. Unlike The Brotherhood, you have God on your side.

Keith shook his head, not knowing what he was getting into. He only knew one thing—he wanted to be famous. "Okay, I'll go. Can I use this thing to call myself a taxi?" He asked while holding his new phone. Livingston pulled his own phone out of his pocket. "I'll do that for you. While we wait, let's go get the camera out of my car. Oh, and before I forget, hand over the station-issued phone. I don't want there to be any way to trace you."

*****

After a restless night's sleep, Jacinda woke to find Jill sitting on the couch with Gregory's laptop. Jacinda sat down and quickly closed the gap between herself and Jill on the couch.

"What are you going to do?" Jacinda asked, in an almost giddy tone.

"I checked his email, but there wasn't much there." Jill gave Jacinda a look that was ripe with scandal.

"You looked at his old email?"

Jill looked embarrassed. "I told you that already". Jill was busy typing away at the keyboard.

"Maybe you did."

Jacinda looked almost uncomfortable. "What are you doing?"

Jill didn't even look up from the screen. "I'm retrieving."

"Retrieving what?" Jacinda demanded.

"Everything, I retrieve lost and deleted information from computers for a living, remember?"

Jacinda felt guilty. "Are you sure we aren't invading his privacy?" She then felt embarrassed for worrying about something as trivial as privacy when the man she loved was missing.

"He's gone Jacinda. Any tiny bit of information may be critical at this point. Besides, I'm not convinced that he's not involved in all of this nonsense. Something in the milk ain't clean, Jacinda. First he disappears, then his father tells you he filed a missing persons report, which he obviously didn't. Something is fishy. , I can't tell you what it is exactly, but something stinks."

Jacinda moved even closer to Jill. Jill flashed the computer screen to Jacinda. "This is his email, right?" Jacinda studied the screen, "Yes, that is his email address. I've already checked it though, nothing really interesting."

"Not yet," Jill said as she typed what seemed to be an endless series of numbers, before clicking *retrieve*. "This could take a while Jacinda. Why don't you go get comfortable?" Jill moved her head closer to the screen. "Jacinda, why are there pictures of you pregnant? You didn't know Gregory when you were pregnant did you?" Jacinda moved her head towards the computer, "No, I didn't know him, but that doesn't mean that he couldn't have pulled them off the internet. I was doing news at the time. Maybe he was just curious what I looked like when I was pregnant. I don't know." Jacinda rubbed her hands together, clearly trying to release nervous energy. She didn't know why she felt so anxious.

"Jacinda," Jill continued, "these pictures were downloaded three months before you even gave birth. What interest did Gregory have in you before he even knew you?" Jacinda's eyes teared up in frustration. "You can't be sure of that. You can't be sure when these pictures were downloaded. Jill shook her head, disagreeing with Jacinda. "No, everything leaves a footprint. Everything downloaded or sent leaves a time stamp on your computer. These pictures were downloaded three months before Kyler was born."

Information continued to scroll down the screen. It all looked like babble to Jacinda, but Jill understood it all. She typed *Jacinda* in the search box, then turned to ask, "What was the name of the Bara thing?"

"BARAchip?" Jacinda asked in confusion.

"Yes, that's it." Jacinda included BARAchip in the search box, and new information began scrolling down the screen. Not only were there a ton of words and numbers--there were pictures. Gregory's computer was retrieving pictures of a baby Jacinda recognized as her own. It was Kyler.

"That's him!" Jacinda cried. "That's him! Look at those eyes. He looks just like me, Jill. That's my son! That's my Kyler! How? Why?"

Jacinda then sank her face into her hands and began to sob. She sobbed until she had no tears left to cry. Jacinda was in shock.

Jill continued to sort through the information. She was now more convinced than ever that Jacinda's precious Gregory had something to do with Kyler's disappearance. But why? Those answers would have to come later. Right now she needed to make sure her friend was okay. She stood from the couch, and walked towards the bathroom door. "Jacinda, are you okay?" When Jacinda didn't answer, Jill slowly opened the bathroom door to find Jacinda shaking on the floor. "Jacinda!" Jill screamed. "Are you alright?"

"Why?" Jacinda repeated over and over again, "why?"

Jill wanted to get to the bottom of things, but she also wanted to diffuse the situation. "Maybe it's not as bad as we think, Jacinda. Let's see what else we can find." Jacinda continued to shake and sob on the cold bathroom floor. When she spoke, it was in such a tiny voice that Jill had to strain to hear her. "We can dig for information that will make Gregory look innocent, but I know he's not, Jill. I know in my heart he's not. It's not even because of the pictures—it's everything. It's just this feeling in the pit of my stomach."

Jacinda's cell phone rang in the living room. Jacinda shot up. "What if it's Gregory?" Jill was right behind her racing to the phone, which was still in Jacinda's purse. "Who is it?" Jill demanded.

"It just says unknown."

"Well answer it!"

"I don't want to talk to anyone."

"What if they know something? Answer it!"

By the time the women stopped arguing, the phone had stopped ringing. "Great," Jill sighed.

The phone started ringing again. The screen flashed *unknown*. "Maybe it's important," Jill said, while prompting her with her eyes to answer the call. Without thinking, Jacinda answered the phone. "Jacinda Kilmeade," She said, in a tone slightly higher than a whisper.

Jill listened intently, trying to hear the male voice on the other end of the phone. Jill could see Jacinda's eyes zone out as she listened. She then heard Jacinda give the caller her address, before hanging up. Jill looked at Jacinda, "Are you crazy? Who did you just give your address to?" Jacinda returned to the couch and pulled her knees up under her chin. She began slowly rocking back and forth. Jill waited for her to speak, but she just closed her eyes and sat in silence.

"Jacinda, I know a lot is going on right now, but you have to communicate with me, sweetie. What's going on?"

Jacinda looked up through damp, swollen eyes. "That was an intern from the station. He said he needed to discuss something with me but couldn't do it on the phone. He asked if he could come over."

"I hardly think you need to be discussing work at a time like this. Why didn't you just tell him no?"

"Because Jill, his voice was urgent. I don't think he wants to discuss work. He told me he had information that will change everything."

"Everything? What could that mean?"

"If you would have asked me last week, I might have had a different answer, but right now—who knows. My world is turning upside down. But I was right about one thing, Jill. My baby is alive! Did you see the pictures? Those pictures are of Kyler; I know it! A mother would know her child anywhere! He's alive!"

CHAPTER 23

Lyla woke in the morning, feeling Kyler rubbing his chubby palm on her cheek. "I hungy," he said, as he nestled his soft head under her neck. Lyla began to stroke his soft, curly hair. "You're always hungry, my love," she said, kissing his tiny hands. Kyler giggled. "Sketti," Kyler demanded before crawling out of bed.

"You liked Miss Marlene's spaghetti, didn't you?" Lyla glanced at the alarm clock, which she hadn't bothered to set. The time was 10 a.m., and Lyla was grateful for the rest. She knew Marlene would probably be at work already, but she quietly opened the bedroom door, just the same. The living room was empty, except for a note on the coffee table. **Make yourselves at home. My home is your home! There are some groceries in the fridge, and I'll run home to bring you guys something for lunch. Your friend, Marlene**

Lyla teared up. After all, she had never been mothered before. She found it so overwhelmingly sweet. She wondered what Marlene meant by bring them lunch. She wondered if she should wait or feed Kyler leftover spaghetti to hold him over. "Sketti," Kyler reminded her, as he pulled himself into the booster chair at the table. Unknowingly, he had answered her question. "Okay, little man. I'll get you some spaghetti. Just let me wake up for a second, will you?" Kyler just smiled and blew her a kiss. He giggled and sang, "Bake up, bake up." Lyla knew that song well; she sang it to Kyler all the time, except she sang it *wake up, wake up*. "I'm waking up, little man. I'm waking up."

Lyla pulled some spaghetti out of the fridge and began searching for a microwave-proof plate. It was then that she heard the key turn in the door. Her heart dropped and she hoped she hadn't been discovered by The Brotherhood. She glanced over the kitchen bar and saw Marlene enter with a small bag. "Good mornin', sleepyheads," Marlene called from the front door. "I'm here a little early But I was just up the street and wanted to drop this by." Marlene held up a small bag. "What is it?" Lyla asked. "It's just something to keep you safe," Marlene answered. "It's no big deal, just one of those pay as you go cell phones. I put fifty dollars on it to start you out, so that should get you a phone call or two. It's just to call anyone you might need to contact, but don't want them to know where you are calling from. I had the man at the desk change the outgoing number to *private*.

Lyla walked towards Marlene and took the bag. "You did all this for me?" Lyla asked, clearly touched. "Well, you and the boy. You never know when you'll need a phone. Anyhoo, I need to get back to work, but I just wanted you to know—and feel free to say no if you don't want to—but my church is having a nighttime service, and I was just wondering if you and Kyler would be my guests.

Lyla felt scared. She had never attended a Christian church. "I wouldn't even know what to wear," Lyla said. "Plus, all Ky's clothes are filthy."

"Well, it's up to you, of course, but you and I are the same size, and I do have a washing machine in the utility room if you want to wash something for Kyler. The kids go dressed real casual. So do the adults. Especially to the night service." Marlene walked over to run her fingers through Kyler's curls. "Hi little fella." "Hi," Kyler giggled.

Marlene turned back towards the front door. "Well, I just wanted to drop that off. I better be getting back to work. I'll be home about six, and I leave for church at about six-thirty, if you're interested in going. Of course, don't you go feeling obligated. Faith can't be forced. I just wanted to invite you, in case you're interested."

Lyla felt grateful for the invitation. For the first time, she knew what it must be like to have a mother. "I'll think about it. I'll let you know when you get home from work. Fair enough?" Marlene just winked and smiled. "Fair enough, hon,"

*****

It had been hours since Jacinda watched the sunrise. Neither Jill nor Jacinda could sleep. Fourteen hours had passed since Jacinda received a call from Keith. She sat on her sofa, her faced stained with tears. So many emotions welled up inside her—so many questions. Who was this man she was married to? How was it possible he had pictures of her missing child? What was so important that Keith, the intern, needed to meet with her immediately? What was taking him so long? She sat with her knees curled to her chest, rocking, in an unsuccessful effort to calm herself. Jill continued scanning Gregory's computer.

The knock at the door startled them both. Jacinda jumped to her feet to answer the door. The plainclothes officer stood with Keith, looking very protective. "Ma'am, this man says you are expecting him. Is it okay that he comes in?"

"Yes," Jacinda said, barely audible. Her crying all but destroyed her voice. "Come in." The officer looked at Jacinda. "I'll be right outside, if you need me ma'am." The officer turned to walk away, as Keith hurried into the entryway.

"Are you okay?" Keith asked, knowing the answer before he even asked the question. "No," Jacinda answered. "I'm not." Keith put his hand on her shoulder. "I'm sorry it took me so long. Can we sit down?" Walking into the living room, he saw Jill pounding away on the laptop. Jacinda introduced the two, "Jill, this is Keith—Keith, Jill." Keith nodded, "Nice to meet you." Jill looked up from the computer. "Likewise."

Jill was so engrossed in finding information on Gregory's computer that she wasn't as polite as she would have been on a normal basis. "Have a seat," Jacinda offered. Keith sat down, but looked very uncomfortable. Jacinda sat straight up, not bothering to rest against the couch. Her discomfort was evident in her body language. "You said you have information?"

Keith didn't know how to approach the situation. How could he possibly tell this woman that he had reason to believe her child was alive and well? That was good news, of course, but what if he was wrong. What if he was offering false hope? Keith, never one for subtlety, decided a direct response was the only way to go.

"Jacinda, this is going to probably come as a shock, but I have reason to believe that your son is alive and in Oklahoma City." Jacinda wanted to cry, but shock wouldn't allow the tears to flow. She simply stared at Keith, unable to form a sentence. Keith continued, "I know what I'm about to say is going to sound crazy, but I believe that I can help you find him. I don't know how yet, but I have a reliable source that says he believes your son is safe. I'm leaving today. I'm going to try to find him."

Jacinda finally found the words to speak. "Oklahoma City? What in the world would make you think that? What source? How? Why?" Jacinda's tears could no longer be contained; they began streaming down her face. Keith continued, "I don't have all the specifics. I hope to find out more as things progress. All I know is I'm supposed to be on a plane and I should receive more information later." Jill looked up from the computer. "This is crazy. How can you come in here and get her hopes up like this? Jacinda says you are an intern at the station. How would an intern have a lead on a child that's been missing for two years? This better not be some cheap ploy to get your name in the headlines."

Keith looked Jill straight in the eyes. "My name is not to be mentioned until we find Jacinda's child. Nobody can find out that we are looking for him. We are up against very dangerous men. Nobody can know I am going to search for him. Nobody. I have to stop by the station and make up an excuse as to why I need to return home for a few weeks. I hope I don't lose my internship, but I'd say it's worth it if I do."

Jacinda didn't know what to believe. She so desperately wanted it to be true, but the story sounded so unlikely. "What do you mean dangerous men? What are you talking about?"

Jill interrupted Jacinda's questioning. "OH NO! Jacinda, you need to see this." Jill managed to recover all of Gregory's deleted emails from the past three years. Jacinda, Keith, and Jill crowded around the laptop, as they began reading each email, beginning with the earliest—three years ago. BARAchip had been introduced to Gregory in the earliest of emails, which meant he lied about not being approached with the idea until recently, which Jacinda already knew. There were also pictures of a very pregnant Jacinda, as well as a picture of Jacinda's late husband. The three read the emails, each one more sinister than the next. One thing was certain: Gregory had his sights set on Jacinda, even before she gave birth. Before Jill opened the next email, Jacinda stood up and ran to her bedroom. She opened her closet, removed a suitcase, and filled it with clothes. Returning to the living room, she was filled with resolve. "Keith, I don't know what's going on, but I'm going with you. What time do we leave?"

Keith looked surprised. "I don't think that's necessary. I promise I will do everything I can do to bring him home safely. If you go, they might get suspicious." Jacinda looked both confused and furious, "Who is *they?*" Keith closed his eyes, searching for an answer. "I'm not at liberty to say right now. In fact, I don't have all the details. I need to stop by the station and wrap a few things up. I'll make up an excuse and take a few weeks off. I'll leave this afternoon." Jacinda wasn't backing down. "You're not going without me, that's *my* baby. I'm going to the station too. I'm going to take a few weeks off, and if they fire me, they fire me. I really don't care at this point. I've clearly been living a lie, anyway. I don't even know what kind of lie, or who's involved, but I'm not going to sit here doing nothing knowing my baby could be in Oklahoma City. I'm going with you."

Keith could tell he was fighting a losing battle. Realizing he had little choice, he gave in. "Okay, I'll go in first, and say I have a family emergency. You can go in later and say what you need to say. We can't take the same flight. I'll fly in first, and wait for you at the airport. Don't pay with a credit card. We need to buy the tickets with cash. Keith pulled 500 dollars out of his wallet and handed it to Jacinda. "This should get you to Oklahoma City." He pulled out a pen and wrote down the number of the untraceable cell phone. "I'll wait for you at the airport. Once you get in, call this number, and we'll get a car." Jacinda handed the money back to Keith. "I have the money. This is my child. I'll go withdraw the money and pay for it in cash." Keith shook his head in disagreement. "No, we don't want any bank records that you withdrew a large amount of cash. You would normally use a card, and we don't want anything to look suspicious."

Jacinda looked at him in utter confusion. "What are we up against? Who are we up against? Who are these people that are so dangerous?" Keith shook his head, "Honestly, I don't know. They won't tell me the whole story. It runs deep, Jacinda—real deep. They won't give me all the specifics, but I think they are trying to protect both themselves, and me. I do know one thing, though. We are being led by the good guys."

Jacinda rubbed her puffy eyes, "Who are the good guys?" Keith knew he couldn't reveal any more information than necessary. "I can't really say, Jacinda. Just trust me. I want to help you." Jacinda felt crippled with shock. "I have no choice but to trust you, Keith. You go to the station, and I'll follow an hour later."

Jill pulled up an airline's website. "There's a flight leaving today at four, and another at seven."
Jacinda thought for a minute. "We don't need to take separate flights. If we pay in cash, we'll be fine. They won't release passenger information. Let's leave at four. We can go into the office an hour apart and meet at the airlines at two thirty."
Keith looked at Jill. "What airline did you say that was?" Jill looked back down at the screen.
"Regional Air." Keith thought for a moment. "Okay. Jacinda. I'll see you at the airport at four. We just can't talk or act like we know each other.
Everybody knows who you are, and I don't think we should be seen together. In fact, try to disguise yourself as much as possible. I don't know, maybe pull your hair into a baseball cap and dress down. You just have to promise me that you won't speak a word of this to anyone, or we could both be in a lot of danger."

Jacinda nodded. "I won't say a word."

Both Jacinda and Keith looked at Jill. "I won't say a word either," she assured them. Keith turned his glance back to Jacinda. "Whatever you do, don't use your cell phone to relay information regarding any of this. Leave your work phone at home, so they can't trace where you are. Your personal cell probably has a monitoring device too. You can't be too careful. I have a cell that's safe. Any call that needs to be made, regarding any of this, needs to be made through my phone. Understand?"

Jacinda nodded. "Understood."

Jacinda looked back at Jill. "What about you? Are you going home today? I feel horrible that you came all this way." Jill nodded. "Yes, I'm going home. But only if I can take Gregory's computer. There is a lot more information I want to retrieve."

Jacinda waved her hand, still in shock. "It's all yours."

CHAPTER 24

Lyla laughed at the mess Kyler made while eating his spaghetti. He was an absolute mess. She's never loved anything, or anyone so much in her life. "It's bath time, little man," she said with a grin. Lyla felt safe here. Perhaps it was the safety that gave her time to reflect on how much grief Kyler's own mother must be experiencing. She wanted more than anything in the world to keep Kyler and watch him grow. She didn't want to miss a moment. But one thing was eating away at her conscience: he wasn't hers. He belonged to someone else. Keeping him would make her no better than the men who took him in the first place. She loved this child more than life itself, but sometimes love meant sacrifice. Somehow, it all came back to sacrifice.

Lyla filled the bathtub, and the messy toddler happily jumped into the water. He loved bath time. Lyla got two cups from the cupboard, so Kyler would have something to play with. It amazed her how entertained he was by pouring water from one cup to the other. After removing him from the tub and drying him off, she realized he had no clean clothes. She found a t-shirt in Marlene's closet and slipped it over his head, onto his tiny body. The shirt swallowed him, but she couldn't help thinking how cute he looked. She gathered their dirty clothes and made her way to the washing machine. After starting the load of laundry, she sat on the couch to cuddle with the toddler. "I love you more than anything in the world. You know, right?" she asked him. "La you," he replied in his angelic tone.

Giving him back to his rightful mother would break her heart, but she knew it had to be done. She just didn't know how she was going to do it. How in the world would she get in touch with Jacinda Kilmeade? How could she convince Jacinda not to tell her husband Gregory? How much information would she have to reveal? She didn't know how she was going to pull it off, but she knew she had little choice. As much as she loved Kyler, his mother did too. She couldn't rob a woman of her only son—her flesh and blood. She couldn't put

Jacinda through any more grief than she has already experienced.

Picking up the phone that Marlene was kind enough to bring her, she called information. "Washington, D.C.," Lyla said to the operator. "Yes, can you please give me the number to the news room of *Your Nation Now*?" The voice on the other line said, "Please hold for that number."

*****

Jacinda and Keith's plan of arriving an hour apart backfired, because Bertha was in a meeting. Both of them sat at their desks, pretending to work. Keith was on phone duty, as usual. He didn't want to answer phones, but at least it helped eliminate the boredom of waiting to talk to Bertha. The phone rang and Keith answered with the standard, "Your Nation Now, this is Keith, how may I direct your call?" The woman on the other end of the phone sounded very intimidated. "Um, yes, is there any way you can connect me to Jacinda Kilmeade?" Keith found this request very strange. Rarely did anyone ask to be connected to a famous reporter; that is what the assignments desk is for.

Unfortunately, everyone who was supposed to work the assignments desk was in the same meeting as Bertha. Keith knew he couldn't connect her to Jacinda; that would go against protocol. "Well, ma'am, I can take a message. Would you like to leave your name and number, and what this is regarding?" The woman was silent before saying, "No, I really can't do that. It's kind of urgent. I was hoping to speak to her, but I understand if…" Something in Keith's gut told him to transfer the call. What could he lose? Nothing was normal these days. Rules were being broken all over the place. Keith paused before he continued. "Hold on one minute, ma'am. I'll see if she's in."

Keith rang Jacinda's desk. She answered, but it was clear that she was beaten down. Her voice was raspy, and it was obvious she hadn't slept in a very long time. "Jacinda," Keith began, "there is a woman on hold for you. She says it's urgent. I'm not saying this has anything to do with what we talked about, but it can't hurt. Do you want me to put her through?" "Yes," Jacinda responded, without missing a beat. "Put her through. I'll take the call." Keith transferred the call and Jacinda answered. "This is Jacinda Kilmeade." The voice on the other end of the phone sounded very torn, very shy. The words didn't come easily, but she desperately tried to get them out in a coherent manner. "Mrs. Kilmeade, you don't know me. Is this a secure line?" Jacinda thought for a moment, her heart began to race, "No, but if you hold on a minute, I can call you from a secure line." Lyla answered almost immediately. "No, I can't give you my number. But if you give me the number to the secure line, I can call you back." Jacinda stood and craned her neck, looking for Keith. Spotting him, she spoke softly into the phone. "Hold on. I'll be right back." Jacinda rang Keith's desk and demanded his cell phone number. "I need the number of the safe cell, please. I think this is important. When it rings, give it to me, and I'll go outside to talk." Keith sounded hesitant. "I'm not supposed to give that number out." Jacinda sounded furious. "What if this is a lead, Keith? I need that number!" Keith hesitantly gave her the number, and Jacinda switched lines without so much as saying goodbye.

Jacinda sounded frantic. "Hello, are you still there?" "Yes," Lyla replied. "Okay, the number is (202) 555-4710. That is a secure line, please call it right away." Lyla agreed, before hanging up the phone. Within seconds, Jacinda was at Keith's desk. She took the phone from his hand and headed out the door. Jacinda stood in the D.C. heat, wondering how long it had been since she'd talked to the woman on the phone. Seconds seemed like hours. She stared at the phone, willing it to ring. Finally, it did. "Hello, this is Jacinda." Lyla was silent for a moment. Jacinda panicked. "Are you there? Hello?"

Lyla responded, "Yes, I'm here. Mrs. Kilmeade, I don't know where to begin. I've been debating on calling you for months. I don't even know how to say this. I want you to know something. Your son is safe."

Jacinda began to hyperventilate and started to sob. She stood outside of the studio and turned to face the brick wall, so nobody could see her in hysterics. Her knees weakened, leaving her in a crouched position on the sidewalk. Jacinda spoke though short breaths and tears. "How do you know?"

Lyla didn't know how to answer her question without implicating herself and making herself out to be a monster. "I know because I've been caring for him since he was born. I can't get into the specifics, but nobody can be trusted. You can't trust your husband. You can't trust your co-workers. You can't trust anyone but yourself and me right now." Jacinda's heart sank. "How am I supposed to trust you? You just said you've had my son since birth. You stole my son from me. How can I trust you?"

Lyla began to cry. "I didn't steal him. You have no idea how deep this runs—how many people are involved. I was just put in charge of caring for him, and I cared for him like he was my own. I love him with my whole heart. I love him, but I know that he's yours, and I can't put you through any more pain than you've already endured. Mrs. Kilmeade, you can't trust anyone. You have no idea how many people are involved, or the reasoning behind it. I want to return your baby, but you have got to promise me that you won't tell a soul. If they find me, they will kill us. We are dealing with very evil people. I don't even know how to go about returning him. I don't know how we can safely do this."

Jacinda's mind was racing a million miles an minute. "Where are you?" Lyla sat in silence. "Are you in Oklahoma City?" Lyla audibly gasped. "How did you know that?" Jacinda answered. "One of the good guys suspected it." Lyla sounded confused. "One of the good guys? What if he isn't one of the good guys, Mrs. Kilmeade?" Jacinda thought for a moment. "Well, if he wasn't, he would have no reason to get me involved. He would have gone alone. Look, I don't know anything right now. But you let me know where you are, and I promise I will keep you safe." Lyla felt overwhelmed, "Mrs. Kilmeade, I need to think. I will call you back, I promise." Without so much as a goodbye, Lyla hung up the phone.

Jacinda crouched by the brick wall, trying her best to collect herself. In the past seventy-two hours, her world had been turned upside down. Everything she believed as truth had been a lie. It was too much to process with so little sleep. She stood up on shaky legs and headed toward the door. Walking into the newsroom, she headed straight for the restroom. Looking into the mirror, she used her hand to brace herself against the wall. It was all she could do to collect herself. *Get it together, Jacinda. Get it together. You're no good to anyone like this.* She dabbed at her face with a paper towel and began to pray. "Please God. Please lead me to my baby. Please protect him. Please protect all of us." After drying her tears and removing her smeared eye makeup, she walked over to Keith's desk, "I'm leaving. I'm going right now. I don't care about informing Bertha. She can fire me. I'm going to go find my baby, but I need your phone." Keith stood up and grabbed both his backpack and the camera that Livingston had loaned him. "Let's go." Jacinda disapprovingly shook her head "Oh no, you're not getting fired because of me, this is my battle." Keith corrected her. "I got myself involved, and I intend to stay that way. I'm documenting everything. Trust me, getting everything on film is the only thing that's going to keep us alive."

*****

Lyla hugged her knees to her chest and began sobbing into her knees. What had she gotten herself into? She knew she would probably spend the rest of her life in prison for aiding in kidnapping. *If everything isn't done perfectly they'll kill all three of us*, she worried, pressing her face into her knees. Watching Kyler play with his toys, her heart hurt even more. *What will I do without you?* She wondered to herself. *Kyler,* she reminded herself, *I've got to do what's best for Kyler. I can't support him, and even if I could—he's not mine. Jacinda will love him just as much. What right do I have to rob her of every happy moment this angel boy creates?* Feeling a sense of resolve, she lifted herself off the couch.

Lyla headed to the kitchen. "Kyler," she said, noticing Kyler never looked up from his toys.

"Kyler, you want some juice?" Immediately, Kyler rose to his feet. Again, the guilt welled up inside of her. He didn't even know his name. He's two and he didn't know his name. He answered to sweetheart, love, and all the other pet names she had bestowed upon him, but the child had absolutely no idea that his birth name was Kyler.

She scooped him into her arms and sat back down on the couch. With Kyler cradled on her lap, she looked deep into his eyes. "Baby, your name is Kyler. Can you say Kyler?" Kyler's attention went back to the toy he had been playing with. "Doy!"

"I see that toy honey, but I need you to listen to me. Your name is Kyler. Can you say Kyler?"

"Kyder," he said, still focusing on the toy.

"Fine, baby. You go play with your toy, and I'll get you some juice." She was certain most two year-olds knew their names and responded when their names were called. *Have I ruined him? Is it too late?* She couldn't worry about the psychological or developmental damage she had caused, or help to create. She couldn't worry about anything but keeping him safe.

If she let her mind stray too much, it would eventually lead to all the consequences involved. Jail time. Death. And those were just the obvious ones. She couldn't get too caught up in the "what ifs." She had to focus. Guilt would only get in the way of the mission, and the mission was Kyler's safety.

CHAPTER 25

Jacinda waited for her plane to board. She pulled the bill of her cap a little lower, hoping to cover her face as much as possible. She hated taking the hat off to get through security, but rules were rules. Luckily, nobody recognized her, and if they did, they didn't say anything. She glanced up at Keith, who was sitting on the other side of the terminal. They were keeping a safe distance, but couldn't stop stealing glances at each other.

Her mind was racing with possibilities. Would she have her baby in her arms by tonight? Would Kyler be safe? Would he feel instantly connected to her, or would she be a complete stranger? She knew she'd be a stranger, but hoped the bond between mother and child wouldn't be forever broken because of a two-year separation. *He won't even know who I am,* she thought to herself, as her hopes began to deflate.

She willed herself to snap out of it. After all, there were no guarantees that the woman who called wasn't some crazy woman getting high off of creating false hope. At this point in her life, nothing was guaranteed. She was sure her husband was responsible for Kyler's disappearance, but she didn't know if he was even still alive. She knew there was a possibility she would be unemployed when she returned. She'd lost her parents, her first husband, her current husband, her baby, and now possibly her job. Despair was a feeling she was intimately familiar with. It was this sense of hope that felt foreign.

Jacinda clutched her purse. Her flight was beginning to board. With one last glance at Keith, she stood to take her place in line. Her jeans, t-shirt, and hat made her feel invisible. She didn't get constant stares of recognition, and for that, she was grateful. Making her way through the gate and onto the plane, she realized there was no turning back. She was on her way to Oklahoma City, and she wouldn't have it any other way.

She took her seat on the plane and watched as Keith struggled to put the camera case in an overhead compartment. He was sitting three rows ahead of her, but she wished he was sitting closer. Besides Jill, she felt that he was the only person she could trust. Getting around the officer standing guard at her house was difficult, but she managed by having Jill create a diversion. She wondered if she should have alerted him, or another member of the FBI. If she were to go missing, the FBI would think she was still safe in her apartment. Of course, she didn't know if she could trust the FBI, and was at odds with that fact. *How can a government entity designed to protect its citizens make me feel so unsafe?*

The fasten seatbelt sign turned on, and the flight attendant began her pre-flight briefing. Jacinda tightly closed her eyes and took in a deep breath. Slowly exhaling, she felt a hand touch hers. Jumping with surprise, she opened her eyes to find an elderly woman to her right grasping her hand. "Don't be scared, hon. You'll be just fine." Jacinda turned to the woman. "I used to be scared of flying, too," said the woman. "But I'm on a plane at least once a month now, and it's something you just kind of get used to." Jacinda forced a smile. "Oh yea, flying makes me nervous."

She didn't mean for the lie to come out, but it was much easier than telling the old woman what was really causing her so much anxiety. The woman had kind eyes, and for a moment that helped Jacinda relax. "I'm constantly flying back and forth," the old woman continued. "I live in Oklahoma, but the grand kiddos are here, and Grandma can't go a month without seeing them-- teenagers or not."

Jacinda eased into a trite conversation, listening to only half of what the old woman was saying. She giggled at the appropriate times, responded appropriately, and tried to conceal the terror that was overwhelming her. All she could concentrate on was the fact that Keith's phone had to be turned off for the flight. *What if the woman who has Kyler tries to call while we're in the air?* Her heart began pounding, and she felt as if someone had pulled a plastic bag over her face. She's had anxiety attacks before, but this was one of the worst.

*****

Lyla checked the clock. "Five-thirty, little man. Marlene should be here soon." Kyler just smiled. "Sketti."

"Oh, really. Is she the spaghetti lady now?" Lyla said with a smile. She produced a smile for the benefit of Kyler, but her insides were being ripped apart. It felt as if her heart were actually being torn from her body. She knew Jacinda was en route to Oklahoma, which meant her days with this precious child were numbered. She didn't even care what happened to her after Kyler was returned to Jacinda. Jail, death--nothing could compare to the punishment of not being able to hold him close to her each and every day. Nothing.

She had so much to figure out. How would she get Kyler to Jacinda? How could she keep both Jacinda and Kyler safe once they were reunited? The Brotherhood will stop at nothing to sacrifice Kyler, and Jacinda has always just been a pawn. Her mind began to race. *What if Jacinda takes Kyler back to D.C., and they kill him. What if she thinks I'm crazy, and unknowingly puts him back in harm's way?* It was then that she realized she couldn't tell anybody where Kyler was until after the day he's to be sacrificed—tomorrow.

*****

Keith and Jacinda loaded their luggage into the back of a taxi. They discussed getting a rental car, but that would involve credit cards and insurance information. The less of a trail they left, the safer they'd be. "Where to?" the driver asked, while peering at them through the rearview. Jacinda glanced at Keith, hoping he had thought this through. Keith leaned forward, "Just take us to the closest hotel." Jacinda's eyes pleaded with Keith. She didn't want to go to a hotel. She wanted to find her baby. Keith looked at her reassuringly. "We still haven't heard anything. We'll go there and wait until she calls again." Jacinda leaned back into the seat and began massaging her stiff, aching neck. She hated carrying anxiety in her shoulders and neck. Her head was beginning to throb, but she wasn't about to let her focus shift from finding her baby.

The hotel was a three-minute drive from the airport. Keith pulled out his wallet to pay the driver, and the two got out of the car. As they were unloading their luggage, Jacinda felt a sense of panic overtake her again. "Check the phone. Are you sure you checked the messages? Maybe she called when we were flying and just didn't leave one. Do you think she just gave up? What if she doesn't call again?" Keith didn't look up from his luggage; instead, he simply headed towards the entrance of the hotel. Jacinda followed behind him, but couldn't stop asking questions. "This is a hotel, you're going to have to use an ID and a credit card." Keith turned, "I have an ID and a credit card."

"Yea, but then they'll be able to track you."

"They aren't going to track me, because they have no reason to think I'm involved."

"How do you know that? And who are 'they'? I

know I've been saying 'they,' but I still have no idea who 'they' are."

Keith turned to face Jacinda. "No disrespect, but you're going to have to calm down if this is going to work. I don't know much, but I can't get into what I do know, because it's really not important at this point. We're here to find your son, and the more focused we are, the better. The first thing we need to do is get into a room and begin documenting everything on camera."

Jacinda looked annoyed. "Documenting? We're in the process of finding my son who was stolen from me two years ago, and you're thinking about a stupid story? A documentary?" Keith was positive he had already told Jacinda this would be the only way to keep them alive—their insurance policy. "Remember, I told you that we had to document everything? It's going to be the only way to keep us safe after we find your son. If the public knows everything, the bad guys are much less likely to kill us."

Jacinda, once again, felt as if she was living inside a crime novel. People were being referred to as *good guys* and *bad guys*. They were waiting for phone calls for their next clue. Documenting everything would save their lives. It's true, her life had been upside down the past two years, but this is the first time she realized that fiction could not possibly be stranger than her own reality.

*****

Marlene opened the door to find Lyla and Kyler sitting on the floor playing with toys. "Well, look at you two! You even have your shoes on, are you going somewhere?" Lyla smiled. "I thought you said we were going to church." Marlene looked pleased. "So you've decided to come along?"

"If it's still okay."

"Of course it's still okay! The more the merrier," she said, as she took a place on the floor next to Lyla and Kyler. "Hi there, little fella. Did you have fun today?" Kyler looked at Marlene and handed her the toy truck he had in his hand. "Oh, you're letting me play too?" Marlene teased. "Wow," Lyla said, looking surprised, "He's sharing with you. I've been trying to talk him into letting me play with that truck all day." Marlene looked playfully at Lyla. "I can get you a little green truck too, if you want one that bad." Lyla giggled. "That's very generous of you, Marlene, but Kyler probably wouldn't share that one with me either. He'd just think he had two." Marlene slowly lifted herself from the floor. "It gets harder and harder to get off the floor, when you get my age. I'm going to go freshen up for church. I'm glad you two decided to join me. Kyler is going to have so much fun playing with the other kids. They have a great daycare there." Lyla felt her heart tightening. "You mean, I have to leave him?"

"Well not for long. We will be in the same building We'll just let him play while we're in the sanctuary. He'd be bored sitting through the service with us."

Lyla felt panicked. In the two years he'd been in her care, he had only been out of her sight while he was sleeping. She didn't know if she could leave him. *What if it's not safe? What if they find him?* The look on Lyla's face revealed her thoughts. Marlene instinctively knew what to say to ease her mind. "Well, I know leaving him for the first time might be hard. But if you want, you can stay and watch him play with the other kids, while I attend the service. At least it will get you two out of the house. And I really think he'll enjoy playing with the other children." Lyla let the statement sink in and suddenly felt more at peace. "Yeah, I guess that would be okay. That might be fun."

Marlene made her way into the bedroom to take a quick shower and change her clothes. Lyla stayed on the floor with Kyler. "What do you think about that Kyler? Do you want to go play with the kids?" Kyler's face lit up. "Pay wi dids."

"Well, all right! We'll go play with the kids. That should be fun. Are you going to share with the other children like you did with Ms. Marlene?" Kyler didn't respond. He simply kept playing. "I'll take that as a yes," Lyla said, as she stood and walked towards the couch. "Pay," Kyler said while patting the floor.

"I can't play anymore, sweetheart. My back hurts. Come sit on the couch with me."

"I pay."

Lyla watched Kyler as he played with the small green truck. "Vroom Vroom," Lyla said, as he pushed the truck along the ground. Kyler smiled with pure delight. "Broom broom," he mimicked. Lyla stood and walked to a small mirror hanging near the front door. She smoothed her hair and gave herself a once over before turning to see Marlene walk out of the bedroom. "Yes, you're still gorgeous," Marlene teased.

"I guess I'm just a little nervous," Lyla admitted.

"Nervous about what?"

"I don't know. About meeting your friends, I guess."

"Oh, don't be silly. Everybody there will love you. You're an angel," Marlene said before turning her attention to Kyler. "And they're just going to want to eat you up with a spoon!" Kyler stood to walk towards Marlene. "Boon." Marlene ruffled his hair with her fingers and turned to face Lyla. "You two ready to go?"

After locking the door, the three headed toward the parking lot. "The taxi?" Lyla asked as she glanced towards the car. "Yup. Big Yellow is what I like to call her," Marlene said with a proud smile. "She's not much, but she gets me where I need to go."

Lyla's mind raced. *Do I sit in the front or the back?*
She knew it was a silly thought, but the last time
she had been in "Big Yellow," she and Kyler both
sat in the backseat. Lyla balanced Kyler's car seat
on her hip as she headed towards the car.
Opening the back door, Lyla secured Kyler into his
seat. Closing the door, she decided to ride in the
front. "Well this feels weird," she said, touching the
dash.

"What? The dashboard?"

"No. Sitting in the front."

"Oh, honey. Did you think I was going to chauffer
you two around? I'm off the clock." Lyla smiled.
"So, then I guess I won't be getting charged?"

"Oh, you'll still be getting charged," Marlene
sassed. "Kidding, dumplin', I'm only kidding." Lyla
smiled. She cherished these few moments when
she wasn't thinking about The Brotherhood. These
moments came few and far between, but they were
divine. Marlene's presence always calmed her,
and for that she was grateful.

MARKED I

CHAPTER 26

Jacinda sat on the corner of the bed, as Keith set up the camera. "I need you to tell your story," Keith said, without looking up from his task. "Tell the camera everything that has happened up until this point. Talk about the abduction, your husband's disappearance, the emails that were retrieved on your husband's computer—everything." Jacinda shifted uncomfortably on the edge of the bed. "I don't even know where to start."

"Start at the beginning. Start with the day your child was kidnapped. Move on to how Senator Kilmeade came into your life. Talk about how he lied about the timeframe the BARAchip was presented to him. Talk about the phone call we received. Talk about everything you remember. Don't worry about babbling or throwing in unnecessary information. We can edit that later."

Still feeling uncomfortable and anxious, Jacinda stood and began pacing the room. "I just need to calm down. I need to relax a second. Can we turn on the television?" Keith looked annoyed. "I know you're upset, but we could receive a phone call at any moment telling us to meet that woman and your son. We need to document everything while it's fresh on your mind."

"We will, I just want to unwind a second. I don't even think I'm capable of being articulate right now. Maybe we can just turn on the television for a second. I just need a minute to relax." Keith knew he was fighting a losing battle. "Fine, let's turn on the TV, and I'll start some coffee. There is a coffee maker in this room, right?" Keith began searching for a coffee maker, while Jacinda switched on the television. Keith turned to see Jacinda; she looked like she had just seen a ghost. "Jacinda? What's wrong?" She didn't responder. Her eyes were glued to the television.

Keith sat beside her and instantly knew why she was in shock. CBN was reporting that the missing child, Billy Morrison, had been located. It wasn't the recovered child that threw Jacinda into a state of shock--it was the picture of Senator Kilmeade. "What?" Keith asked in a tone that begged for answers. Jacinda kept staring at the screen. Both were completely entranced by the newscaster, who explained Billy Morrison was found unharmed, but the shocking news was that he was found with Senator Kilmeade. Apparently, Senator Kilmeade's car collided with another vehicle as he was pulling out of the driveway of a country home. The story became even more sensational when the reporter announced that two men were found dead inside the house that Senator Kilmeade was leaving.

Jacinda flung her body back onto the bed and stared blankly at the ceiling. Keith was at a loss for words. "Well, the good news is they found the child alive," Keith said, trying to put a positive spin on the devastating discovery.

"What's happened to my life?" Jacinda asked without removing her eyes from the ceiling. "How wicked is the man I married? Did he steal the baby and kill those men? What's happening, Keith?" Keith didn't know how to respond. He was just as shocked as she was. He searched for something comforting to say, but that wasn't really his forte'. "So, then Senator Kilmeade is still alive, right?"

"They haven't said, and I don't care."

"You don't care at all? I mean, you don't even wonder?"

"Change the channel, I'm sure another channel will tell you. Or, just keep it here. It's bound to be all they cover. this is huge."

Keith sat silently, listening to the rest of the report. "So he is alive," Keith said, after the newscaster answered his question." Jacinda was still zoning out, staring at the ceiling. "He is what?" She hadn't been listening to the story. "Your husband is alive. He's in police custody. They aren't sure if he killed those men, or if the men were dead when he got there. They said an autopsy will reveal more, but that could take weeks." Jacinda slowly raised her hands to cover her face. "Thank God that little boy was found safe. Thank God Gregory didn't hurt him. Listen to me! Now I'm assuming my husband is a killer. I just don't know what to think anymore. I don't care what happens to him at this point. All I want is my baby. How do we get Kyler back, Keith?"

Keith took his place behind the camera. "We're working on getting your baby back, but first we need insurance that we won't be killed once we find him. Jacinda, I know you're freaking out right now, but you need to follow my direction. I need you to start from the beginning. Tell the camera everything you know—everything you've discovered. If you forget something, that's okay—we'll add it later. Just start from the beginning."

Jacinda tried her best to pull herself together. She placed a tiny microphone on her shirt and stared directly into the camera. "Are you rolling?" Keith nodded his head. "Good. My name is Jacinda Kilmeade. Most of you know me as Senator Kilmeade's wife. The last two years have been—well—they've been crazy, for lack of a better word." Jacinda wiped a tear from her check, and her voice began to quiver. "When my son Kyler was born, he was stolen from the hospital nursery before I had a chance to bring him home. Shortly after, my husband was killed in a hit-and-run. Soon after that, I met my husband Gregory Kilmeade. One thing led to another, and we got married in a very short period of time. After getting married, I was hired at *Your Nation Now*. My first assignment was for a product called BARAchip. It was presented to me as a tiny implant that can be inserted into a child's skin, which would act as a tracking device if the child were to go missing." Jacinda's eyes continued filling with tears. "I found out my husband was pushing legislation that would require all newborns to get the device implanted for their own safety. He told me he had been approached with the technology months after we were married. But through emails, I found out he knew about this technology for much longer than he let on. I also found out that he was receiving pictures of me, via email, long before we even met.

Jacinda began to choke up. She covered her face, "Enough, Keith--I can't do this right now." Keith didn't dare argue. He saw the tears streaming down her face and decided not to push her. "It's okay, we can finish later. Do you need a drink of water or something?"

"No, I need a phone call. I need to know where my baby is. I can't sit around here and wait another minute. It feels like we've been here an eternity." Keith's face dropped. "What?" Jacinda demanded. Keith sat next to her. "If Senator Kilmeade is in police custody, it will only be a matter of time before the FBI knows you're not at your apartment. In fact, they probably already know you're gone. What if they start looking for you?"

*****

Walking up to the church doors, Lyla felt nervous. Everything she was taught to believe told her evil lay beyond the doors, but her heart believed differently. Over the past two years, her inner child was always at odds with her adult self. Marlene turned to face her. "You okay, hon? You look scared to death!" Lyla began twisting her hair with her finger. "I'll be fine, I've just never been in one of these."

"One of these. You mean a church? Oh honey, nobody in there is gonna bite you, I promise." Marlene opened the large, glass doors and Lyla felt a rush of cold air against her face. She instinctively crossed her arms over her chest to protect herself from the temperature. "They keep it pretty cold in here, huh?" Marlene said, as they walked through the doors. "It's not as bad once we get into the sanctuary." Lyla froze in place, "I thought I was going to the daycare." Marlene absentmindedly shook her head. "You are, aren't you? I forgot. It's a lot warmer in there too. We're going to go right down that hall," she said, while pointing to the left. Lyla scooped Kyler up and put him on her hip, as they made their way down the long hall.

When they finally made it to the end of the hall, Marlene touched the doorframe. "Here we are." Lyla clutched Kyler a little closer to her body. Kyler's eyes brightened when he saw the other children and all of the toys lining the walls. "Doys!" Kyler exclaimed. Lyla lifted him off her hip and onto the floor. "You're going to share those toys, right angel?" Kyler didn't seem to hear her, as he scampered off to one of the shelves. Marlene winked at Lyla, "Well that was easier than you thought it'd be, huh?" Lyla soaked in the pure joy on Kyler's face, as he pulled a toy off the shelf. He kept his eyes on a small group of children playing in the corner. "He really does look happy, doesn't he?" Lyla said, with pure satisfaction.

A pretty, young blonde girl met the two women at the door. A white t-shirt and blue jeans adorned her small frame. She had on a bit too much makeup for Lyla's taste, but the red lipstick just accentuated her huge, inviting smile. "Well, hello," said the woman as she approached. Marlene touched Lyla's shoulder. "This is Sandra. She's the teacher here. The kids love her." Sandra smiled, a little embarrassed. "Well I don't know if they love me, but I absolutely *adore* them." Lyla felt instantly at ease. Marlene continued the introductions, "Sandra, this is..." She paused, not knowing if she wanted her real name revealed. Lyla quickly said. "Lauren. My name is Lauren. And that little toy monster over there is my son Kyle." Lyla was so quick to give fake names that she surprised herself. She hated lying, but felt it wasn't yet safe to tell the truth. Sandra eyed Kyler. "Well he certainly is handsome. And the other kids seem to love him." Lyla looked over to find two children standing next to Kyler. Her heart warmed at the prospect of Kyler making friends.

Marlene touched Lyla's shoulder again, as she spoke to Sandra. "She's having a little separation anxiety about leaving her little one. We were hoping it would be okay if she stayed and helped you." Sandra smiled. "Oh, I'd *love* the company! I understand all about separation anxiety. You see that one over there at the table? He's mine. I go to the service on Sundays, but Friday nights, I really just enjoy helping out with the precious little ones." Lyla felt such relief that she didn't face resistance. She had expected Sandra to try and urge her to go to the service. She felt a new sense of excitement that she had never felt before. Kyler was playing with children, and she was talking to someone who seemed genuinely sweet—something she had only experienced with Marlene. *Where were these people when I was growing up?* she asked herself, as she ached for the little girl she used to be. The little girl who would have thrived around people like the ones she'd met recently.

Marlene hugged Lyla. "I'll be right down the hall in the sanctuary, if you need me," she said, before turning to leave. Lyla almost felt like she was being dropped off at daycare for the first time. She felt a twinge of pain in her heart, watching Marlene head towards the door. This was the kind of mother she had always dreamed of; this was a woman who made her feel safe.

MARKED I

CHAPTER 27

Jacinda paced the hotel room, as her thoughts spilled out of her mouth without being filtered. "I need to know, Keith. I need to know what this is all about. I can't just sit here and wait. Gregory's been arrested. You're talking about us being killed. My life has literally fallen apart, and until I find Kyler, I have *nothing*. I don't care about my career anymore. My marriage was a lie. My ex-husband was most likely murdered. And I want answers." Keith sat on the floor with his back resting against the wall. He stood and walked towards his luggage. Pulling out a book, he handed it to Jacinda. "I don't know everything, but I know we're dealing with very dangerous men. Do you remember Senator Mitch Tatum?" Jacinda ran her hand over the face of the book. "Yes. Committed suicide this week, right?"

"No, well yes. I mean, it's the same guy, but I believe he was murdered. He never would have killed himself."

"You talk about him like you knew him."

"I did know him. I mean, I met with him a few times. He tried to explain as much as he could, but he was killed before he could explain everything. That's the book he wrote, though. It explains a lot."

Jacinda opened the book and flipped through the pages. "Keith, I don't have the time or patience to read an entire book right now. Just tell me what it says."

Keith absentmindedly began rubbing his hand over his knee in a repetitive motion, as he sat back on the floor. "It's complicated, Jacinda. I wish I could tell you everything, but it's just so complicated. I just know there is this ancient brotherhood controlling most of the world's corporations and governments. They use symbols to communicate. They're symbols we see every day. Our conscious mind doesn't really pick up on them, because we're desensitized, which is the way they want it. We're constantly seeing symbols such as the pyramid, the owl, and the all-seeing eye, and we don't think twice about them. But to other members of The Brotherhood, these symbols hold power. Or at least they believe them to."

Jacinda interrupted. "What do symbols have to do with my baby being taken?" She seemed frustrated, and Keith knew he couldn't possibly communicate the tidbits of knowledge he had bouncing around in his brain. "Look, I don't know. All I know is there's good reason to believe that this brotherhood has something to do with Kyler's disappearance. The Brotherhood has influence in every major industry, but there are people who have managed to infiltrate it. The man who sent me to find Kyler was someone who has inside knowledge. He won't tell me everything. Not until we return with your son."

Jacinda looked nervous. "Return? So you're saying that this brotherhood, or whatever, has people all over Washington, D.C., and you expect me to *return* with my son? Are you crazy? I don't know much at this point, but I know one thing. After I get my son safely in my arms, Washington, D.C., is the *last* place I'll take him!"

Keith hadn't really thought through the logistics. Jacinda's refusal to return to D.C. made perfect sense, but his orders were to *return* with Kyler. After all, he wants to be the one to break the story, but how can he do that if he doesn't follow orders, and get the information he was promised after his return? "Nobody has to know we are there. There's a safe house."

Jacinda eyed him suspiciously. "A safe house?"

"Yes, there is a house we can go for help. They're the good guys, Jacinda."

She buried her face in her hands. "The good guys? And how do you know that? Is it because they sent you to find my son? If the woman who has my son is on the run, doesn't it make sense that the bad guys would want to send someone to find them?"

Keith shook his head. "I know it seems that way, but these guys were trying to expose The Brotherhood even before they saw Kyler went missing. They were friends of Mitch. They're willing to risk their lives to expose the guys who were responsible for taking your son."

None of what Keith was saying made any sense to

Jacinda. "But why me? Why Kyler?"

"I don't know. The men who sent me know more than I do, but they promised to fill me in when this was all over." Keith felt torn. Should he mention Livingston's involvement? Would that make Jacinda feel more or less comfortable? He couldn't worry about Jacinda's feelings right now. He simply had to get the story. He had to get to the truth.

*****

Marlene, Lyla, and Kyler walked through the door of Marlene's apartment. Lyla felt exhilarated. "That was so much fun!" Marlene continued to the kitchen counter where she placed her purse. "I'm glad you liked it, hon. I didn't think we were going to get Kyler to leave. He was havin' a blast!" Lyla smiled lovingly at Kyler. "Well we didn't without a tantrum. He really was having fun playing with the other kids."

Marlene made her way to the couch and sat down. Removing her shoes, she began massaging her feet. "My dogs are barkin." Lyla eyed her confused. "Your dogs?" Marlene was amused. "You've never heard that before? It means my feet hurt." Lyla giggled. "You have some good ones. Sometimes I think I need a Marlene-to-English dictionary." Lyla joined Marlene on the couch. "Come to think about it, my feet hurt too. I really wish I would have worn more comfortable shoes. I just didn't have time to pack anything."

Marlene wondered if she should press the subject. "So you didn't have time to pack? Then I guess you and Ky leaving was a spur of the moment thing?" On one hand, Lyla wanted to avoid the subject like the plague. She didn't mean to open this proverbial can of worms. On the other hand, she felt so alone. She really wanted to share her story with this lady whom she placed so much trust in. She was just about to open her mouth to speak when she realized—*Danger. Oh my gosh, I'm putting this precious woman in danger. If she knows how much danger she's in, will she be angry? Will she be scared?* The look on Lyla's face prompted Marlene to speak. "I know it's something you may not feel comfortable talking about, but if you decide you need an ear, I'm here. I'm not going to judge you—that's God's place, not mine. But your secrets will stay between us."

Lyla collapsed her upper body onto the arm of the couch and began sobbing. "Marlene, I have so much to tell you, but I'm scared you'll be angry. I'm scared you won't understand. I'm worried you'll be frightened." Marlene inched closer to Lyla, and rested her hand on Lyla's shoulder. "Baby girl, you listen, and you listen good. I ain't scared of nothin'. Fear has no place in my life. I thank God for that every day. The Bible says, 'There is no fear in love, but perfect love casteth out fear.' I give my worries to God, and he happily takes them. My

Savior died on the cross so that I could feel that sense of peace. There is no room for fear in my life--only resolution. We can resolve anything together, with the help of God, but you have to open up."

Lyla looked at her through tear-filled eyes. "What do you mean you give your fears to God? What do you mean, 'He died on the cross so you could feel a sense of peace'?" Marlene leaned back and made herself comfortable. "Well, God gave us the Word, and the power to use it, but unless we know about it, it's useless. That's why I spend so much time studying the Bible. It's the Word of God. God sacrificed his only Son so that our sins could be forgiven. Once Jesus died for our sins, we were given the power to ask for forgiveness. The Bible says, "Give your burdens to the Lord, and he will take care of you.'"

Lyla desperately searched for the peace that Marlene was talking about. "How, though? How do I do it?"

"Well, love. You just have to accept Jesus as your personal savior. You have to believe he died on the cross for your sins. Then, you have to ask him into your heart." Lyla struggled with this concept. "I want to believe. I want to—I do. But how do I? I don't know anything about it. How can I believe something I have no information about?" Marlene just smiled and lifted herself off the couch. Walking to the end table by her recliner, she picked up the

Bible. Handing it to Lyla, she said, "Anything you want to know is in here."

*****

After reading Mitch's book, Jacinda spent the entire night flipping from news channel to news channel. She was restless and wondered if Keith was asleep in the next room. She felt exhausted, as she watched the sun rise, but her mind wouldn't allow her the peace to drift off. She had so many questions and so few answers. She felt as if she were being held captive by a cell phone, completely at its mercy. Until the phone rang, there was no reason to leave her prison of a hotel room. There was nowhere to go. It was a waiting game, and she hated sitting around helplessly. She felt so vulnerable, so worthless.

Mitch's book seemed so crazy, but so clear. How did she not see the symbolism earlier? How did she not question the government, the banks, and the trend towards a cashless society? But what did all of this have to do with her and her son? She insisted Keith leave the cell phone in her room. He tried to resist, but it was useless. Jacinda placed the phone on her pillow, not taking a chance on missing a call. Her entire life centered around this phone, and she couldn't help but worry it might be defective. What if the lady had already tried to call back? She checked the ringer for the hundredth time, to assure herself it was on.

She struggled with her feelings towards her husband. She was desperate to contact him; to receive any information he might have to offer. But she knew he was one of the bad guys, and any information he would offer would be unreliable. How did she feel so numb towards him? How is it that she isn't mourning him, or their relationship? Nothing seemed to matter right now except getting Kyler back. Kyler was all she needed, and without him, she wanted nothing.

She heard a tiny knock at the door. She darted to the peephole and saw Keith standing on the other side. Opening the door, she stood back, gesturing him to enter. Keith made his way to a chair by the window. "I wasn't sure if you were up, so I didn't knock very loud." Jacinda returned to her spot on the bed and sat up against the headboard. "I didn't sleep a wink last night. I can't stop staring at this phone. Why hasn't she called back? What if she doesn't? We can't just sit here, but I don't know what else to do."

Keith nodded, clearly feeling her frustration. "So nothing, huh? It didn't ring once?" Jacinda shook her head, without answering. "Well," Keith said, "maybe she'll call today." Keith stood and headed towards the door. "Where are you going?" Jacinda demanded to know. "The camera, I'm going to get the camera. We should be getting all of this on tape. I have to document everything—not just interviews. I'm just going to set the camera up in case the phone does ring.

Jacinda didn't have the energy to fight. *What could it hurt?* She wondered. He returned in less than a minute. She was glad he propped open the door with the swing lock, because she didn't have the energy to get up to let him back in. Removing the camera from the bag, he set it up on the table. The camera faced Jacinda, and the red light indicated it was recording. Ordinarily, she'd be concerned about her hair and makeup, but that concern was totally absent. She didn't care what she looked like, or what people would think. She didn't even know if anyone would see the footage. She didn't care.

"So I read the book last night," Jacinda said, matter-of-factly.

"What did you think?" Jacinda shrugged. "It was interesting. I probably would have found it more interesting if I knew what it all had to do with my son." Keith didn't know how to respond. He found the book fascinating, but wasn't trying to connect it to Kyler's disappearance when he read it. He was trying to connect it to Mitch's death, so he also read it with purpose. For him, it was clear. A man who knew too much was killed. It made sense. But he knew her experience would be different, because nothing in that book would lead to immediate answers about her son or his disappearance.

"The insignia," Jacinda said without much emotion.

"Huh? What insignia?"

"The *Your Nation Now* insignia. It's a triangle—a pyramid, with an eye. It's two of the symbols mentioned in the book. It figures those two things sit on top of the world. I guess the news program does shape the way the world thinks. It figures George would be part of it." Keith perked up, "George? What do you know about George?"

"Well, I know that he doesn't have any grandchildren, despite the fact he was trying to convince me he did. He let me think his grandchild had been abducted. It was all for the story. He convinced me to let someone else piece together my entire BARAchip story. I just did the voiceover and standup. I memorized a script though, so none of the story was mine. I was just being used."

Keith's mind began to consider the possibilities. "So George made you do a story about a chip?" Jacinda nodded, "it was a chip that was supposed to help parents locate and find missing children."

"Like they have in cars?"

"Yes, something like that."

"So like the chip in Mitch's book—the Mark of the Beast chip."

"Sometimes I thought that, but I never really let myself believe it. It seemed like no bad could come from the technology. Plus, Gregory was helping to push legislation to make it mandatory." Keith leaned forward, "Are you even listening to yourself Jacinda? Legislation to make a chip mandatory? How can that be anything *but* the Mark of the Beast? It's all coming together. Gregory was pushing the legislation. He was found with a stolen child, I mean—I don't know how the two connect, but at least the stolen child part tells me he's not exactly one of the good guys."

Jacinda nodded. "I could have told you he wasn't one of the good guys a few days after he disappeared. After finding the pictures in his email, and knowing he lied to me about when he became aware of certain things, I just knew it. I knew he was involved in Kyler's abduction. I read in Mitch's book about the retreat in California where members of The Brotherhood go each year, and that's where Gregory and my father-in-law were headed. I thought it was suspicious that my in-laws didn't report his disappearance, but I didn't understand why. Now, if what Mitch wrote is to true, it's probably because they are all part of the conspiracy. I just don't understand what the conspiracy has to do with my son."

Keith thrived on puzzles, and this one had all of the pieces coming together. Child location devices, pushing legislation, the mother of an abducted child—it all seemed to be falling into place. "Why did you agree to do the story, Jacinda? I mean, what made you agree to act as a reporter on a piece that you had no part of? What made you decide to be the mouthpiece? Didn't your journalistic integrity tell you that was wrong?" Jacinda nodded. "Yes, it felt wrong, but it also felt important." Keith could tell she wasn't making the connection, but he wanted to lead her to it rather than reveal it to her. "But *why* did you think it was so important? What made you so emotionally attached to the story?" Jacinda's eyes lit up, indicating she was connecting the dots. "Oh my gosh. You're right!"

CHAPTER 28

Lyla slowly entered the living room, not knowing if Marlene was awake or still sleeping on the couch. She was delighted to see Marlene drinking her coffee and reading the newspaper at the kitchen table. Lyla radiated a sense of excitement about her as she made her way to the table. "Well you certainly are in a good mood this morning," Marlene said while returning her smile.

"I am. I did it, Marlene—I did it."

"You did what?"

"I did it. I spent all night reading the Bible, and I did it. I asked Jesus into my heart! I asked him to take my burdens. I asked him to take my pain. I can't describe to you the weight that was lifted, or how many happy tears I cried—I just can't describe it."

"You don't have to describe it, hon. I've been there. I mean, I know everyone has a different experience, but I had the happy tears too. It was just a big ol' emotional release. Well, sweetness. I'm happy for you. I know that is an understatement, but I really am truly happy for you."

"So this is it? Am I going to feel this happy forever? I want to know everything. I want to read more."

"Oh hon, I'm afraid you'll find that Faith isn't that easy, at least not in my experience. You've got to keep reading, keep studying. If you don't constantly read The Word, it's easy to slip, as a Christian. Of course, we're all going to slip. Faith is a journey, not a destination, as you might have heard. Well, I guess the destination is Heaven, so maybe that's not entirely true. Anyhoo, just take it one day at a time and realize that someday, when we leave this world behind, there's a better place waiting."

Lyla looked a little deflated. Marlene sat her coffee cup on the table. "What is it, dear?"

"Well, I just thought I'd feel this way forever. I feel so excited, so free—so loved."

"Well, baby girl, as long as you stick with Jesus, you'll always feel loved. Sometimes you'll feel Him more than others. Sometimes, you'll wonder if He's there at all, but you'll never wonder if He loves you. That you can be sure of. A relationship with Christ is like any other relationship, you've got to keep working at it. You've got to keep communicating. You talk to God, and He talks to you.

Lyla was taken back, "Wait. He *talks* to you? You actually hear Him? He didn't talk to me." Marlene chuckled, "Well, hon. everyone experiences God differently. I feel like God is talking to me when He places something on me. Just an inner-knowingness, like I had when you and Ky crawled into my taxi. I felt that was God talking to me. He just puts things on me, and I know it's Him. But everyone hears God differently. Just like He didn't make any two people exactly the same, I believe He doesn't expect us to experience Him in exactly the same way."

Lyla absorbed Marlene's statement. "I guess that makes sense." She then let her gaze drift to the floor. "If God can talk to you by placing something on your soul, then I think he's talking to me now. There's something I need to tell you." Lyla felt compelled to tell Marlene everything. The truth began flowing out of her mouth without filter, starting from her earliest childhood memories of satanic rituals and abuse. She saw the compassion in Marlene's eyes and kept talking. "It was always like that. I was scared to death of my father." Lyla continued to speak, not even fully comprehending everything she was saying. It was like she was on autopilot, and years of built up secrets and feelings came pouring out on their own. "My mother killed herself when I was nineteen, and Marlene—I didn't cry. I was relieved, is that horrible? I felt less fearful, and I hated myself for that." Marlene grabbed her hand. "Baby, I don't ever want you to think any of that was your fault," she said in a stern voice. "What your mother stood by and let you endure goes against a mother's instinct to protect her child. She was wrong, Lyla. Her wiring was all messed up. No mother who's mind wasn't all crazy would ever stand back and watch her child victimized the way she did. Her killing herself had nothing to do with you, and any feelings you had after the fact were normal. How could you grieve for a woman who let you be tortured? You give that to God, baby. He'll take it all."

Lyla wasn't finished. "That's not even the worst part. The organization my father is a part of, The Brotherhood, stole Jacinda Kilmeade's son. She looked down at the table in shame. "Kyler—they stole Kyler." Marlene looked confused. "Our Kyler?" Lyla nodded. "Yes, but he's not *our* Kyler. He's *her* Kyler." Marlene sat straight in her chair. "Then how did you end up with him?" Lyla still looked ashamed. "They placed him under my care. I was his maidservant, as they called me, and I was to keep him happy until the day he was to be sacrificed—today." Marlene shot out of her chair. "Sacrificed? They were going to *kill* that precious child?" Lyla nodded. "That's why I had to run. I had to save him." Marlene began to pace the kitchen. "So then you're not running from an abusive husband. You're running from a group of people who want to kill that child? They'd probably love the opportunity to kill you too. Lyla baby, you did the right thing by escaping, but now you've got to do the right thing by that baby and his mother. You have to return him."

Lyla knew that was true, but hadn't yet decided how she was going to go about doing it. She let her eyes wander to the paper Marlene had been reading. Pulling the paper in front of her, she began to read the headline: **Senator Kilmeade jailed after being found with abducted child.** This headline didn't surprise her one bit. She had seen her half-brother, Gregory Kilmeade, pass her while she was leaving the country home. They had never formally met, but she had seen enough of him in the press to be absolutely certain it was him.

*****

Jacinda and Keith talked, putting together bits and pieces, trying to form some kind of understanding. Jacinda felt a new rush of energy as she paced back and forth. "It was their plan all along. They knew they were going to steal Kyler, even before I had him. That's why there were pictures of me pregnant. A reporter, they picked a reporter. Who better to tell the world about something like this? And the job—I wondered why someone like me would get hired straight out of a small market." Keith shrugged. "I just thought it was because you were Senator Kilmeade's wife." Jacinda looked annoyed. "Yes, that's what everybody thought, I imagine. It all makes sense now; as much sense as it possibly can make."

"So why did Senator Kilmeade take that child?"

"I don't know; he had the same birthday as my son, though. That can't just be a coincidence."

"So then the day the kids were born is significant?"

Jacinda hadn't yet let her mind go there, but she supposed it was. "Yeah, I guess. I don't know the significance yet, but you're right. There's something to it." They were both startled by the ring of the cell phone. Jacinda dived on the bed to answer it. "Hello!" Jacinda was met with silence at the other end of the phone. "Hello, is anyone there?" A determined voice answered. "Yes, I'm here." Jacinda could tell it was the same lady, but the voice was different. Her once shy, weak voice was now resolute. Keith grabbed the camera. "Put it on speaker," he demanded, but Jacinda ignored him. "Are you still there?" Jacinda asked, her trembling hand gripping the phone like a vice. "Yes, I'm still here. Is this Jacinda Kilmeade?"

"Yes, this is Jacinda."

"Jacinda, I need you to know something. I do have Kyler and he is safe— for now. It's a long story, but there are very powerful men who want to—" Jacinda interrupted her. "The Brotherhood?"

Lyla was surprised. "You know about them?"

"Not everything, but I'm learning. Where is my baby now? How did you manage to get him?" Lyla tried to calm her. "I just need you to know that my father holds a very high position in The Brotherhood. He's the assistant of the guy in charge of everything—Lucio. He's Lucio's assistant. Which basically mean he helps oversee everything. He's a very powerful man. He's your father-in-law."

Jacinda didn't hesitate. "My father-in-law? But he doesn't have a daughter. Gregory is their only child."

"He's Chandra's only child. But he and my mother were in a relationship for years. He—" Once again Jacinda cut her off mid-sentence. "Where is he now? Can I see him? I'll go wherever you want. I'll do anything." Lyla continued to plead her case. "Jacinda, I never agreed with my father's beliefs. When they let me care for the child, I never thought I'd fall in love, but I did. I absolutely love him more than anything in the world, and would die to keep him safe. But I know he's your child. I want to return him, but you have to know how much danger both of you are going to be in." Jacinda didn't wait to respond. "Exactly what kind of danger? And what about you? What's going to happen to you?"

"They will kill me, but that's okay. I've accepted Jesus and have accepted my fate." Jacinda couldn't believe how willing this girl was to die. "Nobody is going to kill anyone. You hear me? I'm not going to let that happen. Now where are you? I'm on my way." Jacinda heard a conversation on the other end of the phone, but couldn't make out what they were saying. "Who is that? Is someone with you?"

"Sorry, I was just asking where we should meet. Yes, there's someone with me, but she's not involved. She's actually been our safe haven. She didn't know anything. She was just helping. But she agreed we need to reunite you with Kyler. We have to. I don't want to lead anyone to her house. I can't put her in that kind of danger. You tell me where you are, and I'll come to you."

Jacinda didn't waste a second. "The Hylan Hotel, room 302—third floor. How fast can you be here?" Jacinda could now hear the conversation clearly. The woman was asking the other person how far the Hylan was. She answered Lyla. "About fifteen minutes, we're not far." Jacinda felt her heart drop to her feet. Would she really see her baby in fifteen minutes? Could this really be happening? "Please, please don't change your mind. I'll be here waiting. Nobody but you knows we are here. It's safe. Please bring him here, and I promise you that I will keep him safe. Please bring my baby." She began to cry. Keith felt exhilarated. He was capturing everything on film. Once Jacinda hung up the phone, he pressed her for details. "Tell me everything the woman said. Don't leave anything out." He walked to the bag and pulled out the small microphone she had been wearing earlier. "Wait. Put this on first."

MARKED I

CHAPTER 29

Lyla sat in the passenger seat of the taxi while Marlene drove Kyler and her to the hotel. Lyla felt a lump in her throat, as she stared at Kyler, knowing she was about to lose him forever. "It's okay, baby," Marlene assured her. "You're doing the right thing. Kyler is going to be well cared for. He's going to be loved. You did your job, Lyla. You protected him. He's going to be safe." Lyla knew she was doing the right thing, but couldn't help but feel devastated. Marlene reached over, leaving one hand on the wheel, and took Lyla's hand. "Let's pray."

Lyla sat holding Marlene's hand, as Marlene guided them in prayer. "Dear Lord, please keep all of us safe on our journey. Please take the grief and worry that Lyla is feeling. Please guide us. Lord. We ask that you impart your wisdom on Jacinda and Lyla so they know the best way to stay out of harm's way, and we want to thank you Lord for leading Lyla to my taxi. I want to thank you Lord for trusting me to help keep them safe. In Jesus name I pray, Amen."

Lyla stared at Marlene. "You mean you're *happy* you're involved?"

"I'm happy I could be part of the solution. I'm also happy that you were brought into my life. You're like the daughter I've always wanted." Lyla felt so warmed by her remark. "Really? You don't *hate* me?"

"Don't you be ridiculous. I love you. I love you, and the Lord loves you. Where do you think you're going to go once you've returned Kyler? Do you think you're going to go knocking on your father's door sayin' 'here I am, please kill me'? No! You're going to stay right here with me, and we're going to keep you safe. You got into the wrong taxi if you think you're just going to turn yourself in to be killed. You've got me now. You've got me, and you've got the Lord. You've been given a whole new chance, darlin'. Don't you see it?"

Lyla sat silently tracing the hem of her shirt with her finger. She hadn't thought much about *her* life, but maybe she was being given a chance. Maybe this *wasn't* the end. She reached over and placed her hand on Marlene's shoulder. "Thank you."
Marlene reached up to touch Lyla's hand with her own. "Don't thank me, hon. Thank the good Lord.

Before Lyla knew it, they were pulling into the parking lot of the Hylan Hotel. Lyla turned to face Kyler, then she turned to face Marlene. "So then I'll see you soon?"

"See me soon? You don't think I'm letting you go in there without me, do you? Good frief, you'd be out

364

of your ever-lovin' mind! I'm going to park and go with you. Do you need a minute to say goodbye to Kyler?"

Lyla felt a squeeze on her heart. "Yes," she said, as she looked back with teary eyes. "I do."

"I'll wait for you two at the entrance. You just come when you're ready." They pulled into a parking spot, and Marlene gave her hand one last squeeze. "You're doing the right thing. You've been through more than most people can even imagine. Even so, this is the hardest thing you'll ever have to do in your life. It's all going to get easier from here. It just will." Lyla had no words. She only hoped Marlene was right.

Once Marlene was out of the car, Lyla unbuckled Kyler from his car seat. She picked him up and held him so close, that his little body shaped to hers. "I'm going to tell you something, Angel. I love you more than I will ever love anything. I want you to know that."

"La bu."

"I know you do, baby. You're going to meet a nice lady. She's your mother. She loves you very much and is going to hold you, play with you, and keep you safe. I may not always be there, but I'll always be thinking about you." She didn't know how to tell the toddler goodbye forever. Not just because she couldn't bear saying it, but because she didn't think he would understand. "You just remember that I love you. I'll always love you." The tears were now streaming down her face, and she was finding it difficult to breathe. It felt as if someone was suffocating her—like she was drowning. She buried her nose in his soft curls. His hair smelled like the baby shampoo that she loves so much.

"I'm a mess," she said, as she sat him down.

"Mess," he mimicked.

"Yes I am. I can't walk in there like this. I have to calm down. She sat in the passenger side of the taxi with her feet planted firmly on the cement. Pulling Kyler onto her lap, she wiped her face with the inside of her shirt. She looked into the backseat. "You'll be needing your car seat; I almost forgot about that." Bumbly Bear was still in the backseat from the first time she and Kyler entered the taxi. With all the toys, he never asked for the bear. The bear's stitches were still torn from where she had retrieved the money. "Bumbly Bear is going to go with you. Would you like that?" Kyler's face lit up as she stood to collect the bear and the car seat. She couldn't look at Kyler—it hurt too much. "Are you ready to go meet you mom?"

"No," Kyler said as casually as if he were answering whether or not he'd like some spinach.

"Well, it's time. She's going to be very nice."

Marlene noticed Lyla struggling with the car seat

and darted across the parking lot to help her. She took the car seat from Lyla/ "I've got this, hon. You just worry about Kyler." Lyla repositioned Kyler on her hip and followed Marlene to the entrance. Lyla walked into the hotel with tunnel vision. All she saw was the elevator. She locked her eyes on the shiny, metal doors and walked towards them. She forgot to breathe. As the doors slid open, she felt dizzy. Marlene put a loving hand on her shoulder. "You okay?"

"I don't know," Lyla responded, honestly.

"One foot in front of the other," Marlene instructed.

Once the doors slid shut, Marlene turned to Lyla. "What floor did she say?"

"Three—the third floor. Room 302."

Marlene pushed the button and they felt themselves begin to rise. As the elevator came to a stop and the doors began to open, Lyla hugged Kyler tighter. "One foot in front of the other," Marlene reminded her. They stepped out of the elevator and made their way down the long hall. Without Marlene's simple instructions, she probably would have remained motionless in the elevator. She continued putting one foot in front of the other until they reached the door that read 302.

*****

Jacinda kept checking her watch as she paced

back and forth across the room. "It's already been thirty minutes. What if they aren't coming?" Keith was still behind the camera. "Maybe there was traffic; they're only fifteen minutes late." Before she could respond, she heard the knock at the door. Running to answer it, she completely forgot to look out of the peephole. Opening the door, all she could see was her son. Reaching for him, she tried to talk, but only a high-pitched squeal escaped her lips. After hugging the toddler to her chest, her knees failed her. She collapsed to the floor, holding Kyler safely against her. It could have been minutes or seconds since she had first reached for him, she couldn't remember. At that moment, nothing mattered—nothing but feeling her child next to her body. Her baby was safe. He was safe, and he was perfect.

She had dreamed about this moment for two years, but never did she visualize it like this. She couldn't speak to comfort him, she couldn't say anything at all. She just kept kissing his head while she held him close. Kyler looked up at Lyla, reaching for her. He began to whine. "Oh my gosh," Jacinda said. "He doesn't know me. He's scared of me. My baby is scared of me." She felt as if someone had just punched her in the stomach, as she allowed Lyla to take the toddler, in an effort to calm him down. "I'm so sorry," Lyla said. "I'm so sorry. He's just not used to you. It won't take long."

Lyla was now feeling less for herself, and more for

Jacinda. She couldn't imagine what Jacinda must be going through. It wasn't fair that this woman was robbed of two years with her baby, and it wasn't fair that he didn't know who she was."

Jacinda found the strength to rise to her feet. She reached out to touch Kyler's hand. "I'm your mommy. I love you more than anything. I know you don't know me, but I love you more than anything I've ever loved before." Kyler nestled his head in the crook between Lyla's neck and shoulder. He never took his eyes off Jacinda. Jacinda slowly reached to touch his hand. "Do you think I could hold you?" Kyler still looked reluctant. Jacinda looked at Lyla. "He really trusts you." Marlene stepped through the doorway. "I'm afraid we're going to draw attention if we stand here. Do you mind if we come inside?"

Jacinda felt foolish for not assuring their privacy before making such a scene. "Sure, of course. Come in," she said, as she stood against the wall. "I'm sorry. I wasn't thinking." All three women and Kyler made their way into the room. Marlene looked up at Keith. "Why are you filming?" Jacinda didn't wait for him to answer. "Insurance," she assured them. "Showing the world the truth is the only way to keep us safe." Her eyes stayed locked on Kyler. "Please, will you let me hold you? I won't hurt you. I know I scared you, baby. Kyler looked at Lyla, and she assured him by nodding her head. "It's okay, baby. She's your momma. She loves you." She handed the toddler to Jacinda, hoping against hope that he wouldn't reject her again.

Holding her son in her lap, Jacinda couldn't stop staring at him, while rocking her body back and forth. "You're so beautiful," she said. "You are even more beautiful than I imagined." Jacinda looked to Lyla. "Does he talk?"

"Oh yes," Lyla assured her. "He's just being shy."

"Tell me everything," Jacinda insisted. "What does he like? What does he do? What have I missed?" Lyla tried to answer the question without crying. It wasn't until she swept her hair away from her face, that Jacinda noticed she looked like Gregory. "You *are* Gregory's sister," Jacinda said, sounding amazed.

"Maybe by blood, but I've never met him. I'm nothing like him or my father. I mean, I look like them, but that's where it ends.

Keith got a little too close with the camera. "Can they have a little privacy please," Marlene snapped.

"Privacy is the last thing they need right now ma'am. If we all want to stay alive, we need the opposite of privacy—we need exposure. Look, I don't want to do it in front of the kid, but do you think we could go to my room and do an interview? Documenting everything is the only thing that's going to keep us safe." Lyla found that logic a little crazy. "You're kidding right? The only thing that will keep us safe is hiding. If they find us, they're going to kill us."

Keith kept the camera focused on Jacinda and Kyler. "No, you're wrong," he said, sounding a little arrogant. "Telling your story to the world is the only thing that is going to keep us safe. You do want us to be safe, don't you?" Marlene interrupted. "Won't exposing them on camera be writing their death warrant?" Keith stayed behind the camera. "No, if any of us die, it gives us credibility. They're going to want to make us look crazy, not credible." It made sense to Lyla, when he put it like that.

"You know, you might just be right," she acknowledged.

"So, can we go to the next room and do an interview?"

"Sure, I guess," Lyla said while looking to Marlene for assurance. Marlene nodded her head and Lyla felt a little more self-confident about her decision. "Okay, fine, but not in front of Kyler."

CHAPTER 30

Lyla returned from her interview to find Kyler asleep on the bed next to Jacinda. Marlene opened the door for Keith and Lyla, but made her way back to the chair. "He just zonked out," Marlene said with a smile. "Jacinda rocked him to sleep." Jacinda looked up through joyful eyes. "I didn't want to put him down." Keith walked over to Jacinda and sat next to her. He tried to keep his voice low.

"There's a lot more to the story than we guessed. Lyla said Kyler was supposed to be sacrificed today." Jacinda audibly gasped. "For what? Why would they do such a thing?" she asked, clearly horror-struck.

Lyla answered. "To consecrate the ground for their lord, who is prophesized to be born tomorrow—the day after Kyler was to be sacrificed." Jacinda still looked shocked. "But why? Why Kyler?"

"It's all going to sound very random and cruel, but they needed a child that was born during the transit of Venus. The mother had to be a child of God, and announce BARAchip to the world. They looked at pregnant reporters all over the country, and you were the one they felt was best suited." Jacinda's feelings had been confirmed. "So then Gregory had been watching me. Our marriage was no accident?"

"I'm afraid not. Gregory plays an intricate role in all of this. Like me, he was born into it. I've never met him, but I know our father is very active in The Brotherhood, and Gregory was brought in years ago."

Jacinda desperately tried to absorb all of the information. "So you say you were born into it; how do you fit into it now?"

"I don't. I escaped. I did it for Kyler. Now, if they find me, they'll kill me for betraying them."

"So, do you believe in their mission?"

"I didn't really know what to believe, until I met Marlene. Thanks to her, I found Jesus and I've never been more at peace."

"So you're a Christian?"

"I can't imagine being anything else, now. It's something I knew nothing about less than a week ago. Everything is happening so fast."

"Do you know why Gregory stole the other child?"

"No, but I saw him approaching the country home we escaped from, as we were leaving."

Jacinda looked to Keith for answers. "Why? Why did he steal that other child?" Jacinda thought for a moment and wondered if her friend Jill had retrieved anything on the computer that would shed any light on their questions. She didn't want to put her in danger and quickly dismissed the possibility of contacting her by phone.

Keith was still documenting the conversation with the camera. "Are you guys ready to expose them?" Lyla turned to face Keith. "It's not that easy. You don't know them like I do."

"That's exactly why you're coming with us," Jacinda responded.

Lyla tried to hide her excitement. The thought of being with Kyler even one more day thrilled her to the core. "You mean, you want me to come?" Jacinda's eyes locked with Lyla's. "Lyla, you risked your life to save my child and return him to me. What you did was selfless. I can tell that he loves and trusts you. I'm going to put every bit of energy

I have into exposing the monsters that stole my baby and killed my first husband. In order to do that, I'm going to have to do a lot of footwork—a ton of research. If everything you say is true, it needs to be brought to light. I have to stop the world from accepting this chip. The truth needs to be told. Who else can I trust to help me with Kyler while I'm doing all of this? I already know you're willing to lay down your life for him."

Lyla sat next to Jacinda and touched her hand. "I will, Jacinda. I'll die for him. You don't know what it means to me to be able to help you with him, even if it's just for a little while. Plus, I'll tell you guys everything I know. Hopefully I can be useful."

Keith couldn't believe his luck. In order to get the story, he'd be waging war with an ancient evil society. Perfect. Livingston told him to return with the child, but it was clear they would be stopping by Jill's first. After all, her phone was probably bugged. Livingston was just going to have to wait. Marlene walked towards Lyla. "Are you sure about this?" Lyla stared into her kind, brown eyes and responded, "I've never been more sure of anything."

Marlene hugged her close, "It looks like the LORD has called you. I'd go with you guys, but I've got a son and a grandbaby to think about. I'd go if I thought you needed me, but I'm afraid I don't have anything to offer the group. I feel honored that God even let me play a small part in all of this. It's a lot of information to deal with, so I'm going to give it to God."

Lyla hugged Marlene tightly against her. "I'll never forget everything you've done for me and Kyler. I can't thank you enough."

Marlene pulled away to look her in the eyes, "Remember what I told you, hon. Don't thank me, thank the good Lord. This was all part of His glorious plan.

Jacinda looked lovingly at her sleeping child, as anger rose inside of her. She had to expose The Brotherhood, not only for her late husband and her son, but also for herself—for the world. She couldn't know everything she does now and stand passively by waiting for evil to dominate the planet. "This is going to be dangerous," she said, looking at both Keith and Lyla. "Are both of you dedicated enough that you're prepared to die?" Lyla nodded her head. "Absolutely." Keith shook his head from behind the camera. "No, but I'm willing to document you two being dedicated enough to die." Jacinda shot him a disgusted look. "I was only kidding—kind of," he assured her. "I'm just here for the story."

Jacinda knew it was true. He'd do anything for the story, so she knew he was solid. Feeling more determined than she's ever felt in her life, she lifted herself off the bed. "Well then, first stop is California. Then we'll take it from there. I need to know what Jill has recovered, and I'm not taking any chances over the phone. Hopefully, after we have that information, we'll know where to go from there. Keith peeked out from around the camera. "So let me get this straight. Most of The Brotherhood is *in* California, and you want to go there. Do you have a death wish that you'd like to share with the group?" Jacinda shot Keith an annoyed look. "Are you in or out?"

"I'm in," Keith assured her. "I think you're crazy, but I'm in."

Jacinda looked at Marlene. "Can you take me to the bank?"

For the first time, Keith moved the camera from his face. "You can't go to the bank. I already told you The Brotherhood will be suspicious. They'll be able to track you."

Jacinda dismissed his concerns. "I'm quite sure The Brotherhood is already suspicious. And by the time they'll be able to track me, we'll be gone. I need to go withdraw enough money to support this mission. It sounds like it's going to be long and expensive." Keith had a hard time arguing with her logic.

Jacinda turned her attention from Keith to Marlene. "So, would you mind?"

Marlene winked. "I'd be happy to help any way I can. Let's go." Jacinda turned to Lyla. "You'll take care of Kyler while I'm gone? I'll be back in thirty minutes, tops. Once I come back with the money, I'll come get you guys, and we'll head to California. I just hate letting Kyler out of my sight for even a second."

"I'll guard him with my life," Lyla assured her.

Jacinda headed towards the door. "So the adventure begins," she said, sounding resolute.

"Yes," Keith agreed, hesitantly. "So it begins."

Lyla lay next to the sleeping toddler, as she watched Marlene and Jacinda leave the room. Keith was sitting next to her, but Kyler was all that mattered. She thanked God that today wasn't going to be her final goodbye. She'll get to be with the child she's grown to love as her own, at least a little longer. She buried her nose in his soft curly hair and kissed his head. The sweet smell of baby shampoo filled her nostrils. She didn't know what Heaven would be like, but for the time being—this was the next best thing.

To Be Continued in Marked II: The Resistance

Now available for download!

Chapter 1 preview:

Chapter 1

Keith crossed the California border, momentarily removing his hand from the steering wheel to pump his fist.

"Yes, another state down!"

Keith looked in the rear view mirror at Jacinda. She looked so happy sitting in the backseat next to Kyler, her two-year-old son. In an attempt to make up for the years she had lost with him, she couldn't stop kissing his hands, and lovingly stroking his hair. Jacinda was captivated by the beautiful toddler, and knew she could be totally fulfilled sitting next to him forever. It didn't take her long to learn the tickle monster game. Each time she tickled him, he giggled uncontrollably. As the tickling stopped, he would look at her a moment before saying, "Ticko monner!" Once he said the magic words, the tickle monster would attack. It had always been Kyler's favorite game, and it was now Jacinda's favorite thing in the entire world. Kyler finally had a tickle monster that never tired of playing the game.

Lyla sat next to Keith in the passenger seat. She hugged her knees and rested her head against the window. She was beautiful, and that fact didn't escape Keith.

"Are you getting hungry?" he asked her, in an awkward attempt at conversation.

"Not really," she replied, "but I can eat whenever you guys are hungry."

How can anyone be so passive? He wondered. She hadn't so much as asked to use the restroom since they'd left Oklahoma for California. She simply used the restroom when someone else demanded a pit stop.

Keith glanced back at Jacinda. "I still can't believe you bought a van! Couldn't we have at least traveled in style?" he asked in jest. "I don't know, maybe an SUV made in this decade, perhaps?"

Jacinda met his eyes in the rearview. "You know as well as I do that everything made in this decade is computerized. I'm not taking any chances of them tracking us down."

"Fair enough, but couldn't you have at least bought one that wasn't all white? I feel like I'm driving a bunch of convicts around! I am. I'm driving a convict van; all we need are bars on the windows. Do you see the way people are avoiding us?" Keith teased.

"Added bonus," Jacinda replied.

Keith looked down at the fuel gauge. "Couldn't you have at least bought a hybrid? We've had to stop for gas every ten seconds."

"It's a good thing you haven't been paying for it," Jacinda quipped, never taking her eyes off Kyler. She dabbed at her face with a tissue, as beads of sweat rolled down her forehead. The man she'd bought the van from had said the AC was in great condition, but the cool air barely trickled out of the vents. The shoddy air conditioning couldn't compete with the scorching July heat.

"Speaking of money," Keith continued, "I still can't believe they let you withdraw that much money at one time! I thought there would be a two-day waiting period or something. It's insane they let you just walk out of the bank carrying that much cash."

Jacinda withdrew every dime the bank would allow. She recalled the overwhelming anxiety she'd felt on the way to the bank just one day earlier. There were so many unknowns. *Would her account be frozen? Would someone at the bank notify The Brotherhood? Would they let her withdraw enough money to live on until she could ensure their safety?* She knew The Brotherhood would do everything in their power to hunt them down. She was fully aware of how widespread The Brotherhood's influence was, and realized that any paper trail would lead them directly to her and her son. Everything had to be paid in cash—everything.

Until The Brotherhood was exposed, Jacinda Kilmeade refused to leave so much as a blip on the radar. Two days ago, she never could have predicted she would be in a twenty-year-old van heading to California with an intern, her precious son, Kyler, and the woman who had raised Kyler since birth. If she had learned anything in life, it was to expect the unexpected. Two years earlier, her son had been kidnapped and her husband killed. She had to start her life over, but had never given up hope of finding her son. She learned very quickly that tragedy could strike without warning. She knew nothing in life was guaranteed, and treasured each and every moment.

Jacinda began to doze off, but was startled awake by the sound of a blaring car horn. She looked up to see a vehicle full of teenage girls giggling and waving at Keith.

"I take back everything I said about this van; it's a total chick-magnet!" Keith announced, only half-kidding.

"Eyes on the road, Romeo! You're carrying precious cargo," Jacinda reminded him, although she couldn't help but giggle. Giggling wasn't something she'd felt like doing for a very long time. She cherished these moments. For the first time in over two years, her heart wasn't aching for her son, because he was peacefully sleeping beside her. Her heart should have been aching for her husband, Gregory, but somehow she managed to block out every emotion but anger when she thought of him. She was still enraged that Gregory had played such a prominent role in her son's disappearance. As far as Jacinda was concerned, Gregory could sit in jail forever. In fact, prison seemed entirely too compassionate.

Jacinda didn't have time to sort through her anger; she was on a mission. Exposing The Brotherhood was the only thing that mattered. It was a feat that no one had ever successfully accomplished. The Brotherhood had messed with the wrong woman— the wrong mother. Every bit of grief and anger she'd felt over the past two years had transformed into focus and determination. Everything she had left in the world was right there in that van, and she had no intention of losing any of it. A reporter and an intern were about to take on The Brotherhood with a baby and nanny in tow. She vowed to do whatever it took to expose The Brotherhood's wicked agenda. To call it an adventure of a lifetime would be a foolish understatement.

*****

George, the director of *Your Nation Now*, loved his yearly visit to Rhapsody Grove. He loved rubbing elbows with the powerful and elite. He looked forward to mingling with world leaders; it made him feel important. In the grand scheme of things, he did play an important role in the coming New World Order. George was the news director of the highest rated television news program in the country. He had the final say on the stories that aired. George had been pushing The Brotherhood's agenda for years.

While he played an integral role in publicizing The Brotherhood's propaganda, he knew anyone could fill his position. He was merely a pawn. He understood he was expendable, which was why he did everything The Brotherhood demanded. This visit to the grove was different than previous retreats. When *Your Nation Now* had failed to air footage of BARAchip, he had been treated as a traitor upon arrival. Despite explaining the story was complete when he'd left for the retreat, he was being punished for not personally ensuring the story aired.

George couldn't wait to be a part of the action at the grove, which was why he'd headed to the retreat before Jacinda's BARAchip package had aired. It was that careless choice that had landed him in the *sweat shack*. The sweat shack, named because of

the sweltering July heat, was where The
Brotherhood imprisoned their traitors during the
retreat. They didn't let defectors know they'd been
discovered until they arrived. Once the traitor
checked in, they put a sack over his head, secured it
with a rope around his neck, and locked him in the
tiny 12X12 foot shack. Some prisoners described
it as a place to think, others, a place to die. Either
way, George didn't feel he deserved such harsh
treatment after years of faithful service. He'd
handled the BARAchip story exactly as they had
demanded. He'd even hired Jacinda Kilmeade for
the sole purpose of showcasing BARAchip
technology to the world.

It wasn't his fault the tape had faded to black right
before the story was set to air. Of course, once
Bertha had told him about the tape, he'd known the
responsibility would fall squarely on his shoulders.
After all, he should have seen the project through
from beginning to end. He shouldn't have left D.C.
until his mission was complete, and the story had
aired. He felt so careless for trusting such an
important mission to lackey producers. *Which one
of them messed it up?* He wondered. It didn't matter
who was responsible; it was George who would
suffer the consequences. He feared he was a dead
man.

George sat in the sweat shack thinking about

everything he'd done to help shape public perception. The scorching July temperature made the air in the shack feel suffocating. The heat of the stale air burned his lungs when he breathed. The stench of rotting wood filled the tiny room, and he wondered if bugs and rats were biding their time to feast on his body. *How dare they treat me like a traitor! Sure, it was irresponsible to leave before the story aired, but I thought everything was handled.* George had believed his job was complete. He'd figured it was in the bag, but the only thing currently in the bag was George's head. Literally. He had never felt such discomfort in his life.

Just when he was beginning to lose every last bit of hope, the door opened. He couldn't see anything, but was able to detect the sunlight that streamed in from the open door. *Thank God*, he thought. *I'm getting out of here.* His hopes were dashed when he heard the thump of a body hit the floor. A man screamed for help. Three seconds later, the room went black.

"Hello," George said. "Who's there?"

"Who are you? Who's in here with me?" the man inquired between sporadic breaths. "How long have you been in here? Will they come get us soon?"

George closed his eyes. Closing his eyes when he

felt helpless was a habit. He listened to branches crack as their capturers walked away from the shack. Certain they were alone, he answered as calmly as possible.

"It's George Dittmeir. News Director of *Your Nation Now*." George was far from calm, but knew any outward expression of panic would only throw the man deeper into hysterics. "What's your name? Who are you?" George asked.

"Tony. Tony Randall," the man replied.

George sat a little straighter. "*The* Tony Randall? Louden Records Executive, Tony Randall?"

"Yeah, man. That one. How long are they going to keep us in here?"

"I don't know," George responded honestly. I've heard that some people are put here to think about what they've done, while others say they're sent here to die. Let's hope we're here to think."

Tony remained silent for a moment before asking, "So, what are you in here thinking about?"

"I messed up a story," George confessed.

Tony didn't skip a beat. "The BARAchip story?" George simply nodded, forgetting Tony couldn't see the gesture.

"That's way worse than what I did," Tony said, half chuckling with relief.

"Well?" George asked. "What *did* you do?"

"I fell in love."

"They put you in the sweat shack for falling in love?"

"Not exactly, but falling in love was what got me into this mess."

"So?" George prompted. "What did you do?"

Tony didn't respond immediately. George wasn't sure if Tony was thinking or just avoiding the question altogether. "I guess we're not getting out of here alive, anyway," Tony said. "We might as well confess our sins, right?"

"Right," George responded, although he was holding out hope The Brotherhood hadn't sentenced him to death by way of the sweat shack.

"You ever heard of the Twenty-Seven Club?" Tony asked.

"The what?" George asked.

"The Twenty-Seven Club, man."

"No, I guess I haven't."

"Have you ever noticed how many musicians die when they're twenty-seven? I'm not saying all of 'em made a pact, but a lot of them did. You got the teenagers and twenty-one-year-olds dying to get a record deal. They'll do anything to get signed."

"Okay," George responded, unsure of where the conversation was heading.

"Well, some of 'em, and I can't say for sure which ones, but some of 'em agreed to sign a contract with Lucifer."

"You mean, they signed a contract with the devil?"

"That's exactly what I mean."

"Get out of here; that's just a figure of speech. They didn't really make a deal with the devil."

"Oh, really? So when the devil collected their souls at twenty-seven, it was just a coincidence? I only witnessed two of our artists participate in the ritual. They didn't really sign their names on a dotted line. It was a little heavier than that."

"Okay, I'm listening," said George, indicating he was still interested.

"Well, my girlfriend, Chyanne, agreed. I signed her when she was only eighteen years old. She was still wet behind the ears. Her career never really took off. She only had one top-forty hit in her three-year career, but The Brotherhood offered her more. They offered her all the fame and success she wanted. She just had to sell her soul. She's only twenty-one, man. She's not even convinced she has a soul to sell, but she wants to be rich and famous more than anything in the world. She'd do just about anything to live that lifestyle. But she didn't know what she was messin' with. She didn't realize that the devil always collects. She came home all excited that she was going to be the *next big thing*. She said all she had to do was show up somewhere and promise her soul. I think she actually thought *she* was conning *them*.

"I couldn't let her do it, man. I couldn't lose her in six years. I love her too much to live without her. So, I told her. I said, you've got no idea what you're messin' with, baby girl. Once you make this pact, you can bet Lucifer will collect. You can't live on the devil's dime and not expect to pay with your soul. I told her about the two other artists I watched sell their souls. Annette Patrick and Dendy Miller. Both of them were super ambitious kids with stars in their eyes. Both died at twenty-seven."

George took a moment to process the information. "You know, I never really thought about it, but a lot of really great musicians did die at twenty-seven: Robert Johnson, Brian Jones, Jimi Hendrix, Janis

Joplin." He paused, trying to think of more, but Tony beat him to it.

"Curt Cobain, Shannon Hoon, and Amy Winehouse. I could go on and on, but what's the point?"

"All of them? They all sold their souls?" asked George.

"How should I know, man? Some of them just died. It could have been a coincidence. I can only confirm the ones I saw. I only witnessed two. I heard about others, but I couldn't swear to nothin'. Once the second artist died at twenty-seven, I knew we weren't playin' games, but I was too far in. I was making so much money. I had houses all over the world. Still do. But not her, man, I couldn't let them take her."

"So?" George asked. "What happened?"

"I told her. I told her the truth. I begged her not to do it. She told me I was crazy and stormed out of the house. I figured she'd go somewhere and cool off, but she never came back. That was about a week ago. I guess she told 'em. Why else would I be in this room with this bag over my head waitin' to die?"

The two men sat in silence for what seemed like an eternity. George finally spoke. "Twenty-seven, huh?"

"I'm tellin' you, man, if you ever get out of here, look it up. I'm not sayin' they all sold their souls, but I know for a fact two of them did. Once they turned twenty-seven, the devil came knockin'."

MARKED II

Crossing the Arizona Border, Keith momentarily took his hands off the wheel to clap. "Yes, another state down!" Jacinda sat in the backseat, next to her two year-old son, Kyler. In an attempt to make up for the two years she lost with him, she couldn't stop kissing his hands and lovingly stroking his hair. Jacinda was mesmerized by the beautiful toddler and knew she could be totally fulfilled sitting right here next to him forever. It didn't take her long to learn the tickle monster game. Each time she tickled him, he giggled uncontrollably. As soon as she stopped, he'd look at her a moment, before saying, "Ticko monner!" Once he said the magic words, the tickle monster would attack. It had always been Kyler's favorite game, and was now Jacinda's favorite thing in the entire world, aside from her son, of course. Kyler now had a tickle monster that never tired of playing the game.

Keith looked at Lyla, who was sitting in the passenger seat. She was beautiful, and that fact didn't escape Keith. "Are you getting hungry?" he asked her, trying to make conversation. "Not really," she replied. "But I can eat whenever you guys are hungry." *How can anyone be this passive?* He wondered. She hasn't so much as asked to use the restroom since they've been en route to California. She simply uses the restroom when someone else demands a pit stop.

Keith looked at Jacinda in the rearview mirror. "I still can't believe you bought a van! Couldn't we have at least traveled in style?" he asked, smiling at her in the mirror. "I don't know, maybe an SUV made in this decade, perhaps?" She met his eyes in the rearview. "You know as well as I do that everything made in this decade is computerized. I'm not taking any chances of them tracking our whereabouts."

"Fair enough. But couldn't you have at least got one that wasn't all white? I feel like I'm driving a bunch of convicts around! I am. I'm driving a convict van. All we need is bars on the windows. Do you see the way people are avoiding us?" Keith teased.

"Added bonus," Jacinda shot back.

"Couldn't you have bought a hybrid? We have to stop for gas every ten seconds," Keith said, while looking at the fuel gauge.

"It's a good thing you're not paying for it."

"Speaking of money, I'm still in shock you were able to withdraw that much money at one time! I thought there would be a two-day waiting period or something. It's insane that they just let you walk out of the bank carrying that much cash."

Jacinda laughed, "Me too! I didn't even have the foresight to bring anything to put it in. I literally walked out of the bank with bags of money!"

"Speaking of foresight, I must have ESP, because I've actually referred to you as *money bags* before. I'm pretty sure it was just a premonition."

"Jacinda shot him a forced look annoyance. "Or, it was just you being snotty."

"It could have been that too," Keith agreed.

Jacinda had to draw out every dime the bank would allow, because after today, everyone would be looking for her. Knowing how far-reaching The Brotherhood's tentacles were, she knows any paper trail will lead them right to her and her precious child. Everything must be paid in cash— everything. Until The Brotherhood is exposed, Jacinda Kimeade won't leave so much as a blip on the radar. Two days ago, she never would have predicted she would be in a fifteen-year-old van heading to California with an intern, her precious child, and the woman who has been raising her child since birth. If Jacinda has learned anything in life, it's to expect the unexpected. Life is unpredictable, and you adapt, or you die—period.

Jacinda was startled when she heard honking. She looked up to find a car full of teenage girls giggling and waving at Ketih. "I take back everything I said about this van. It's a total chick-magnet!" he said, only half kidding.

"Eyes on the road, Romeo! You're carrying precious cargo!" Jacinda reminded him, although she couldn't help but giggle. Giggling was something she hasn't gotten to do in a very long time, and she cherished these moments. For the first time in two years, her heart wasn't aching for her child, because he was peacefully sleeping next to her. Perhaps her heart should have been aching for her husband, but somehow, she's managed to block out every emotion towards him but anger.

Jacinda didn't have time to sort through her emotions; she was on a mission. Right now, only one thing mattered—exposing The Brotherhood. It was a mission that no one has ever accomplished, but they messed with the wrong woman, the wrong mother. Every bit of grief and anger she's felt over the past two years, has now transformed into focus and determination. Everything she has left in the world is right here in this van, and she has no intention of losing any of it. A reporter and an intern are about to take on The Brotherhood, with a baby and nanny in tow. She'll do whatever it takes to expose The Brotherhood's wicked agenda. To call this the adventure of a lifetime would be an understatement.

MARKED I